Chev's Mate
INVI WRIGHT

COMPLETED WORKS
by Invi Wright

***

<u>STANDALONE</u>
The Nanny

Aine

Lord of Dread

<u>THE FEMALE SERIES</u>
The Female

Her Males

Their War

Chev's Mate

Queens (coming 2025)

<u>THE CURSED KINGDOMS SERIES</u>
The Cursed Kingdom

The Shattered Kingdom (coming 2025)

TRIGGER WARNINGS CAN BE FOUND ON:
inviwright.com

THANK YOU

***

The largest thank you possible to my husband. You gave me the confidence and support to pursue writing, and none of this would be possible without you.

Also, to my Patreon subscribers: Brianna Kathleen, Lexie Terry, Lindsay, Leilani S., Vanessa Turpin, Kimberly Belbot, Sharon H., Gigielle, Lora Beth Farmer, Bhavini, and Patience Isch. Your support is the sole reason I'm able to do this, and I can't properly convey in words just how much you mean to me. I hope you enjoy this story!

Chapter One

VANESSA

I HIDE MY shaking hands behind my back as I stare at the portal, struggling to work up the courage to step through.

It looks rather inconspicuous at first glance, like nothing more than a doorway leading into a dark room. When it turns on, though, the blackness shifts into a blue, luminescent haze. There's a low buzzing, too, but it's so quiet, I'd never notice if I weren't paying such close attention.

"You're all set, Vanessa," the guard on my left says.

He's a shifter. I can tell by his bulging muscles and the way he tugs angrily at his jeans. Shifter males typically wear leather skirts, but they're expected to wear traditional clothing around non-shifter women. They hate it.

It's a rule meant to make women feel comfortable, but it doesn't really work.

I was owned by a horde of violent ogres before the war, and I'm happy never seeing a half-naked man again. Still, even when clothed, being near men makes my heart race and my back sweat. The fear of what lies between their thighs is ever present in my mind, and no amount of clothing is ever going to fix that.

But I'm determined to overcome my fear.

It's been six years since the demon wars, and I've spent almost five years in rehabilitation facilities. I've attended thousands of therapy sessions and have thrown myself into every trade program offered. I want my life to mean something, and when I saw an open facility manager position, I just knew I had to apply for it.

My life is going to mean something. I'm making sure of it.

I'll be assigned to a rehabilitation facility, and I'll be the voice of the women inside. Even after all these years, there are still so many women who rely on the therapy and trade programs they offer. It's doubtful they'll ever choose to leave, which I can't blame them for.

It'll be my job to ensure their needs are being met and to communicate with the shifters and elves who manage the programs. I'll be making a difference.

The portal continues to buzz, the blue haze pulsating. It's been programmed to take me to the shifter headquarters. To Echo's office.

I've met her twice during my interviews, but she still makes me nervous. While she's never been anything short of kind, being in her mere presence is overwhelming. She was never purchased, never mistreated by men, and she was raised with confidence. She speaks louder than I'd ever dare to, and she carries herself in a way I can only dream of doing myself.

Not to mention her influence.

Her brother is Chev, who everybody knows is the leader of the bear shifters. He worked directly with the demons and elves to execute the retrieval of the purchased females. He and Echo are the reason I'm no longer owned by those men.

It's intimidating.

I swallow past the lump in my throat, knowing I need to leave.

I can't be late for my first day of work. I was provided a female escort for both of my interviews, but now that I'm officially an employee, I have clearance to travel alone. It's terrifying.

The two guards in the portal room stare at me, their eyes darting questioningly between me and the portal, but they make no moves to intervene as I square my shoulders and lift my chin. It's now or never.

I step into the blue haze, my heart pounding as I'm teleported to Echo's office. I pause to catch my breath once I'm on the other side. I don't think I'll ever get used to that feeling, and I succumb to a full-body shiver as I catch my bearings.

The buzzing from the portal vanishes as it's shut down, and I pat my hips and smooth down the front of my sweater. I wasn't sure what to wear, but everybody was dressed casual during my interviews. I hope my black sweater and long skirt are appropriate. I typically wear baggy clothing, something to cover the generous curves most nymph women are burdened with, but today's clothing is tighter.

I'm already regretting the color, though. My hair is light, and it stands out against the black fabric. I pick one of the long strands out of the fibers and clench it within my fist.

"Vanessa!"

I plaster a wide smile on my lips as I turn toward Echo's receptionist.

She's a friendly woman, a deer shifter with delicate features and a kind smile, and she tucks a piece of auburn hair behind her ear as I approach her desk. I can't remember her name.

"Good morning," I say by way of greeting.

Her smile widens. "Echo stepped out for an urgent meeting, but she should be back shortly. You can wait here."

She gestures for me to sit in one of the chairs beside Echo's office door. I take the one farthest from the portal.

The reception area is small, with only a desk, a portal, and three chairs inside. It's made cozy with large plants and bright-blue furniture, though. I quite like it, and I shove my shaking hands under my thighs as I peer around.

The shifters prefer to live among nature, and Echo clearly attempted to replicate that here. Besides the large plants stuffed into every corner of the room, there are framed images of forestry hung on the walls.

I wonder if they're of the shifter realm. I've never been there, but I've heard great things. There's a rehabilitation facility on their lands, but I wasn't lucky enough to be placed there. I got stuck in the elven realm, which was still nice.

I was told the elven lands are most similar to what my home used to look like, but it only served as a reminder that my home no longer exists. The nymphs were decimated during the female decline, and our land was ravaged.

It's nothing more than ruins now.

I tap my foot against the ground, nervously waiting for Echo to arrive.

She's kind, and she likes me. I repeat that to myself while I wait. There were thousands of applicants for this role, and the small voice in the back of my head tells me that I was only hired because I was rescued from the ogre realm. The shifters want to use me as an example of how successful rehabilitation can be.

It's a painful thought, one I try hard to ignore. I got this job because I deserve it.

"I swear, I'm about a second away from cutting off Chev's—" I stand as Echo bursts into the room, her eyes quickly shifting from her receptionist to me. "Vanessa! You're here!"

Echo scrambles to collect herself, her angry expression shifting into a welcoming smile. She's wearing a wide, leather band around her chest and a matching leather skirt, the traditional female shifter attire.

They call it their 'leathers,' and they're incredibly passionate about them.

All shifters have a red design on one of their thighs that depicts the animal they transform into, and Echo's is a bear. It fits her. The bears are known to be the loudest and most brutal of the shifters, and Echo's personality reflects that.

Above the animal design is their mate marking, but Echo's is covered by her skirt.

It's well-known what they look like, though. All shifters are born with a thick, white line on one of their upper thighs, and the marking curves over their pubic bone before traveling along the top of their intimate parts.

It turns black when they meet their mates, and the shifters are notoriously protective of them. They take matehood seriously, and their marks are reserved solely for their other half.

"I'm sorry I'm late," Echo says, hurrying to unlock her office door. "Have you been waiting long? I was meeting with Chev, and he was in a talkative mood."

I smile, hoping she can't see my nerves. "I understand. I haven't been waiting long."

I was supposed to meet Chev during my second interview, but something came up at the last minute and he couldn't attend. I'm okay with that. I've seen photos of Chev, and despite the hard work I've put into being comfortable around men, I'm still terrified of the shifter male. Everybody talks highly of him, and many see him as a hero, but I can't get past his size.

I much prefer small men, ones who look twiggy and unthreatening.

Chev is not that.

Echo opens her door and gestures for me to enter, and I quickly do so. Her office is just as bright as her reception area, and

I glance at her cluttered desk before sitting in one of the chairs in front of it.

"I have some documents I'd like to review with you," Echo explains, sitting behind her desk. "Afterward, I'll give you a tour of the building and show you to your office. We encourage all new hires to use their first week getting acclimated to the building and the rehabilitation facility they've been assigned to."

I nod, beyond happy to hear that. I was worried they'd load me immediately with work and deadlines.

"Sounds good," I say, straightening my spine. "I'm excited to get started."

I mean it, too. I'm passionate about the females, and working with Echo is a dream come true.

I thought my life ended the day I was purchased. The ogres did unspeakable things to me, and even when I was rescued and brought to the elven facility, I couldn't imagine a life for myself. I sat in my room, curled up in bed, waiting for the ogres to steal me back.

At one point, I was hospitalized and given a feeding tube, but I'm working hard not to be that woman anymore.

Echo walks me through her paperwork. I struggle to understand some of it, but she's patient when I have questions. Most of it seems straightforward, and I happily sign my name at the bottom of each page.

She makes copies for me.

"We're going to start you off in the demon realm, specifically Wrath," Echo says. She puts the copied paperwork into a folder and slides it across her desk. My hand shakes as I pull it into my lap.

Wrath? I frown.

Everybody knows the facility there is a joke, only placed so the shifters aren't accused of playing favorites. The King of Wrath was the demon who discovered the cure for the female decline, and he and his mates were the ones who kickstarted everything. There are hardly any females in their facility, and the Wrath Queen, Charlotte, already acts as the facility manager.

I'll have no work.

I want to make a difference, and that isn't going to happen in Wrath. I let out a slow exhale, trying and failing to hide my disappointment. This is a joke. I should've known they wouldn't put a rehabilitated female in a serious role.

They don't think I can handle it.

Echo places her hand over mine. "Is everything okay?"

Her palm is warm, and she brushes her thumb across my wrist in a comforting gesture.

I gulp, hesitating. I probably shouldn't tell her I'm disappointed. I don't want to sound ungrateful, even if I am, and I don't want to make a bad impression on my first day. This isn't what I hoped for, but it's better than nothing.

I moved out of my facility months ago, but the female community I now live in is boring. Ten communities have been built, and they're essentially a woman-only retirement home. I loved it for about three months, but there are only so many bottles of wine I can drink and shows I can watch. I need stimulation.

Echo squeezes my hand, and I let out a low sigh.

"Everybody says the facility in Wrath is small and empty." I hope this shows my concern without sounding whiny.

Echo nods, confirming my statement. "That's true," she says, "which makes it a great facility for learning. We start all new hires there, and once they've grown comfortable with the processes and work, we transfer them to a facility with more need."

Oh.

"I should've started with that," she continues, grimacing. "My apologies."

I relax, beyond relieved to hear that. Echo chuckles and pats my hand before pulling away and leaning back in her chair.

"Let me show you around," she says, standing. "Chev still wants to meet you, so don't be too surprised if he pops his head into your office sometime later today."

I lick my lips and rise, clutching my paperwork to my chest.

"I told him to wait until you're settled, but he's impatient," Echo continues with a roll of her eyes.

I'm not excited to meet Chev, but I can't turn him away. He oversees everything, and he's an active member of the organization. I'll have to face him at some point.

I'll do my best to limit our interactions, though.

Echo leads me out of her office and through reception. Both of my interviews were conducted here, and I'm excited to see the rest of the building.

Her office opens to a large, spacious room full of desks. I tighten my grip on my paperwork as I exit the quiet security of her reception area. I knew her office was in the heart of the building—it makes sense—and I try not to look too scared as I eye the men and women bustling around.

They look distracted, but many shoot me friendly smiles as they pass.

I think I'm going to puke.

"This is a secure building," Echo explains. "The doors are guarded, and the only portals are in Chev's and my offices. They're also guarded."

She gestures toward a pair of shifters strolling the room. They're men, and they're large—probably bears. They must be guards.

It's nice to know that not just anybody can enter the building. My nights are haunted by the ogres who owned me, and I still fear them finding me and stealing me back.

Echo walks into the room, and I wipe my sweaty palms on my jeans before following. Several shifters are working here, their leathers giving them away, but I spot a few elves and other breeds I don't recognize.

It's hard to tell what everybody is from only a glance, but the strength of the power they emit is suffocating. It's impossible not to notice when they walk past, and I wonder what they must think about having a weak nymph in their workspace.

I keep my eyes peeled for Chev or demons as Echo leads me around. I'd rather die than have to communicate or be alone with either of them, but I'm interested in seeing them in person. There are rumors that the King of Wrath and his mates are frequently spotted here.

He has three of them: an incubus, a fate, and a human.

I'd love to meet the human, Charlotte. She's the only female in the group and, along with Echo, she led the efforts to save us. She's an inspiration, and everybody in the elven facility I was in looked up to her.

I was so excited to meet Echo, and I'm pretty sure our entire first interview was spent with my jaw on the floor. It feels almost surreal to be surrounded by such influential people, let alone getting to work with them.

Echo turns down a hallway, and the foot traffic thins out.

"Your office is this way," she says.

I'm relieved it's out of the way, and I clasp my hands behind my back as she leads me down another corridor and eventually comes to a halt in front of a door. There are several lining the hallway, probably all offices.

My door is a dark wood, and a black number twelve is engraved in the center of it. I commit that number to memory.

Echo claps. "This is it!"

I smile, my pulse racing as I push open the door and step

inside. My office is small, barely fitting a desk and a filing cabinet, but it's perfect. There's a large window along the back wall, letting in so much sunlight, and I happily spin around and take it all in.

Echo said we're encouraged to make the space our own, and I very much intend to do so. I'm going to fill it with plants and posters. I'm not sure which posters I'll hang, but I enjoy the look of the human ones from before the decline. They were creative.

"The closest portal is the one in Chev's office," Echo says. "I'd recommend using that one when you need to travel." She peers into my doorway, a soft smile toying at the corners of her lips. "He's rarely here, so you shouldn't run into him too often."

I dip my chin, hoping my nervousness isn't too noticeable.

"Good to know. Thank you."

Echo nods. "Make yourself comfortable. I'll come and check on you in a few hours. The password to your laptop is on the sticky note there." She points to my desk. "And the files on the Wrath facility have already been downloaded."

I turn and glance at the laptop sitting on my desk. It's sleek, and I'm excited to use it.

"Do you have any questions?" Echo asks.

I shake my head, and she disappears. This is truly happening.

Chapter Two

VANESSA

I PINCH MY nose, more than a little overwhelmed.

I've been working here for almost three full days now, and I'm starting to worry the files I'm expected to review are endless. I've been staring at my laptop for hours, trying and failing to absorb every little piece of information I can find about the Wrath facility. I failed to realize just how many files I'd have to familiarize myself with, and it's intense.

I know I'm not expected to get through everything right away, but I'd still like to make a good dent before the week ends. I want to impress—especially before I leave for Wrath tonight. I could commute here from my new placement in Wrath, but most facility managers choose to live and work out of the realm of their placement. It makes sense since I'll be spending most of my time there. The portals are easy enough to use, but they take a lot of energy to operate.

It's not as if I'm unfamiliar with living on facility land, and I admittedly enjoy the security and safety that being there offers. It's the one good thing about being placed in Wrath. I know I'll be safe.

I tap my foot against the ground as I click through the files on my computer. I find one discussing meal plans, and I rest my chin in my palm as I scan it. I try to remain focused, but my eyes continually flicker toward the door.

Chev hasn't visited me yet, but I know it's inevitable.

I want to get this introduction over with, and not knowing exactly when he's coming is driving me insane. Every time I get in the groove of things, I hear a sound in the hallway and clam up.

I'd much rather have a set time for his visit, but I know better than to complain about how he runs his company. If Chev wants to be a pop-in kind of guy, I'm not really in a place to ask him to change.

At this point, though, I'm unsure if he's even coming. The day is almost over.

I don't want to do this again tomorrow. Although maybe if I'm lucky, he'll never stop by. I intend to begin working out of the Wrath facility next week, so he's running out of time to make his introduction. I doubt he ever visits the Wrath facility, so once I'm there, I'll be free of him.

That, admittedly, sounds nice.

I sigh, moving on to my next file.

Two more hours, and I'll be heading to Wrath. I'd be lying if I said I weren't nervous, but I think I'm equal parts excited. My things should've been brought over today, and Echo told me there'll be somebody waiting to show me my new home when I arrive.

I'm sad to be leaving the friends I've made in my small community, but I'll have the weekends to visit them.

My computer screen dims. I frown, confused as I try to figure out what's happening. Technology isn't a luxury the ogres provided, and while I learned the basics from the trade programs I participated in, I received little to no instruction on troubleshooting.

The screen is still readable despite being dim, and I grin proudly when I notice the red power indicator. It says my computer is low on charge, and I fiddle with the plug shoved into the side of the device before following the cable to the outlet.

It's not plugged into the wall.

If being a facility manager doesn't work out, I've got a career in technology I can push toward. The elves have several technological-focused trade programs in their realms, and I've heard they're relatively easy to get into.

I crawl under my desk and stick the plug into the outlet, proud of my problem-solving. I'm careful not to shock myself, constantly wary after an incident a few years ago. I tried plugging something in while still touching the metal prong, and my entire arm went numb.

I spent an hour entirely convinced I was going to lose it.

The computer beeps, signaling it's now charging, and I knock my knuckles against the floor with a triumphant smirk. Today's a good day.

My self-victory dies as I hear my office door open, the creak loud. My pulse skyrockets, and I take a second to calm down before moving. It's probably just Echo coming to check in on me. She does so once or twice a day.

"Vanessa?"

I freeze, my muscles tensing. The voice is low and masculine, and it sends unwanted shivers down my spine. I recognize it from the news programs, and I clench my fists as I work up the courage to stand and confront Chev.

He saved the females. He's a good guy, and he's safe.

It's not uncommon for rescued females to grow overwhelmed and hide, and I don't want him to think that's what I'm doing. I'm scared, yes, but I refuse to let my fear rule my life. I've earned this job, and I've worked hard to overcome my fears.

Chev's footfalls sound heavy as he enters my office.

I hear only three steps, which I hope still has him at a reasonable distance from my desk. I know I can't hide from men forever, but being in an enclosed, private space with one still pushes the limits of what I can handle.

The longer I hide under here, the worse it'll appear, though. Clenching my jaw, I crawl out from under my desk and stand. *Oh. No.* My heart stops, and I place a hand over my chest as I stare at the man before me.

Chev's just as large as I feared, and he's a spitting image of Echo, with his curly, dark hair and vibrant-green eyes. He's wearing his leathers, and every exposed muscle on his body grows rigid as he looks at me.

His eyes dart along my face before lowering to my feet and bouncing back up. I'm horrified, unable to move.

Chev blinks, a look of complete shock taking over his features before his lips spread into a genuine smile. I don't return it. I was removed from the nymph lands when I was a child, but I don't need the stories of my people to recognize the pulsating claim within me.

It calls to Chev, making me feel like a rubber band pulled too tightly.

He's my mate, and judging by the look on his face, he knows it.

"Vanessa?" His use of my name has shifted from a worry-filled question to a deep purr, and I imagine if I weren't so fucking uncomfortable, I'd enjoy it.

He steps forward. I step back.

We do this again.

And again.

Chev clears his throat. "My mate."

He doesn't seem to recognize my discomfort, and I hold out my hands as I hurry to the other side of the room. I'm not interested in having a mate. I have no desire for intimacy, love, or anything that comes with a mate bond. I want to be independent, free of ever needing a man again.

I gasp, the sound ragged as it leaves my throat. "No."

Chev stills, his head cocking to the side as he stares at my palms. His chest expands as he breathes, and I'm disgusted as he openly scans my figure. I purposefully wear modest clothing, but his gaze makes me feel naked.

I hate how he looks at me, evaluating my body with such open excitement. I curl in on myself, not wanting his eyes—or any part of him—on me.

"You're my mate," Chev says.

I shake my head, denying it. "No, I'm not."

"Yes, you are," he insists. He grabs the front of his leathers and yanks them up, exposing himself. "Look!"

I scramble backward, my shoulder slamming into the wall. *What's he doing?* He takes a hold of himself, and I'm filled with horror.

I'm going to vomit. I knew this was too good to be true. When I was first rescued, I thought it was a cruel joke. The ogres loved to do that, loved to make us believe things were getting better just so they could watch our bodies and minds break at their hands once more.

It was a cruel form of torture. You eventually learn not to get your hopes up, and I was stupid to do so here. The shifters may have removed us from our owners, but at the end of the day, males are males. They only have one thing on their mind, one goal, and Chev is showing me his.

"No, no! Not that!" Chev sounds panicked. He shoves his length to the side with enough force that he winces, hiding it from my view as he points to the mate mark next to it.

His is a light gray.

"You're my mate, Vanessa," he says. "I can feel it, and you've darkened my mark."

I turn away, watching out of the corner of my eyes as he finally lowers his skirt. Men exposing themselves to me is nothing new, and it always ends the same way. I want to hurt him.

The way Chev stalks toward me is proof enough of his intentions. The shifters have always placed too much importance on their mate bonds, and while their obsession is cute from a distance, I just know it's absolutely suffocating from the inside.

I don't want a mate. I don't want a male.

"Leave," I say, struggling to work up the courage to speak. "I don't want this."

The therapists inside the facilities always say we're entitled to speak our minds. If we don't want a man, we have every right to say so. We're not property, and they can't force us. Not anymore.

"No." Chev doesn't hesitate to reject my request. "You're my mate."

My heart is beating so fast, it's a miracle I'm still standing. I scan the room, hoping to find a weapon to defend myself with. I refuse to become an abused, kept female again. I worked hard to overcome it, and I won't let Chev take my freedom from me.

"I am your nothing," I insist, subtly inching toward the office door. "I am not your mate."

Shifter males are territorial, but I bet Echo can help me. Her office is on the other side of the building, but I'm willing to bet I'm faster than Chev. He's large and strong, which doesn't always correlate to fast.

I need a head start, and what lies underneath his leathers is the perfect target.

Chev takes a cautious step in my direction, his shoulders

hunched forward in a clear attempt to appear small. I muster every bit of courage I have as I let him approach.

He coos. "It's okay, my mate. I'm not going to hurt you."

He holds out his arms, and the second I feel them begin to close around me, I raise my knee and slam it as hard as I can between his legs.

Chev groans and folds in on himself, and I waste no time darting toward the door. I want to draw attention to us, and I scream as I sprint down the long hallway. I was happy with the seclusion of my office, but now I wish it were in a busier area.

Loud footsteps thunder behind me, encouraging me to pick up my pace as I hear Chev closing the gap. He's faster than I thought he'd be.

I open my mouth to let out another scream, but the noise is stolen from my throat as a heavy arm wraps around my midsection and pulls me back against a hard chest. My heels drag against the floor, and I scratch at Chev's bicep as he forces me into my office.

I thrash and try to pry him off, tears streaming down my cheeks as I struggle to breathe. Chev releases me the second we're back inside my office, and I flatten myself against the farthest wall as he locks the door. Why's he doing this?

"Fuck," Chev says, running his hands through his hair. "Fuck!"

He turns and reopens the door a second later. I'm still flattened against the wall, too frantic to feel relieved, as he storms out of the room. He slams the door shut behind him, and my knees wobble as I rush toward it.

Is he still out there?

I place my ear against the door, listening for any sounds of life. My ears aren't nearly as good as that of the strong breeds, but I can hear heartbeats from close proximity. There's nothing but silence, but it doesn't calm me.

I doubt Chev will be gone for long. This job isn't worth my freedom, and I need to disappear before he returns. There aren't many places for females to escape, but I've heard rumors of lands where shifters don't have jurisdiction.

The door handle doesn't budge when I try to pull it open, and after three consecutive attempts, I realize it's locked. Chev locked me in here? How? The lock is on *my* side of the door.

I kick at the wood, not caring that the action makes my toes sting. I'm faintly aware that I'm hyperventilating as I yank at the door repeatedly, trying and failing to break the lock.

Why would he trap me in here? It's probably because he knows I'm going to run.

What if he tries to kidnap me, forcing me into some obscure, hidden area within the shifter lands? It'd be easy for him to do. Chev's the leader, and he has nobody to answer to. There's nobody to stop him.

Chapter Three

VANESSA

I IGNORE THE blisters forming along my palm as I yank at my office door, my desperation to leave growing by the second.

My panic is all-consuming, and I struggle to regulate my breathing as I continue pulling at the knob. Chev probably wedged something against the door, preventing it from opening, and I grimace as I give another unfruitful yank. I have no idea how long I've been locked inside here, probably no longer than five minutes, and I let out a frustrated shout as I kick the wood.

It hurts my foot.

"Help!" I scream.

Nobody answers, and I grimace before trying again.

A wiser person probably would've accepted that nobody was around to hear them, but I refuse to give up. It's only a matter of time before somebody walks down the hallway and hears my angry shouts.

The shifters really chose the thickest wood money could buy, so I'm sure my screams aren't traveling far.

I scan the room for something I can use to break the door. I tried doing it with my fists, but all that's earned me is a sore wrist and bruised knuckles. My palms are sweaty and sticky as I pull open my dresser drawers and look for something, anything, I can use.

This room is empty, and I doubt the laptop or charging plug I've been given will be of any help.

Wait. I can message Echo.

My computer chair tips over with the force I use to shove it out of the way. It takes me three tries to unlock my computer, my shaky hands and frazzled mind causing me to type my password in wrong the first two times. I tap my foot impatiently against the floor as I navigate my way to my messages, angry with both myself and the computer for its slower-than-instant speed.

I think I might be hyperventilating again, and I freeze when I hear something in the hallway. Footfalls. Two pairs of them.

I'm back at the door a second later, banging against it with a scream. It's about time somebody made their way here. I grow louder when the feet stop just outside my office door, and I listen carefully to the sound of something heavy being slid aside.

I knew Chev propped something up against the door.

It's pushed open, and my lips curl into a relieved smile before I see who's standing in the hallway. Chev is back, and he's not alone. The large man beside him has entirely black eyes and hair, and I immediately recognize him from the news.

He's a demon, the King of Wrath. Aziel.

I step back into the room, my heart dropping. What are they doing here?

Aziel looks me up and down as Chev did earlier, but I'm happy to note there's no sexual nature to his gaze. If anything, he looks bored, which I take as a good sign. I like when men aren't happy with what they see. It means they'll leave me alone.

"Who's this?" he asks, turning to Chev.

I curl my fingers around the fabric of my shirt, my eyes

darting nervously between the two men. Why did Chev bring Aziel here? Does Chev know I'm being placed at the Wrath facility?

I hope not. I don't want him to know anything about me.

Chev shifts his weight from foot to foot. "This is Vanessa," he says. His tone is soft, regretful even, but I know it's a lie. "She's my mate."

I don't want him. I don't want a mate.

Chev's muscles flex, and his hands fidget at his sides. He wants to touch me, grab me, and it's taking everything in him not to do so. I wonder what's stopping him. He's stronger than I am. We both know it, and I know shifters feel ownership over their mates.

It's probably because of Mammon. The Queen of Greed has been trying to turn the elves and other blessed breeds against the shifters and demons. She's publicly spoken out against them since the demon war, and if she catches wind of Chev forcing himself on a female, she'll have all the ammunition she needs.

She wants to absorb Wrath and the shifter lands, forcing Aziel and Chev to submit to her. That's probably the only thing holding Chev back.

He may pretend to be a good man, but at the end of the day, he's part animal. He runs on instinct, and that instinct is no doubt telling him to take me.

Something inside me whispers something similar, whispers for me to take him, but it's easy to ignore. My mind has been broken and reformed what feels like a million times, and I'm good at denying my wants.

Aziel looks confused, his eyebrow furrowing as he looks between my red, splotchy face and Chev's nervous one. The shifter tries to make eye contact with me, but I refuse to give it.

That's only going to encourage him.

"Oh," Aziel says, his words slow as he tries to read the room. "Congratulations?"

I struggle to find my voice, my fear making it impossible to think. Going silent is a defense mechanism, and no amount of intense therapy has been able to break me from the habit. Instead, I shake my head. My blonde hair whips around my face, and a low whine slips from Chev's throat.

The noise calls to me, the repressed part of my soul desperate for him, but I ignore it.

I don't want a mate.

"She denies me," Chev says.

Aziel looks shocked. "She smells like a blessed breed. Does she not feel the bond?"

He steps toward me, but he freezes when I scurry back. It's the same dance I did with Chev, but Aziel doesn't seem particularly keen to play as he returns to his original position by the door. He already has a full harem with his three mates, and I can tell he's not interested in me. It makes me happy.

"I accidently uncovered my penis," Chev whispers. He sounds ashamed. I don't believe it. "I was too excited, and I scared her."

Unwanted tears fill my eyes. For a brief moment, I thought he intended to rape me. I'm still not entirely convinced that he doesn't.

Chev whines again. My body recognizes it and urges me to comfort him, but I refuse. I've mindlessly followed my instincts one too many times, trusting men because they seemed nice and I was desperate for a friendship. Some stupid bond isn't going to make a fool of me.

"Is this what you brought me here for?" Aziel asks.

Chev nods. "Yes."

Aziel straightens his spine and turns toward Chev. He looks pissed, and I step back as the full strength of his power reaches me. It makes me want to drop to my knees and submit, but I refuse. The therapists say we aren't supposed to do that anymore.

"You said this was an emergency," Aziel seethes. "You physically took my child out of my arms and demanded I bring you back here."

Chev doesn't seem to care about the anger pouring from the Wrath as he grunts and wildly gestures in my direction. I eye the distance between them and the door.

I doubt I could make it past Chev, let alone Aziel. The demons can teleport, making my speed useless. He can catch me in a heartbeat, even if I have a decent head start.

"This *is* an emergency, Aziel," Chev argues. "I've found my mate, and she's scared of me."

My head pounds. I don't like when men talk about me like I'm not here—like I'm some object and not a real person.

Aziel runs a hand through his hair. "This is *not* an emergency."

He turns toward me. I flinch, staring at the milky spit-up on his shoulder so I don't have to look into his angry eyes.

"You're expected to arrive at my facility in a few hours, aren't you?" he asks.

I hesitate before giving a jerky nod.

Aziel frowns. "Well, I suppose I can take you now."

He holds out his arm. I don't move.

"Chev can't teleport, and I'll let the portal operators know not to let him enter the facility," he says. "I'll speak with Echo tonight and let her know the situation. I imagine she'll want to talk with you."

There's no reason for me to believe Aziel. I know that, but I still find myself inching forward. He's mated to Charlotte, the woman who spearheaded this entire thing, and I'd like to believe that means something.

Plus, I'm desperate to get away from Chev.

The shifter looks angry, his arms crossed over his chest as the vein in his forehead pulsates. The infuriating part of my soul that recognizes him as my mate urges me to remain by his side, but I won't give in to it.

I don't trust Aziel, but I don't have many other options right now. I'd rather go with him than stay here with Chev.

Chev steps between Aziel and me, his wide stance screaming trouble. Aziel doesn't seem concerned, but he's not in a position to be. The shifter is no threat to him, not like he is to me.

"Vanessa," Chev says. "I'm so sorry I scared you. I was excited to show you my mark, but I know I shouldn't have come on so strongly. Can we talk? Please? Aziel can stay in the room."

A hopeful smile spreads over his lips, but it falls when I shake my head.

Even if he's being genuine, it doesn't change the fact that I want nothing to do with him. I don't trust males, and I especially don't trust ones who think they have some fated ownership over me.

"I don't believe in mates," I say.

Chev blinks, cocking his head to the side. The words don't seem to process in his head, and I can practically see the gears turning as he tries to make sense of my statement.

"I'm aware mates exist, and I'm aware you're mine, but I don't want one," I explain. "I have no interest in males—no interest in you." Chev winces. I continue. "I don't want to see you again."

I wonder if Aziel can smell my fear, and I take a tiny step away just in case. I'm uninterested in provoking him with my negative emotions. I've heard rumors that he's calmed considerably since finding his mates, but you can never be too careful.

Chev clears his throat before shaking his head, denying my words.

Aziel takes this as his cue to leave, the man disappearing into thin air. Chev doesn't seem to notice he's gone, but I do. Aziel was the only form of protection I had against Chev.

My hands begin to shake, and I hide them behind my back as I square my shoulders and try to make myself as big as possible. Nymphs aren't skilled fighters, our talents revolving more around nature and creating life, but I'll do my best.

Chev can't teleport, so if he wants to take me out of here, he'll have to bring me to a portal. There are only two on this level, and guards surround both. I'll scream for help the moment we're within hearing distance.

I won't be taken without a fight.

I barely have time to react to Chev's widening eyes, his face morphing into that of his animal just as a hand lands on my shoulder and the world around me vanishes. The touch is firm, but it's quickly pushed to the back of my mind as my knees buckle and another arm wraps around my waist to keep me from tumbling over.

I'm vaguely aware I'm flailing as my stomach flips, and I clutch the arm supporting me. What's happening? My eyes see nothing, but when the world around me spins and begins to realign, I shut them so I don't get sick.

I'm being teleported.

Chapter Four

VANESSA

THE WORLD MATERIALIZES, and I brush off the arm supporting me before planting my hands on my knees. I'm dizzy, and I squeeze my eyes shut as I struggle to wrap my mind around what's just happened.

Aziel steps away from me, giving me plenty of space. I appreciate it.

"Are you all right?" he asks.

I don't immediately respond. Is he referring to my dizziness or my encounter with Chev? Either way, my honest answer is *no*. I'm about as far from all right as one can get.

"Put Chev on the block list," Aziel says. He's not speaking to me.

My legs are shaking, and I push off my thighs and force myself to stand up straight. I'm in a hallway surrounded by light-blue walls, the color immediately recognizable. All rehabilitation facilities have similar décor.

"Am I in Wrath?" I ask.

Aziel nods, and I shift my attention to the guard he just spoke to. It's a demon, that much is evident by his black eyes and long limbs. Demons have distinct features, and this guard ticks all the boxes.

"If he tries coming through the portal, escort him out immediately," Aziel continues to say.

The man nods, his hair bouncing around his head. "Yes, sir."

He spins and leaves, probably to inform the other guards. I stare at his back as I work up the courage to face Aziel. I haven't been touched by a man in years, and even though I know Aziel was only trying to help, I want to scrub the skin he came in contact with.

I just barely resist the urge to scratch at it as I finally turn toward Aziel.

Demons typically exude power, a sickening scent that overpowers senses and urges weaker beings to submit, but Aziel holds his in. It's surprising. Demons place a lot of importance and self-worth on the power they emit.

Aziel subtly wipes his hand on his pant leg, and I can't help but notice it's the same hand he touched me with. I don't take offense. If anything, I find it comforting. He's disgusted to have come in contact with me, and that's all I ever want from men.

I swallow past the lump in my throat, and Aziel pushes his hair out of his face with a quiet sigh. I'm pretty sure he's staring at me, but it's hard to tell when his eyes are entirely black. I've never seen a demon in the flesh, and it's quite unnerving.

My mind is still fuzzy from the teleporting, but it's getting better with each passing second.

"We're happy to have you here," Aziel says. "Your things were brought over this afternoon, and your office should have everything you need."

I open my mouth, about to say something, before snapping my jaw shut with a quiet click. I don't know what to say. I don't even know if I still want this job. All I want to do right now is curl up in a small ball in a spot where Chev can't find me.

He has access to the entire rehabilitation network, including the facilities and the files. He's probably reading about me right now, learning my history with the ogres and my years since I was rescued. The thought makes me sick. I don't want him to know anything about me, especially the horrid details of my abuse.

Aziel gestures for me to follow him.

"Silas was going to give you a tour, but we're already here, so I might as well do it," he says.

Silas? It takes me a second to connect the dots. I'm not familiar with Aziel's harem, but I'm pretty sure Silas is one of his mates. He's a demon, a fate, but I don't know anything else about him.

"I'll alert Echo of the issue once we're finished," Aziel continues. "She'll help keep Chev away from you."

Hearing that is nothing short of sweet relief.

Aziel begins walking down the hallway, and despite my hesitation, I find myself quickly following him. The corridor he teleported us to is small and empty, but we almost immediately turn into a busier one.

Several females mill about.

There are not nearly as many as I'm accustomed to seeing in the facility where I was rehabilitated. That place was jam-packed—still is—but this facility is bare bones.

"Chev is a good man," Aziel says. "But he made a mistake today, and I assure you he'll be punished for it."

He smoothly avoids two females who come scampering down the hall toward us. They eye him, their gazes heavy, but Aziel doesn't spare them a second glance. I like the way he ignores women. It's rare to see, and it's comforting. I don't believe demons have fated mates the way shifters and nymphs do, but he acts as loyal as one.

I should ask him to bring me home—back to the female community I've been living in for the past several months. I wanted this job so badly, but I'm not sure it's worth it if it means being vulnerable to Chev. I can hide in Wrath most of the time, but there will be days when I need to visit the headquarters. He'll be there, and I doubt he'll leave me alone.

I don't do it, though. That would be letting Chev win. I won't let one male ruin what I've worked so hard to achieve.

I'll push Chev out of my mind and continue as if I never met him. He'll eventually have to accept it, and I'm sure with his title and importance, he'll be able to quickly find another woman to whom he can give his affection.

Yes. That's precisely what I'll do.

Aziel doesn't try to make any further conversation. He's curt but polite as he gives me a tour of the facility, and I appreciate it. He'll occasionally pause to introduce me to a staff member, but the introductions are quick.

Everybody is kind, and my anxiety lessens with each minute I spend here.

"This will be your office," Aziel says, coming to a halt in the middle of a hallway. He pushes open the thick, wooden door on our left, and I lean around him to peer inside. The space is fully furnished, and I can't help but wince as I take it in.

Aziel gestures to the giant bouquets covering almost every inch of the room. "Charlie insisted on the flowers. She read that nymphs enjoy nature."

It's a lot, and I plaster a weak smile on my lips. Nymphs love nature, but we tend to prefer it in its natural state. Cutting flowers is a borderline sacrilegious action, but there's no way Charlotte could've known that.

"Will you thank her for me?" I ask.

If I weren't so out of sorts, this many cut flowers would likely bring me to tears. I do a good job holding back my discomfort, though. At least, I think I do. Aziel sucks his cheeks into his mouth as he evaluates my reaction, and after a moment, he slides his gaze to the vases.

"I'll tell her no more flowers," he says.

I open my mouth to argue, not wanting him to think I'm ungrateful, but his back is to me before I get the opportunity.

"I'll show you to your home and leave you to get settled," he says. "It's a bit of a walk."

His pace is fast, and I struggle to keep up. Is Aziel always this curt? I don't dislike it, but it's not the most welcoming. I'm beginning to wish I would've gotten my tour from Silas, after all.

I trail my fingers along the walls, letting the emotions they hold fill me. My nymph abilities are weak, but I can still feel the history that lives in the things I touch. It only works when the stories are strong and hold powerful emotions, which these walls most definitely do.

Flashes of sorrow and anger are the first to fill my body, but they're almost immediately replaced by curiosity and excitement. These are the most recent emotions, which is encouraging. Good things are happening here.

Thoughts of Chev try to force themselves into my mind, but I refuse to indulge. I can't let myself, at least not now.

"Are you sure Chev won't be allowed access?" I ask.

I mentally curse myself the second the words slip from my lips. I've heard the rumors about Chev and Aziel. They're close, the two almost always spotted together. I've also heard Aziel is one of the few non-shifters who has access to Chev's lands, the demon allowed to enter and exit as he pleases.

Aziel slows before coming to a halt and turning toward me. His face is blank, making it nearly impossible to read his emotions.

"Chev will be banned from using the portal within this facility and any in the immediate area," Aziel says, his blank expression shifting into one that looks almost like pity. "Chev is a good friend, but I won't compromise your comfort for his. He wouldn't do it for me."

I nod.

I don't want to be a burden, but I can't work here if it means Chev has unrestricted access to me. The mate bond is sacred to shifters, and I'm sure he's been waiting a long time to find me, but I'm not interested in any sort of romantic relationship.

I don't see that changing, either.

I want to spend the remainder of my life alone, free to make decisions and be my own person. Never again will I allow myself to be at the mercy of a man, and that's precisely what a mate bond is.

Alpha males are dominant, and Chev is no different. There's a slight possibility I'd consider him if he were a mild-tempered animal, like a deer, but he couldn't be further from that. His bear will want to control and own me, and that's something I'll never be in a place to give.

My head aches the more I think about it.

Aziel leads me to the back entrance of the facility, and I wince as he pushes open the doors. Sweltering heat hits me, the temperature in Wrath warmer than it has any business being. I've never been a fan of the heat, but I'm excited to visit the lava fields.

The climate inside Wrath is unique, and Aziel's land houses some of the largest lava fields in existence. Nymphs are tied to nature, and I'm interested to see if I feel an affinity toward lava the same way I do with woodlands.

Aziel guides me away from the facility and down a worn path leading into the woods. I thought my housing was on the facility property.

"This land is safe," Aziel says, seemingly sensing my nerves. "The facility is gated, and the lands are monitored."

I suck my lips into my mouth, not responding. It's comforting to know the house is within the gated area, and I want to see it and understand precisely how far it is from the facility before making any judgments.

After only three minutes of walking, I'm sweating. I wipe my forehead, mentally cursing the punishing sun. Aziel huffs and wipes at his own face, which is interesting. I thought he'd be all for the warmth.

We continue forward, and I admire the large trees lining the small path. It's truly beautiful here, and I shut my eyes as I let the energy of the woods fill me. I love it.

After five minutes, I finally spot a building. It's a large, two-story brick house, complete with a wooden porch and giant windows. I stare with a slackened jaw as we approach it. Is this where I'm meant to stay? I assumed I'd get placed in a small building, maybe even a studio. This is an entire house.

I quicken my pace, eager to see more.

"Guards are assigned within hearing distance," Aziel says. "They won't hear anything said at a conversational tone, but any yelling will alert them."

That's a comfort.

Aziel gestures to a small shed to the left of the house. "There's a golf cart you can use to travel to and from the facility. Please don't run over any guards. They're not targets, and they will get angry."

Of course they aren't. Is somebody using the golf carts that way? What even is a golf cart? I've gathered that it's some sort of vehicle, and I struggle to hold back a giddy smile. I've never driven before, but it's always been something I'm interested in.

I hope it goes fast.

We walk up the porch steps.

"A shadow has been assigned to keep the house clean and the kitchen stocked," Aziel says. "She's quiet, and she'll be in and out while you're at work."

Aziel hums and looks toward the sky. I stare at the front door, still amazed this is where I'm to be staying. It makes the option of quitting and hiding away significantly less appealing. I want to live here.

I clear my throat. "Thank you for all of this."

Aziel nods before checking the time. The way his eyes widen is borderline comical.

"Fuck," he huffs. "I'm late to meet with Gray." I'm pretty sure Gray is his incubus mate. "I need to go, but I'll stop by in a few days to see how you're adjusting."

Aziel vanishes a second later, his body disappearing into thin air.

I stare at the spot where he was just standing before turning back to the house. The large front door entices me, and I drag my fingers through my hair as I stare at it. This day hasn't gone as planned, and I squeeze my eyes shut as thoughts of Chev threaten to work their way to the forefront of my mind.

I can't think about him or our bond.

I fight to keep my mind clear as I push open the front door and step inside the house.

The décor is minimal, and I eye the potted plant in the entryway before closing the door behind me. The interior is open, and I can see the kitchen and living room from where I stand. There is no formal dining space, but that's fine by me.

It's not like I plan to host any dinner parties.

The furniture is cozy. There's a gray couch large enough to sprawl on, and I'm pleased to see a full, floor-to-ceiling bookshelf and a TV. To the left is a stairwell, and I cross my arms over my chest as I move to the second level of the house.

On the left is a bathroom, the sink visible from where I stand, and I peek in before approaching the closed door on the right. It's made of thick wood, and I hesitate before pushing it open.

It leads to a bedroom, and I stare in awe at the king-sized bed in the center of the room. I've never slept in a bed larger than a twin, and I smile as I run my hand over the light-green silk sheets. My bags are on the floor, both open and empty. My things must have been put away for me.

I could get used to this.

There's a private bathroom inside, and I eye the bathtub and large vanity. This place is fantastic. I've always loved bathroom products, and I can't wait to begin my collection.

Through the bathroom is a walk-in closet, my things already unpacked and hung up inside.

I do another lap of the house before collapsing on the downstairs couch.

My thoughts threaten to return to Chev, and I turn on the TV to distract myself. I'm only thinking about him because of the bond, but I know that with time and distance, I'll be able to push him entirely out of my mind.

If there's anything I'm good at, it's avoiding my problems and pretending they don't exist. My dilemma with Chev will be no different.

Chapter Five

VANESSA

I DON'T THINK I've ever moved so quickly before, and I pray I don't trip as I round the tight corner that leads to my office. I take the turn a bit wide and barely avoid running into a guard, but he's a demon and jumps out of the way well before my reflexes have me adjusting my steps.

"Sorry!" I say, continuing forward.

He probably thinks I'm weak and clumsy, which, while accurate, isn't exactly the perception I want the guards to have of me. Either way, it's a problem to worry about another day.

I'm running late.

It's been a long day, and while I love it when the women stop me in the hallway to talk, sometimes it makes me painfully late.

Another guard steps out of my way, already laughing. "Vanessa's in turbo mode today!"

Todd is one of the only guards I've grown to enjoy being around during the two weeks I've been working out of the Wrath facility, but even he isn't going to slow me down. Not today.

I ignore his joke, desperate to get to my office before Echo does.

Another guard offers a smile as I pass by. I've met everybody who works here at this point, and they're all friendly. I'm making a genuine effort to learn every face and name in the facility, and I think the females appreciate that I've scheduled one-on-one time with each of them.

Facility managers usually hold group sessions, but I want to provide an environment for women to voice their concerns more intimately. My office is always open, and having individual meetings shows that I genuinely care. I'm not just in this for the paycheck.

I've already got a notebook full of ideas and improvements we can make, and thankfully, most are small and easily doable. The females here don't want much, but I believe the things they feel are lacking are reasonable to get for them.

I just hope Aziel will, too.

He pops in for a minute or two most days, usually just to make sure the place hasn't burned down, but there hasn't been time to sit down and discuss the specifics of what I'd like to do. I had to go through his assistant to get a monthly check-in penciled into his calendar, but that's not for another week.

Even then, it's only for fifteen minutes.

That will be a point in and of itself to discuss. If we want to make timely decisions, I need him to dedicate more time to the facility—or hire somebody who can.

From what I understand, this was originally Charlotte's job, but the rumor floating around Wrath is that Aziel and another one of her males are refusing to let her work. Everybody's quiet about it, but it seems this happens every time she falls pregnant.

I'm not too fond of it, but I'm doing my best not to judge. I would never be happy in a relationship where my significant other controlled my life so completely, but to each their own. If she wants to be an incubator, that's her prerogative.

That doesn't change the fact that Aziel is too busy to be doing this, though, and we need a dedicated person to oversee the facility. There's only so much I can do, and there's not enough time to sit around and wait for Aziel to approve my proposed changes.

I just need to find a way to express this without sounding rude.

Aziel seems reasonable, but my fear of men makes speaking on sensitive topics like this hard. A voice in my head tells me he'll punish and hurt me for making him angry, and it's nearly impossible to ignore sometimes.

I push open my office door, grimacing when I see Echo sitting in the chair opposite my desk. She's doing something on her phone, but I don't look at the screen.

"I'm sorry I'm late," I say, stepping into the room.

"It's not a problem." Echo puts her phone away. "How are you feeling? I know this has been a hard few weeks for you."

I shrug, not sure what to say. Echo's been beyond patient with me, and she's gone out of her way to keep me and Chev apart. Aziel's remained true to his promise and Chev hasn't been allowed to step foot on the property, and Echo's been coming to Wrath to meet with me instead of making me come to the headquarters.

I was finally beginning to move past everything with Chev when he popped up on the TV two nights ago, his damn face restarting all the progress I'd made. I can't get his image out of my head, and he's all I can think about when I lie awake at night.

Word has spread that he's found his mate, but nobody knows it's me. They also know she's a rehabilitated female and he scared her away, and it's getting a lot of press. Half the people hate him for having been rough with his mate, and the other half couldn't care less. They think it was a misunderstanding and his mate should forgive him.

They think I'm a bitch for turning down the almighty Chev.

I disagree.

Mammon has even taken it upon herself to issue a statement. She and her followers are calling Chev names I feel uncomfortable repeating.

It makes me feel bad for him, which isn't an emotion I want to have. Pity is dangerous, and this distance between us has been good. I don't think Chev is a bad person, and I'm able to recognize that his actions during our meeting were motivated by panic and fear.

He wasn't trying to show me his penis when he lifted his leathers, and he didn't even seem to realize it was out until he saw my fear. He was overwhelmed and frantic, and I don't think he deserves to be persecuted so intensely for it.

I don't know how the details of our encounter got out. I sure haven't told anybody, and I highly doubt Aziel or Chev would. If I weren't so afraid of being named, I'd do my best to correct the news outlets that speak so poorly about him.

My belief in the rehabilitation system is unwavering, and I don't want this unfortunate event to hinder all the fantastic work the shifters have been doing. They've saved the lives of millions of females, mine included, and it's shocking how easily the news channels have turned against them.

Mammon must have significant connections.

"I'm feeling okay," I tell Echo, finally answering her question. "I'm adjusting."

I'm painfully aware that Chev is her brother and anything I say to her may get back to him. I need to be careful with how much information I share.

My fingers twitch with the urge to check my phone and look up the most recent articles written about Chev. It's hard to ignore his existence when his face and name are plastered everywhere, and my self-control is proving to be nonexistent.

I found myself looking at photos of him while I was in bed last night, and I'm disgusted with the direction my thoughts took me. I haven't felt arousal in years, but the mere images of him had me clenching my thighs with need.

I even caught myself trailing my fingers along my legs, an action I'm horrified about. Distance is supposed to help me forget Chev, not make me fantasize about his touch and body.

"I appreciate you checking in," I tell Echo. "I've learned a lot these past two weeks, and everybody here has been kind."

Echo smiles, looking pleased. "I'm thrilled to hear that."

I wonder what she thinks about this whole Chev situation, but I highly doubt she'd give me an honest answer. Echo is painfully diplomatic.

I should consider scheduling an appointment with my therapist. I thought I could handle this on my own, but I fear I'm beginning to spiral. Every thought somehow revolves back to Chev, and it's only getting worse.

I haven't seen my therapist in months. I stopped going shortly after moving to the female community. I didn't want to use up resources others need so much more than I do. There are only so many trained trauma professionals around, and with the sudden influx of females, they're stretched thin.

I know my therapist will make time for me if I need it, but I'm hoping I can avoid it for a bit longer. The shifters keep records of everything, and I'm sure Chev and Echo are closely monitoring me. I don't want them to see I've contacted my therapist and think I can't handle my job.

"And you're getting along well with Aziel?" Echo asks. "I know he can be a bit…particular."

I shrug. "He's fine. Busy, but fine."

Echo doesn't look surprised to hear that. I'm sure it's not the first time it's been commented on, and I doubt it'll be the last.

"Good." Echo brings her hands together in a quiet clap. "Was there anything you wish to discuss with me? I have nothing pressing, so I'm all ears."

I shake my head. "Nope. Everything is good here."

Echo pauses, giving me a moment to change my mind, before standing. Her visits are always brief, probably because of how busy she is. I doubt she meets with all the facility managers like this, and I'm sure I'm getting special treatment because of my connection with her brother.

"I'll be off, then," she says.

"It was great seeing you." I rise and walk her to the door. "Thanks for stopping by."

She leaves, and I rush to eat lunch before my next meeting. There have been some concerns with the guards' proximity to the bathrooms, which is a problem I can fix without Aziel's permission.

The women want the guards to stand farther down the hallway, which is an easy solution. I paid a visit to the particular bathroom earlier today, and I must admit the guards stand a bit too close for comfort.

I'm sure they can hear everything happening inside the toilets, which is precisely what the females would like to prevent. Nobody wants their bathroom habits to be overheard, and it's understandably causing a bit of stress.

"Shit!" I hiss, choking on my food.

My throat burns as I struggle to clear it, and I pat my fist against my chest several times. I've been loving cooking for myself, and I found several cookbooks inside the kitchen I've been working my way through. The shadow who cleans my home also keeps my pantry stocked with the best ingredients.

I feel like royalty.

A small part of me wonders if I'm getting this treatment because I'm Chev's mate, but I'd like to believe it's because Aziel's naturally a generous person. The demons, specifically the Wraths, are rumored to go above and beyond with their facilities.

Everybody knows it's because they feel guilty for not saying anything to help the females when they first discovered the cause of the decline, but they've never been asked directly about it. After meeting Aziel, I don't think I'd ask. He's easily one of the most intimidating men I've ever met, and everybody says his two other demon mates, Gray and Silas, are the same.

It makes me feel bad for Charlotte, but that's not my relationship to dissect.

I finish my food with only a few minutes to kill, and I curse myself when I can no longer resist the urge to look up Chev. It feels like there's a new article written about him every hour, and I torture myself by reading every single one.

The story hasn't changed, and I find myself uncontrollably angry as I read the cruel words. They label him a fraud and say he's undeserving of his position, all of which I disagree with. A few articles even call for him to step down and let either Mammon or Echo take over his position, and when I come across those, I have to set my phone on my desk and take a few deep breaths.

I know it's the mate bond making me feel this way, but it doesn't stop me from wanting to argue every little thing these reporters incorrectly say about Chev. Not caring about my trauma or fear, it urges me to seek him out.

The mate bond is fully convinced he's the one person who will fix everything for me. I wish that were true.

As much as I love the idea of finding love, I've long since accepted that it's not in the cards for me. I'm too broken for those emotions, and the best thing I can do for myself and the world around me is to focus my efforts on helping other women.

It gives me purpose and keeps my mind busy, which helps to quiet the raging anxiety constantly threatening to consume me.

I glance at the clock. I needed to leave two minutes ago, but I click on another article instead. This one's got a video attached to it, which I can't possibly ignore.

One more, then I'll go. Just one more.

Chapter Six

CHEV

GREEDY. FUCKING. BASTARDS.

I shove at the hand on my chest, angry my guards are again rejecting my attempt to see my mate. It's been almost three weeks. Three excruciatingly long weeks since I laid eyes on Vanessa, and it's eating me up inside.

The guards act as if I'm some horrible monster for daring to ask if my ban has been lifted. I do it every morning—it's the first thing on my agenda when I arrive at work. I'd rather embarrass myself and look desperate than miss the day Vanessa decides to lift my ban.

"Not today, Chev," Tony says.

I smack at his hand, only slightly settled when he winces and removes it from my chest. Tony's a demon, so he doesn't understand what having a mate bond is like. He'll never feel the pull, so he's in no place to judge.

Shifters used to monitor the portal near my office, but Echo had them replaced with demons. Tony's from Wrath, and I can tell by looking at him that he'd be harder to fight than the shifters who were here before. That's probably the point.

I stare at the portal, desperate to walk through it, before returning to my office. I'll try again tomorrow.

It's only a matter of time before Vanessa allows me to see her.

I fully understand how badly I messed up when we first met. I've heard it from my family and friends, and I've even received a visit from a worked-up incubus I've never met before. Word spreads quickly, and nobody is pleased with my actions.

I came on too strongly and ruined everything. I've imagined what it would be like to meet my mate hundreds, if not thousands, of times over the years, and in none of those fantasies did I imagine she'd be frightened of me.

Her rejection of the mate bond was a complete shock, and I was a fool to think showing her my mate mark would help things. I didn't even realize I was partially erect or exposing myself, and by the time I did, it was much too late to take it back.

And, fuck, do I wish I could.

I just need the opportunity to fix things.

Vanessa's my mate, the female who is perfect for me in every way. Once I speak with her, I'm sure she'll understand and forgive me. I know she has severe trauma, and I have no intention of rushing her into something she's not ready for.

I'm not a very patient man, but I will be for her. My days and nights are haunted by the sight and smell of her fear, and I'll never be the cause of it again.

I'm no better than the men who abused her, and I didn't even find pleasure in hunting down and executing the ogres who once owned her. Echo tried locking Vanessa's files, denying me access to valuable information regarding my mate, but she wasn't fast enough.

I haven't looked through any of the notes uploaded from her therapy sessions or health assessments, but I've diligently read everything else. I immensely enjoy learning about her.

She'll be pleased to learn the ogres who once harmed her are dead. It messes with the process my people have worked tirelessly to implement, but I don't care. The bodies have already been found, and nothing came of it. A few dead ogres are nothing new, and they hardly turn any heads.

I push open my office door and sit behind my desk. Echo will undoubtedly be here soon to yell at me about something or other, and I hum quietly to myself as I turn on my computer and look up Vanessa's name in our system.

I've been blocked from messaging her, and it seems that hasn't been changed.

My mate still doesn't wish to see me. She's a blessed breed, so I know she feels the bond as I do. It's only a matter of time before her urge to seek me out overshadows her fear. I can't wait, and I snatch my newest hobby off my desk before rising and heading toward her old office.

Shifters sidestep around me, all too nervous to meet my eye. I'm happy not to have the distraction of their conversation.

Vanessa's office still smells faintly of her, and I shut the door to keep the air in before sitting at her desk and flipping open my book. I don't know much about nymphs, but I found a wonderful book on them in Silas's library. I'm determined to get through it before he notices I've stolen from him and comes to collect.

I find the page I last left off on, already giddy. The more I learn about my mate, the more my excitement grows.

The nymphs are a fun breed.

I'm ashamed to admit I've never paid too much attention to them before finding Vanessa. They're not physically strong—even the males weak and small—but now I find the nymphs to be nothing less than fascinating. They love nature, which is ideal, considering my home is in the middle of wooded shifter lands.

The females are occasionally gifted with affinities, too. They usually tie into emotions or nature, and I wonder if Vanessa has any. I'm sure she'll tell me everything there is to know about her once she realizes I'm the man she's meant to be with.

The next section offers a physical description of nymphs, but I skip over it. The author of this book clearly has a sexual interest in them, and I don't want to read something that's going to make me angry. I'm sure he'll have written something crude about the nymph female's shape or size, and I don't care to read it.

Nymph women have always been highly sought-after. Their delicate nature and giving personalities were a perverse fascination for many of the males who purchased females for pleasure. The thought of Vanessa being abused by them fills me with an uncontrollable rage, but I do my best not to let it consume me. That's best done by avoiding the sections of the book that objectify them.

Nymphs don't like violence, so I will be calm for my mate.

A knock on the office door draws my attention, but I ignore it. It's probably Echo coming to lecture me about being in Vanessa's office. I'm going to pretend I'm not here until she goes away. Sometimes it works.

The door slams open, the thick wood smacking against the wall.

It's Aziel, and I smoothly hide away the book I stole from Silas. Aziel welcomes himself inside Vanessa's office, and he pretends not to have noticed the book as he shuts the door behind him and looks around.

"How's she doing?" I ask.

Aziel cocks a brow. "Hello to you, too."

Vanessa's office has a pretty view, and Aziel peers out her window. The view from my office is even better, and I think Vanessa will love it. She can sit on my lap and admire it while I work. Then she can admire me.

"Well?" I ask. "How is she?"

Aziel rolls his eyes. "She's adjusting well," he finally says. "She's been busy, and the women seem to like her."

I nod, happy to hear it, as I trail my fingers aimlessly over my mate mark. It's slowly darkening, but not nearly as quickly as I'd like. Had I made a better first impression, there's a chance it'd be black by now. Vanessa and I would be in a good place, and instead of the news talking about my mistreatment of my mate, they'd be celebrating us.

"Has she asked about me?" I ask.

I have a feeling I already know the answer, but I'm a glutton for punishment.

Aziel shakes his head, giving me my answer even before his lips form the word *no*.

My bear urges me to seek Vanessa out and hide away with her, and it's getting harder to fight the urge. What if she's in danger and I can't reach her in time? Despite my trust in Aziel, a part of me is angry with his involvement in keeping her from me—even if I know he's doing it at her request.

Aziel steps closer to me, and I frown when I catch a hint of my mate on his clothing.

He visits his facility most days, but my bear doesn't seem to understand or care that he's not doing it to spite me. I'm starting to see my dearest friend as competition, and for once, I'm grateful Aziel is stronger than I am. I'd hate to lose control and accidentally kill him.

Aziel seems to sense my growing anger as his nostrils flare and his eyes narrow. His body grows rigid as he prepares for a fight, and a second later, the full extent of his power fills my lungs. It doesn't intimidate me the way he wants it to.

If anything, it only seems to worsen my misplaced fury.

I stand to match his height. "She's *my* mate."

Aziel nods, quickly agreeing. "I have no interest in her, Chev."

The part of me that knows and trusts Aziel believes him, but the irrational part of me that seems to grow with each day does not. He's a threat, the male keeping me separated from the woman I'm destined to be with.

"Let me into Wrath." I grab my stolen book and drop it onto the desk. It lands with a heavy *thud*, and I quickly open it and point to the section on nymph abilities. "Nymphs have bad ears and eyes. Not as bad as humans', but not as good as mine or yours. I will watch from a distance. She won't see me." I'm practically begging. "I'll stay outside the facility gates, and I won't bother her."

Aziel sighs and shakes his head, but I continue before he fully rejects me.

"I'll wear the Wrath clothing," I say.

I prefer my leathers, but I'll do anything for Vanessa. I'm confident she won't see me if I watch from the woods beyond the facility. Even if she does happen to look in my direction, my clothing will blend in and she'll think I'm a guard. I'll stay far enough away that she won't be able to tell it's me.

I'd never do anything to make her uncomfortable, but I need to be near her to focus. I'm not effective when my bear and I are at such ends, and this will help me get my mind back on track.

And ensure Vanessa is safe.

Nobody is better equipped to protect her than I am.

"Chev…" Aziel sighs, visibly conflicted. "You're asking a lot from me. She doesn't want to see you."

I know she doesn't, but I also know Aziel is going to give me what I want. I'm his only friend, and as much as he likes to put on his tough exterior, I know he has a soft spot for me. He wants to see me happy, and I will only be happy when I can watch my mate.

"I'm very sneaky," I assure him. "I'm not going to interfere with her life or work. I just want to be in the area."

Aziel laughs as if I've just told him the best joke, but I don't see what's so funny. I gave Charlie refuge when she came to the shifter lands, and I found her very interesting. I spent most of my days spying on her, and she never noticed me.

"I would do it for you," I continue.

It's a lie. I wouldn't, but Aziel doesn't need to know that. If Charlie came to my lands asking for refuge, I'd do everything in my power to assure Aziel never saw her again. I'd be successful, too.

Aziel pinches his nose, and I know he's giving in. He's weak. "You have to promise not to be inappropriate. Your dick stays in your pants, even if you think nobody can see, and no trying to sneak into her house while she's at work."

I work my jaw side to side, angry with what he's insinuating, before nodding. I made mistakes during my first meeting with Vanessa, but I would never be so callous around her again. I'd never invade her space like that, especially when I know how scared she is of me.

And to bring up my penis feels like a slap to the face. It's common for shifters to relieve themselves in the woods, and I'm tired of Aziel acting holier-than-thou because he prefers to do it in the privacy of his home.

"I would never dream of doing those things," I say. "I will have my belongings brought to Wrath this evening." Aziel opens his mouth, but I continue before he can reject me. "Have the shadows ready a bedroom for me. I want to be in the one with the window that faces the facility. I will be living with you until Vanessa decides to come home with me."

This is what's best for everybody involved.

I clear my throat. "If you try to deny me, I'll never speak to you again."

Aziel rolls his eyes and runs a hand through his hair. He can pretend not to care all he wants, but we both know I'm his only friend. He needs me.

"Yes?" I ask.

I trail my fingers over the surface of Vanessa's desk, nervous as I wait for Aziel's response. I need to be close to Vanessa, and I have no intention of intruding or forcing myself into her life. Watching from a distance will be enough for me. I'll wait until she's ready.

Aziel nods, and I rush to grab his arms so he can teleport me to Wrath.

He instinctively smacks my hands away, but I quickly return them to his shoulders. He's tense, and I squeeze his muscles before remembering that demons don't like touch as much as shifters do. My people love intimacy, even if it's non-sexual. Aziel doesn't enjoy it.

"Don't make me regret this," Aziel threatens.

I give him another squeeze. "I won't."

Chapter Seven

CHEV

VANESSA IS BEAUTIFUL. All shifter males say this about their mates, but I am being especially true.

I stand deep in the woods, hiding partially behind the thick trunk of a tree. I'm sure Aziel has dozens of guards watching me, the nosy fuckers probably under strict orders to ensure I'm not pushing any of the boundaries Aziel and I agreed to.

I'm giving them nothing to report back on.

My mate hums under her breath as she steps out of her house with a ring of keys swinging around her thin finger. She's wearing loose clothing, but they do little to hide her frame. She has generous curves, and everything she wears displays them. I know it's not her intention, though, so I don't look. Her long blonde hair is tied up behind her head, which I like because it better lets me see her face.

Nymphs have delicate features, and my mate is no different. I love her.

I can't help but anxiously fist the bottom of my shirt as she approaches and climbs into her golf cart. I hate that fucking vehicle, and I hate even more that Aziel gave it to her with no regulations. She always drives it at full speed, and my heart physically stops every time she turns too quickly and the wheels leave the ground.

I'm beginning to worry she's never driven before, and the delighted squeals she releases whenever she almost crashes the cart are the only thing keeping me from going to Aziel and demanding that he take it away. He can say it needs maintenance—and then conveniently never return it.

Vanessa full lips pull into a wide smile as she climbs in the cart and turns it on. I tug at the uncomfortable Wrath clothing I'm forced to wear before stripping bare. This is the only time I'm allowed to expose myself, but it's for a purpose. I don't want to rip my clothing, and I set them on the ground before shifting into my animal form.

It's freeing, and I allow myself a few moments to stretch my limbs and lower back. It feels good, and a low grumble pours from my throat as I pick up the clothes with my teeth and begin following Vanessa.

I keep far enough away that I won't be seen, and I happily trot along the fence as she makes her way to work. She continues humming to herself, my female finding a love for the music I hear blaring out of her home every night.

Aziel forces me to stop watching her when it grows dark, so I don't hear too much of it, but I love the few minutes of her scream-singing I get most nights. She didn't close her curtains last night, and I got to watch her dance around her kitchen while cooking.

She cooks frequently, and I've already made plans to expand my kitchen. I want her to be pleased with my home, and after seeing her move around the kitchen here, I know mine is lacking. I don't have enough counterspace or cabinets, but those are things I can fix easily.

I'm also relieved she eats meat. The book I studied said many nymphs are vegetarian, but after watching my mate prepare and devour a large chunk of thigh yesterday, I'm confident she will love ucka. I'll catch the biggest one I can find, and she will be quite pleased.

Maybe if I'm lucky, she'll even let me feed the meat to her.

The thought excites me, so I force myself to stop thinking it. I've been trying my hardest not to let my arousal get the best of me. I don't think Vanessa would appreciate the physical reactions I have to the thought of her. Shifters place significant value on physical intimacy, but I've already accepted we won't have that type of relationship. I'm okay with it.

Aziel's guards pointedly avoid looking in my direction as I follow my mate through the woods, but I can tell they know I'm here. They stiffen when I grow too close, and a few even go as far as to shoot me warning looks behind my mate's back. I'm not intimidated.

Aziel might be stronger than I am, but the guards are nothing more than chew toys.

Wrath is unbearably hot, and I pant into the air as Vanessa slows to a stop outside the back doors of the facility. She haphazardly parks her ungodly vehicle off to the side before hurrying inside, her pace fast. She's always in a rush, but I don't feel bad for her. She spends a lot of time on her phone in the mornings, constantly distracted by the small device as she gets ready for the day.

My mate makes herself late.

Naughty girl.

She spent almost an hour on her phone this morning. I'd kill to know what she was looking at, her nose scrunched and lips pursed as she glared at the screen. It was unbearably cute, even if she was clearly upset. I like to think she was playing a game, and that little pout is the face she makes when losing.

Vanessa greets the guards by the back entrance, her friendly smile growing as they open the doors for her. I watch as she disappears into them, already dreading the long wait until she leaves for the day. The doors are shut behind her, and I wait several more minutes to ensure she's not returning before dropping my clothes and shifting back into my skin form.

I hate the Wrath clothing, and I huff as I tug the insufferable items on. I know I agreed to this, but I still hate it. I hate feeling constricted, and I hate how my entire day revolves around secretly watching my mate travel to and from work. I want more. I want to talk to her, to hear her friendly greetings and see her smile directed toward me.

The guards openly stare at me now that Vanessa is gone, and I shoot the ones at the back door a dirty look before turning and beginning my walk to Aziel's home.

Charlie wasn't happy when she heard Aziel had agreed to let me stay with them, but I think she's warming up to me again. I don't like it when she's angry with me, even though I know I deserve it. Still, she's been kind enough to let me work out of her office while I'm here. It's especially great because I don't have to travel to the headquarters and see Echo.

My sister is too meddlesome.

Children scream as I push open the front door to Aziel's home. The house is large, but their voices bounce off the walls and echo down the hallways. I barely step foot inside the foyer when I'm attacked by Cassia. The tiny wrath wraps her stubby limbs around my leg, and she sinks her teeth into the outside of my thigh as I head to Charlie's office.

The woman in question is making breakfast in the kitchen, and I tiptoe through the room. Cassia continues chewing my leg, and I shake her off before setting her on the table along the way.

"A deposit for you," I joke to Charlie.

She's still angry with me, but the corners of her lips twitch upward as she fights back a smile. I stare at her stomach, evaluating her growing bump, before grabbing an apple off the counter and continuing to her office. I'm behind on work, and I do my best to push thoughts of Vanessa aside so I can focus. It's nearly impossible, but I manage to get a good amount of work done before lunch.

A shadow brings me a plate of ucka, and I mindlessly eat while I continue working.

This is the most focused I've been in weeks, and I know it's because I'm finally getting to see Vanessa. My bear has been a wreck for weeks, and he's finally quiet. Mates put our animals at ease.

Even if our relationship is unstable, my bear is pleased knowing she's alive and only a few miles away.

I find myself tapping my fingers to the beat of the song she was humming earlier as I respond to my messages. Some are over a week old, which is unforgivable. Mammon might be correct in saying I should step down. It's hard dividing my time between my pack and the females, and now that Vanessa is part of the mix, my productivity is at an all-time low.

I'm not adequately fulfilling either of my responsibilities.

My computer begins to ring, and a request for a video chat pops up with my sister's name. I purse my lips, my chest deflating as I accept the call. Echo's ugly face covers my screen a second later, and she's already scowling as she launches immediately into one of her lectures. I feel bad for the mate she ends up with.

"Chev…" She pauses and pinches the bridge of her nose. "Where are you?"

I shrug, not wanting to tell her the truth. She's been exceptionally protective over Vanessa, and she'll kill me if she learns I'm in Wrath.

"I will ask this one more time, Chev. Where the fuck are you?" Echo repeats, seething.

My spine straightens, my bear not appreciating the challenge. Echo may be my dearest sister, but I'm still in charge. She *will* show me respect.

"I am in Wrath," I say, "and unless you have something important to discuss, I have work to return to."

I can practically taste Echo's anger. She scoffs, and her eyes dart toward something— or someone—behind the computer. My lips curl, furious she's tricking me.

"Who's there?"

Echo seems taken aback by the sharpness in my voice, and she rolls her eyes before spinning the computer around. I relax once I see it's just Aziel and Gray. They're sitting in the chairs on the other side of her desk. Gray winks and gives me a tiny wave, and Aziel offers a slight nod.

"Why have you called me?" I ask as Echo reappears on my screen.

Instead of answering, she shares her screen to show me a message I sent out only minutes prior. I'm increasing the clothing budget for the remainder of the year, a decision I've carefully considered. The females still living in the facilities are issued essential, everyday wear, but I think they should be allowed to purchase a few additional items they pick out themselves. They will be given an annual budget that will cover four or five moderately priced items.

I frown. "Yes? What's wrong with this?"

"Where do you expect this money to come from?" Echo asks. "It's not sustainable."

It doesn't need to be. Wrath and Lust have been footing the bill for almost the entire cost of the rehabilitation programs. The trade programs do generate some revenue, but the organization as a whole is operating at a loss. No part of it is sustainable, but we aren't anticipating it will run indefinitely.

The goal is to reach a point where the facilities are no longer needed. The day we shut down will be a happy day because that means females are safe and comfortable to exist in the world again. My mate is an excellent example of how far they can come.

"Lust will pay," I say. I haven't spoken to Gray about it, but he's never turned down my budgeting decisions before. His kingdom is beyond wealthy, and he believes in offering the females pleasures just as much as I do.

We spend the next forty-three minutes arguing, the four of us divided. Aziel takes Echo's side in the issue, but Gray is on mine. I can always count on the horny incubus to take my side, and I end the call feeling victorious.

Gray's willing to pay, *and* my plan allows us to employ more females. People will have to design and make the additional clothing, and we have an entire fashion-related trade program ending in a few weeks. Those females will be ecstatic to have a job so soon after finishing.

I return to work with a giddy smile, and I make it through a sizable portion of my inbox before Aziel wanders into my office. He looks tired, and he reeks of my mate.

"You look like shit," I say.

Aziel wordlessly tugs off his shirt and tosses it in my direction. I don't enjoy how he saturates the fabric, but it will settle my bear to sleep with something that smells of Vanessa.

"Your mate is quite outspoken," he says, sitting opposite my desk.

I grin.

"She practically bullied my assistant into putting a meeting on my calendar," he continues, running a hand through his hair. "Then she spent the entirety of it lecturing me on how busy I am."

I bark out a laugh, pleased to hear it.

"You *are* busy," I point out.

Aziel shrugs, looking away. "She made good points."

Of course she did. My mate is the most intelligent person we've ever hired, and she's a great asset to the Wrath facility. Aziel sucks in a slow breath and kicks out his foot. He's not happy, but he never is. I'm used to it.

"Charlie's been asking to return to work for weeks," he says. "She says we're suffocating her, and it seems I can't manage her workload as well as I thought I could." He stares at the ceiling, where Charlie's footfalls can be heard. "It might not be a bad idea to let her return to work."

Charlie will be happy to hear that.

The office doors open, and Cassia comes shuffling in. Her chubby arms and legs are drowning in pajamas too small for her rapidly growing limbs. She's bigger every time I see her, and she storms into the room like a woman on a mission.

Her eyes dart between Aziel and me, and I shrink away when they linger on me for a second too long.

I love children, but I prefer avoiding this one. The tiny wrath has two very sharp teeth just starting to grow in, and I don't enjoy how she's always trying to use my legs for teething.

She heads toward me as if she can read my mind, and I refuse to show her my fear as I lift her onto my lap. I'm pleased when she doesn't bite me. She wants to play with the items on the desk, and I move my computer out of her reach and push Aziel's shirt out of the way so she doesn't get her scent on it.

"Send a photo of Cassia and me to Vanessa," I tell Aziel. "I want her to see that I'm good with children."

Aziel laughs. "Absolutely not."

I frown, bouncing Cassia with my knee until she loses interest and leaves. She seems only to like me for three-minute increments. It's my bear that attracts her. She senses that I'm a predator and she wants, even at her young age, to challenge me. Once she realizes I'm not going to try to fight her, though, she has no desire to be around me.

She's going to be a terror when she's older.

The other two children are upstairs with Gray, and they scream whenever the incubus does something to excite them. Charlie's with them, too, her giggles loud.

"I think Vanessa will like working with Charlie," I say, returning my attention to Aziel. "Echo told me Vanessa gushed over your female during her interview."

Aziel already knows my opinions on his decision to pull Charlie from work, so I won't voice them again. Charlie loves her job, finding purpose in helping the females, and I don't think it's right for Aziel to pressure her into leaving solely because she's pregnant. I understand his fears, but Charlie is a capable female.

And I enjoy working with her. She's fun to be around, and she's best at keeping her males in line. They're overbearing when she isn't around.

They turn every meeting into an argument between themselves, wasting time and energy when everybody knows they're going to go home and ask Charlie what she wants them to do. It's easiest to cut them out of meetings and go straight to the decision-maker.

"Charlie's excited to meet Vanessa," Aziel admits, glancing at the clock. "Shouldn't you have left already?"

I follow Aziel's line of sight, panicking when I realize I'm running late. I never lose track of time, not when it comes to my mate. I grab Aziel's shirt and rush out of the office. His laughter travels down the hallway behind me, but it goes in one ear and out the other as I rip off my clothes and transform into my bear form.

I have a mate to escort home.

Chapter Eight

VANESSA

I'M BEYOND EXHAUSTED.

Still, despite knowing I should be getting ready for bed, I find myself desperately reading article after article about Chev. People are still angry with him, but things are finally starting to die down.

He's still making up a significant number of headlines, but there are a few about other topics mixed in. Seeing people forget Chev's wrongdoings makes me feel better than it should. I want to hate him for how he treated me, but I'm having trouble finding the emotion.

I flop down on my couch, my annoyance building as I skim through a particularly scathing article about Chev. It's written by a news organization backed by Mammon, so the bias is to be expected. The Queen of Greed openly hates the shifters, especially since her mate died on Chev's lands.

I finish the article before shifting gears. I've stumbled upon several online communities of people lusting over Chev. I hate them, but I've spent nearly all my free time scrolling through them these past few weeks.

His admirers—men and women alike—openly discuss their

wishes to be his mate. They're uncomfortably vocal about their desires and fantasies revolving him, and I fear they're going to be full of spite when they discover I'm his mate.

The hatred will only grow when they learn I've rejected him.

They'll probably start hypothesizing over who his chosen mate will be. He'll have to pick one. He's the alpha of his pack, and he'll be required to father children at some point. I'm sure several women will offer.

I navigate to their online forum, and I suck my lips into my mouth as I see what they have to say. Their words make me angrier than they should, but only because I hate the thought of other people fantasizing about Chev. Our mate bond is possessive, and my heart lurches whenever they say something vulgar—which is frequently.

The women in the group are still guessing who Chev's mate could be, but they've almost entirely skipped over me. I'm a nymph, and apparently, that puts me out of consideration. Almighty Chev would never be mated to such a weak woman.

It hurts my feelings more than I'd care to admit, but I continue scrolling.

Today's most popular posts are about Chev's absence from the Seeker headquarters and another, more vulgar one about the markings on his thighs. I want to read through the one about his thighs first, but I restrain myself and click on the first post.

People love spotting Chev, and they're concerned by the lack of images these past few weeks. Most assume he's returned to the shifter lands until everything with his mate dies down. Echo and the few others close to him have refused to speak up and share any information about his whereabouts, other than to briefly say he is alive.

I know he's alive. Our bond is weak, but it was still triggered when we laid eyes on one another. I'd know if he died. It would be a soul-deep longing, and a piece of myself would permanently disappear. I don't feel that, so I know he's alive.

I hope that's all our bond shares. Some mates can feel one another's extreme emotions, mainly negative ones, like pain and fear. I don't believe it's common among nymphs, but it is among shifters. I don't want Chev to feel my emotions.

Some women in the group guess that Chev is staying with Aziel, a potential option I don't like to consider. Aziel's manor is close to the facility, only a few miles from the gated property. I know he and Chev are friends, but I hope he didn't open his doors to my mate.

The mere thought has my heart racing with fear, and I peer at my windows as I contemplate the possibility. If he was let into Wrath, it's only a matter of time before he finds his way to me. Shifters don't just give up on their mates, and Chev will be looking for me.

Does he know where I live?

I keep my eyes and ears open whenever I travel to and from work, but I haven't seen anything amiss. I like to think there's no way I'd miss a giant bear following me home through the woods.

I click out of the thread when the conversation turns sexual. The women begin discussing how much they'd love to be Chev's mate and how they'd never run from him. That quickly dissolves into them sharing painful details of all the things they'd let him do to them.

Most of the women in the group are younger than me, so young they were still teenagers when the shifters took over the Seekers facility. They were too young to be sold, and they never truly experienced what it was like to be a purchased female. They don't know, so how can they relate? I repeat that to myself as I climb off the couch and head upstairs to bed.

I'm happy there's a younger generation of women who are so

open to men. It's good. It's progress. But it still makes me so fucking angry. Chev is my mate, and even if I don't want him, that doesn't make him any less mine.

It's irrational and unfair, but it's how I feel.

Thoughts of Chev with other women consume me, and I'm hardly aware of a thing going on around me as I change into pajamas and pace the length of my room. I don't want to read anything more this group has to say, but I also don't want to read the negative things the news organizations spew.

I'm desperate, and I drag a hand through my hair as I find myself looking up images of him. There are hundreds, if not thousands, of them available. He's one of the most popular men across almost every realm, and his face is probably one of the most recognizable.

I wonder if he's ever been with another woman.

I'm sure people throw themselves at him, probably offering things I'll never feel comfortable giving. He's a healthy adult man, one I'm sure has sexual needs. Has he taken any of those women up on their offers?

Shifters pride themselves on waiting for their mates, but not all. Their reproductive systems still work, and the men are pumped full of testosterone and other hormones that make them crave release. Nothing is stopping a shifter male from fucking a woman, maybe other than tradition.

My palms are sweaty, and I wipe them on the soft cotton of my nightgown before taking a seat on my windowsill. I'm too worked up to go to bed, infuriating thoughts of Chev swirling around my head and refusing to let me have just a moment of peace.

I zoom in on a picture of his thigh, borderline desperate to see the mark that haunts my every waking moment. Given the sheer number of images of him, I thought there'd be more of his animal and mate markings.

Instead, I have to zoom in on grainy images, which isn't satisfying. It doesn't scratch my itch, and I let out a quiet groan as I scroll through picture after picture. I just want to see his mate mark. It's high up on his thigh, so close to his groin, and I place a hand over my chest when emotions I don't want to feel begin swirling inside me.

Chev is so muscular, and I should hate it. I know I should, but all I can think about is how he would feel under my hands. I want to touch his legs, his torso, his shoulders, and every other part of him.

I hate how needy he makes me, and I curse the damned bond as I get up from the window, turn off the bedroom lights, and slide into bed. There's a video of Chev fighting, one I return to almost every night when my desperation peaks. He looks so powerful in it, and I can't stop myself from fantasizing.

There's nothing wrong with fantasizing. Chev will never know, so I don't see the harm.

Chapter Nine

CHEV

VANESSA HAS ALREADY left the facility by the time I arrive, and I curse myself for being late as I run to her home. Her golf cart is parked by her porch, and I pout as I shift into my skin form and redress. I've missed her, and I have nobody to be angry at but myself.

I wander behind her house, deep enough in the woods that she won't be able to see me if she looks out her windows. Her curtains are drawn, and I lean against a tree and fiddle with my phone, mindlessly scrolling through the newest articles written about me. I hoped they would grow better with time, but they're worsening. Mammon is working hard to discredit me, and it's working.

It's only a matter of time before I'm asked to step down. I'm good at my job, and I've efficiently implemented many of the changes I promised to achieve. The females are rehabilitating at incredible rates, and we're seeing even more success than initially planned. It's not enough, though.

I disrespected a female, my own mate, and I'm being punished for it. People have lost trust in me, which I honestly can't blame them for. Echo will take my place, but she is a good leader. The women will be in capable hands.

I kick at a random rock and glance at Vanessa's back windows. She's nowhere to be seen, my mate hidden inside her home. I'm disappointed, but it's okay. I'll be back tomorrow morning. Vanessa's always more lively in the mornings.

I scroll through another few articles, but I lose all interest the second Vanessa's bedroom light flickers on. *Yes*. My mate strolls inside the room, her pace slow and sleepy. She worked a long day today, and I'm sure she's exhausted.

Before I can follow what's happening, she throws her phone on the bed and rips off her shirt. I gulp, my eyes landing on the smooth skin of her belly and chest. She's wearing a modest bra, but it's enough to crush me.

I lick my lips, knowing full well I should leave. I can't get my muscles to follow the command, though. I scan the area to ensure nobody else is around to see her, and I quickly strip and shift into my bear form. I hear better in this form, and I listen for guards as Vanessa walks around her bedroom.

I'll kill anybody who gets too close.

My butt snaps several twigs as I plop down, and I fight my bear's instinct to howl as Vanessa moves closer to her window. He wants to inform her of our presence, but I refuse. She'd be upset to learn I'm here, and I selfishly don't want her to stop undressing.

I slap my tail against the ground as she begins removing her pants.

She undoes her buttons, but I huff and look away the second her light-blue underwear comes into view. I want to see her so badly, but not like this. I won't do this. I won't be this man.

I fight every instinct to look as I shift back into my skin and redress. My clothing is tight and uncomfortable, and I curse Aziel for supplying me with such constricting items. I miss the freedom of my leathers.

Aziel's shirt is folded and tucked carefully aside, and I hesitate before putting it on. It still smells of Vanessa, and I quite like it. I planned to sleep with it tonight, but I've never been known for my self-control.

It's not a shifter's best quality.

I force myself to stare at a tree for several minutes, giving Vanessa enough time to redress. I bet she'd change quickly in leathers. She'd be easier to undress, too, but I know not to expect that. My mate may never want me to remove her clothing.

When I turn back to her window, I'm relieved to see she's redressed. She wears a black nightgown, the cotton fabric clinging to her every curve. She might as well be naked.

Despite my hatred for Wrath clothing, I quite like this.

It leaves much to the imagination, while also leaving nothing. I can see every slope and curve of her body, and I do my best not to stare at her full breasts or wide hips as she picks up her phone and paces the room.

Her face is red, which is intriguing. What's she looking at that's got her so emotional? Occasionally, she turns in a way that her phone faces the window, and I inch closer to see. It's still not enough—I can't quite make out her screen—and I climb onto the lower branches of a tree to get a better view.

This is inappropriate. I know I'm going too far, but I have to see what she's doing. The new angle is better, and I slam a hand over my mouth when I finally glimpse her screen.

Me. She's looking at photos of *me*.

My bear forces loud vibrations from my chest, and I have to swallow down air to get them to stop. I can't be too loud. Vanessa may be a nymph, but her hearing is good enough to detect my damn bear making his annoying fucking mating noises.

I grab the branches of the tree I'm sitting in, squeezing so hard, I think my fingers are bleeding. Even that isn't enough to stop the noises from pouring out of my throat. It's practically a purr, and my heart drops into my stomach when Vanessa turns toward the window.

My bear finally stops, but I fear it's too late. I know Vanessa can't see me, but I still shrink behind the foliage to be safe. Did she hear me?

She places a hand over her chest, her fingers curling and digging into the soft flesh of her throat. She may not be a shifter, but her body will respond to my bear's call. My fears are confirmed as she trails her hand down her torso, her skin turning red.

My noises made her aroused. This is not what I want.

I have half a mind to run to her door and admit to what I've done, but that will only make things worse. She'll know I was watching her, and she'll never want to see me again.

Vanessa stares out her window for a few seconds, her eyes darting around before she returns her attention to her phone. She sits on the windowsill and leans against the glass, giving me a perfect view of her screen.

Her screen, which is covered in images of me.

She scrolls through them, and I let out a whispered curse when she clicks on one of the more salacious ones. It's of my thigh, the one that holds my animal and mate mark. She's looking to see them, but she won't find anything on the internet.

I've never concerned myself with my attire or the way I move. Nobody in the shifter realm has ever looked at me inappropriately, so there was no need. Everybody has a mate, and if my intimate parts are exposed every once in a blue moon, it doesn't matter.

Being thrust into the public eye was a shock, and for a while, I was unequipped. People were sneaking photos of me, purposefully trying to get glimpses of my bare body. There was an interest in my mate and animal markings, and even more so in the skin that lives above them.

I was horrified, but Silas helped remove the images of my intimate parts—even the blurry ones. Suddenly, I wish they were still available.

Vanessa uses her fingers to zoom in on the image, my female staring intently at my upper thigh before scrolling higher. Precisely what part of me is she hoping to view?

She moves away from the window seat, and she shifts her weight from foot to foot before turning off the main light in the room. I can still make out her form as she crawls into bed and slips under her covers.

My mate lifts her knees, the sheets rising and forming around them, and I practically fall from my branch with how much I lean forward. What is she doing? I'm not a stupid man. My aroused mate is lying in bed, her legs spread, looking at a photo of me.

Even if she did hear my bear's mating call, she wouldn't be driven to these lengths. This is her own doing.

Vanessa continues scrolling through her phone. I can't see her screen, but I'm confident she's looking at photos of me. Her hand gradually disappears underneath the covers, and I slam my palm over my straining length when her eyelids flutter shut.

My mate is touching herself to me.

She throws her head against her pillows and slides her hand lower, and I force myself to leave my tree. I want nothing more than to stay, but I won't do that. I'm better than that.

I find enough enjoyment in knowing she still feels desire. It's not uncommon for rehabilitated females to refuse any form of intimacy, even from oneself, and I'm happy Vanessa doesn't seem to face the same objections.

She lowered her arm quickly, and with confidence. She's familiar with pleasuring herself.

My body aches, but I ignore it. I don't want anybody to know what I witnessed tonight, mainly because it's nobody's business, and I force my thoughts toward boring topics as I return to Aziel's home.

Charlie and her mates are in the family room when I arrive, and I pop my head in to announce my arrival.

"I am here," I say. "I'm going to bed."

I keep my lower half hidden behind the doorway, but Gray still smirks at me. I'm sure he can smell my arousal. It's probably pouring off me in waves.

"Is that Aziel's shirt?" Charlie asks.

I glance at myself, frowning as I search for the right words.

"Chev ripped his shirt in the woods today," Aziel smoothly lies, pulling Charlie onto his lap.

She squeals and grabs at his hands, and I leave before their touching grows inappropriate. They hump every night after the children go to bed, and I'm eager to retire before their noises reach my ears.

I never imagined Gray could be so mean. He was kind when he touched me during the Lust ceremony, whispering promises that my mate would still love me and that our actions wouldn't ruin me. It's shocking to hear him on the other end of the spectrum, but I suppose versatility comes with being the King of Lust.

I shake my head, forcing thoughts of that night to the back of my mind. What happened that evening isn't a secret, but I'm unsure if Vanessa knows. I'm not sure if I want her to. Shifters save themselves for their mates—we always have—and I don't want her to think I am an overeager man who couldn't wait.

I *can* wait. I will wait forever if I need to.

My bed is freshly made, and clean clothing for tomorrow is laid out on the sheets.

I quite like the treatment I receive from the Wrath housekeepers, and I smile as I pick up tomorrow's clothing. The outfit is more or less exactly what I wore today, and I test the stretch in the pants before putting the clothes aside.

I'm still painfully erect, and I force myself into a freezing shower until I've softened. It takes longer than I'd like, especially when my mind continues wandering back to Vanessa. She's masturbating to images of me, to images of my thighs and markings.

I'm aroused within seconds of leaving the shower, but I refuse to indulge as I climb into bed.

Every brush of the sheets feels fantastic, but I ignore it as I lie on my back and stare at the ceiling. I promised myself I wouldn't fantasize about Vanessa, but it's impossible not to when the image of her touching herself is permanently etched into my mind.

I lie in bed, wide awake, for several hours before giving up and wrapping a hand around myself. It feels good, and I pray Gray can't hear me as I run my fist from base to tip. I'm on edge already, and I know I won't last long.

I jerk myself quickly, and I slam a pillow over my face to muffle my moans.

My hips twitch and roll to meet each of my strokes, and I hate myself for the way I imagine it's Vanessa wrapped around me. I imagine touching her, tasting her, fucking her.

I cum within seconds, and I'm disgusted with myself for being so weak. I pull the pillow off my face with a low sigh. I'll be better next time.

Chapter Ten

VANESSA

THE GUARDS OUTSIDE Charlotte's office are new, and they both stand stiffly in the hallway outside her door. It's no secret her mates are anxious about her returning to work, and they assigned special guards to watch over her. These men are large, and they don't joke around as the other guards often do.

I try not to look too nervous as I approach them, and I force myself to smile as they turn in my direction. The facility has been buzzing with news of Charlotte's return, which should have been this morning.

"Morning," I say to the guards. "Is she in?"

I didn't want to bombard Charlotte the second she walked through the facility doors, especially since I'm sure there are several people eager to greet her. Everyone who works and lives here has nothing but good things to say about her, which is comforting.

The guard closest to me nods. I wait for him to say more, but he doesn't. Wonderful.

I smooth down the front of my dress and push my shoulders back before knocking on the door. I'm beyond excited to meet

Charlotte, maybe even more so than I was to meet Echo, and my heart is pounding with nerves.

What if she doesn't like me? I know she's close with Chev, and what if she judges me for turning him away? I can only imagine the things she's heard about me.

"Come in!"

Charlotte's voice is muffled as it travels through the door, and I debate pretending I didn't hear it and running away. I can come back later, preferably when I've had more time to prepare. I'd probably do it if it weren't for the guards standing on either side of me. They wouldn't hesitate to tell Charlotte I was here, and then she'd think I'm odd.

The wooden door is heavy, and I blow out a tuft of air as I push it open.

I've never been inside Charlotte's office, and I take a moment to look around the basic furniture and décor before locking eyes with the woman behind the desk. Charlotte stands as I enter, a broad smile spreading across her lips. She's wearing a long, black dress, the fabric just tight enough to show her small baby bump.

She's shorter than I anticipated, and she tucks her brown hair out of her face as she welcomes me inside.

She greets me. "Vanessa. I was just about to come see you."

I smile, hoping my voice doesn't crack. "Good timing, then. I'm sure you're busy, but I just wanted to stop by and introduce myself. I'm excited you're here, and I'm sure Aziel's told you about my badgering."

Charlotte bursts out in laughter, but she just as quickly clamps a hand over her mouth.

"What he calls *badgering*," she teases, "I call *determination*. My mates are old as dirt and stuck in their ways, so don't let them get you down. I've heard a lot of great things about all the work you've gotten done these past few weeks, and I'm happy to meet you."

I'm sure my cheeks are beet red, and I hope it isn't too apparent as I bite back a smile. Aziel is impossible to read, and I'm pleased he told Charlotte he thinks I'm doing a good job. Echo tells me my work is impressive, but I think she'd compliment me even if it weren't.

"Thank you," I say. "It's truly an honor to meet and work with you, Queen Charlotte."

It is, and I'm not ashamed to admit it. The work she's done for women is beyond impressive. She fought even when it put her in danger and meant betraying the ones she loved most, which not many people have the strength to do. Without her, I'd still be stuck in the ogre realm.

Charlotte smiles. "You can call me Charlie—everybody does."

"Charlie," I correct myself. My cheeks grow warm, and I shift my weight from foot to foot. That's so informal.

Charlie's smile grows. "How are you liking it here? Are you adjusting well?"

Does she know about Chev? I assume she does. I'd be shocked if she didn't. It's all over the news, and Aziel probably told her the first night I arrived.

"I love it here," I say. "It's been a big change, but I'd say I'm adjusting pretty well. I'm working on booking some new daily activities for the women, so that's been keeping me busy."

It's a project I've been working on since my second day here, but it took forever to get Aziel's approval on the budget changes. He seemed to think our daily schedule is fine as is, but that's not what the women here are saying. They're bored, and they're incredibly vocal about it.

I'm booking a few rotating instructors for fitness classes, which I think the women will enjoy. The facility I was originally put in had a weekly self-defense class I loved, and I'm eager to bring it here. Most of the women seem interested, too.

Charlie nods, probably having already heard about my idea from Aziel. I fear I overstepped and was too aggressive during our meeting, but he didn't seem upset. I'm hoping he doesn't hold a grudge.

"How exciting!" Charlie says. "I doubt my mates would let me participate *in my condition*, but I look forward to watching."

She overenunciates her words and gestures to her stomach, making light of the pregnancy. I take that as my opportunity to look. I've never seen such a happily pregnant woman before, and it's refreshing. When I was with the ogres, pregnancies were treated as a shameful secret.

Infants were taken away almost immediately after birth, so women were afraid to get attached to the child growing inside them. Everybody pretended the pregnancy didn't exist, and once the woman gave birth, the child was never spoken of again.

I'm thankful I never had to experience it firsthand.

"Well, I'll leave you to get settled." I pause and clear my throat. "I don't want to intrude, but what will your hours here look like?"

If I'm lucky, I get maybe thirty minutes a week from Aziel. I anticipate Charlie will be more available, but I know she's pregnant and her mates aren't excited about her being here. I'm hesitant to begin relying on her if she's going to up and disappear once her pregnancy progresses.

"I'm committing to a minimum of two hours a day," Charlie says. "I'd like to do more, but I promised my mates I wouldn't overexert myself. Human bodies aren't necessarily equipped to grow demon babies, so pregnancy can take a lot out of me."

I nod. "I can imagine."

If Chev and I ever had children, I wonder how my body would

take it. Nymphs are weaker than shifters, but we're stronger than humans. I don't think I'd have any issues.

Not that I'm planning on ever having children or accepting Chev, though.

"I'll see you around, then," I say, heading toward the door.

Charlie returns to work, and I rush out of her office before I begin rambling and say something I regret. I don't think I embarrassed myself too badly, and I feel I hid my nerves moderately well. Charlie seems nice enough, and I look forward to working with her. I can already tell I'll get way more done with her on my side than I did with Aziel.

Chapter Eleven

CHEV

PAIN WAKES ME up, and I immediately know it's from Vanessa.

I'm out of bed in a heartbeat, my bear bursting from my skin as I lunge for the bedroom door. A loud snarl I'm unable to control spills from my throat as the pain in my shoulder grows, the feeling slight as it travels through the mate bond.

My thigh tingles, almost even burns, as my mark calls out to me. I'm hardly aware of anything happening around me as I barrel down the hallway, desperate to find Vanessa.

Charlie rounds a corner, her eyes wide as she spots me, but she's smart enough to jump out of the way. Her fear must travel to her mates because, within seconds, the smell of demons surrounds me.

There are flashes on either side of me as Aziel, Gray, and Silas try to teleport into my path, but I'm moving too quickly. Silas manages to appear in front of me, but it's a mistake.

I bite the limb he throws in my direction, and I use it to toss him against the nearest wall. There are shouts, many of them, but they go in one ear and out the other as I tumble down the stairs. My paws slip against the steps, my bear form unaccustomed to using stairs, so I practically roll down them. I don't care.

I need to find Vanessa.

I slow as I run through the corridor the children play in, narrowly avoiding running into them. Even Cassia moves out of the way, a scared scream tearing from her throat. I'll apologize and let her chew on me later.

I'm faintly aware of Aziel yelling my name, but I ignore every one of his calls as I finally burst out of the house. I break the front door in the process, the wood splintering as I slam my body through it. I'll fix it later.

The pain in my shoulder remains, and it's all I can think about as I take off in the direction of the female facility. My bond guides me toward Vanessa, and I run to her as fast as possible. I've never felt her pain before, so I know it must be severe.

Vanessa should still be in bed, but she's in pain. Something is wrong.

My bear releases another howl into the forest, the loud noise echoing as I hurry to my mate. I want everybody to know I'm coming. Whoever has hurt Vanessa will die today, and I want them to know it.

When the fence surrounding the facility enters my line of sight, I lower my head and slam into it. The metal forms around my skull before breaking apart. It hurts. Fuck, it hurts, but it's not unbearable. I would crush a thousand fences for my mate.

"Chev!"

Aziel appears in my path.

He may be my dearest friend, but at this moment, he's nothing more than an obstacle keeping me from saving my mate. I charge, fully intending to crush him, but my feet are swept out from underneath me by a tricky fucking incubus.

Gray yanks my ankles, and he tumbles alongside me as I fall. I'm immediately trying to get back up, and I snap my teeth in his direction when he throws his torso over me to try to keep me down. Gray is brave but weak, and I kick my hind legs into his belly just as Aziel joins in to help him.

Aziel is strong, and he successfully manages to pin my bear. I snarl, my spit hitting him in the face and mouth as I wiggle and kick, trying and failing to break free.

Silas appears near my head. "Vanessa's okay!" He grabs my jaw and forces me to look into his eyes. "I was just at the facility. She's taking a self-defense class with the other females, and she made a wrong spin and twisted her arm. She tore the muscle, but she's okay."

He's covered in blood from when I bit him, but his injuries seem to have healed. He holds out a phone, and an image of Vanessa is on the screen. She's sitting on the ground, leaning against a tree as she holds an ice pack against her shoulder. She looks confused.

I'm sure she wasn't expecting a bloody Silas to appear and take a photo of her.

My bear is skeptical, and I huff as I lean forward to smell Silas. He wears my mate's scent, and I wiggle closer to ensure it's fresh. I know the fate doesn't like me, but he still brings his body closer to mine.

Yes.

The smell is fresh.

I'm too worked up to shift back into my skin form, but my bear no longer tries to fight. Aziel releases me before lunging at Gray, his body shaking. Aziel seems just as agitated as me, maybe even more so, and he buries his face against Gray's neck. Gray glares at me. I don't care.

I try to stand, but I'm unsuccessful. I hurt myself falling down the stairs, and smashing my head against the metal fence didn't help. I shouldn't have done that.

A tense silence stretches over the four of us, and it continues until a panicked Charlie comes bursting into the area. She narrowly avoids a large tree as she whips around in her golf cart, and she accidentally runs over Gray's ankle in her path toward me.

The incubus curses, clutching the limb to his chest, but I'm not worried. He's well-fed, and he'll heal quickly.

"Chev," Charlie gasps, throwing herself in my direction. "What's happening?"

Silas swoops in and pulls her away from me. It's a smart decision, and I wiggle even farther away. My bear is unpredictable, and he won't hesitate to bite her if she gets too close. I settle next to Aziel, trusting him to stop me from doing anything stupid, and I lie on the ground as I wait for my body to heal. I'm comforted knowing Vanessa is okay, and I'll have Aziel check in on her later this morning, this evening, and before bed.

Gray places a hand on my back, mindlessly trying to stroke my fur, and I grumble until he pulls away.

I am no pet.

It takes several minutes until I have enough strength to shift back into my skin form, and I lie face down on the ground as my head heals. Somebody covers my lower body with fabric, and I groan into the dirt to say *thank you*.

Another several minutes pass before I manage to sit up. Aziel and Gray are leaning against a nearby tree, and Charlie and Silas sit in the golf cart. All four are staring at me.

"Why are you still here?" I ask.

Silas scoffs. "Would you rather we left you alone and vulnerable?"

Charlie elbows him, the action subtle. "Is your head feeling better?"

She climbs out of the golf cart. Silas doesn't stop her from approaching me this time, but I can feel three pairs of demon eyes watching my every move as Charlie roughly grabs my head and forces me to look down. Pointy fingers sift through my hair, searching and prodding at all my sore spots.

Charlie sighs as she looks them over, and now that my senses have cleared, I can finally smell the blood that covers me. About half of it belongs to Silas and Gray, but the other half is mine. It pours down my head and shoulders, and I frown as I wipe at the wetness on my forehead.

"You're about healed," Charlie says.

She returns to Silas. I eye the fate, scanning his arm. His shirt sleeve is missing, but the spot where I bit him looks fine. I look at Gray next. His stomach and chest are covered in blood from when I kicked him, but he seems okay, too.

Aziel was unscathed.

"I'm sorry," I mutter.

Gray shrugs, always quick to let things go, and Silas hums. Aziel doesn't respond, but I'm not surprised. His tense muscles and blown-out pupils make it clear that he's still struggling to hold back his wrath.

Play-fighting is usually enough to rile him up, but I wasn't playing. I attacked his mates and scared his children. I'm impressed he didn't kill me when he had me pinned earlier. That's some very exciting growth on his end.

Gray's shirt is covering the lower half of my body, and I hold it against me as I stumble to my feet.

"Come on," Charlie says, patting her golf cart.

Gray, Aziel, and I climb on it, joining her and Silas. The wheels struggle to support our weight, and Charlie complains as she brings us back to the house. We move at a snail's pace, and we receive many concerned looks from the guards and housekeepers.

Gray and Aziel are gone the moment we're back, the incubus pulling his mate upstairs. Silas hands me a pair of clothes before

Charlie forces me into the kitchen.

Their children peer at me from behind the kitchen doorway. I begin my apologies with the tiny, brown-eyed incubus. He's the most easygoing of the three children.

"I'm sorry, David," I whisper. "I didn't mean to scare you."

He frowns, still hiding behind the doorway, before slowly inching forward. His gaze continually darts toward Silas and Charlie, likely looking toward them for confirmation that I'm safe. I swoop down and pull him into a hug once he's near, which spurs on Valeria. The twins are always competing, and she sprints forward the second she sees me holding her brother.

"Valeria!" I gasp, lifting her with my other arm.

She touches my head, and I force myself to smile as her eyelids flutter shut. She's too tiny to see a fate without direct skin-to-skin contact. She can still enter the fated world, but I don't think she sees anything worth knowing. She won't until she's older, but this is still good practice.

I hate it. Shifters don't like fates, but I'll make this exception for her.

Valeria opens her eyes with a huff, and I grimace as she kicks me and wiggles in my arm.

"Okay, okay." I groan, setting her down.

She storms out of the room, clearly angry. I don't understand, and I turn toward Silas for help. He's fighting a smile as he hands Charlie some ice for my head.

"You're heavily involved in her life, so she probably didn't see anything," he explains. "She gets angry when that happens. We're working on it."

I think that's the most Silas has ever willingly spoken to me.

"I'll get her," David says, also wiggling to be put down.

I set him on his feet, and he quickly disappears after Valeria. Cassia is next. She's easy to please, and when she charges for me,

I push her to the ground. I feel horrible doing this, but she loves it. She screams out in laughter as she falls onto her butt, and when she tries getting back up, I push her down again.

Shifter children aren't violent, and I hate when I have to bully Cassia. She jumps back up, and I let her bite my kneecap before pushing her away with my foot.

"That's enough," I say. "You lose."

Charlie snorts, and Cassia tries to growl at me. The noise sounds silly coming from her throat. She's not a shifter, or any sort of animal, but that doesn't stop her from trying to imitate me. We make eye contact, and I make a big show of dropping my gaze to the floor.

My submission seems to lift her spirits as she squeals and runs toward Silas. He snatches her up and carries her from the room, heading in the direction where David and Valeria are screaming at one another.

"Sit," Charlie orders, pointing to a chair.

I do, and she drops a bag of ice on my head. It's too hot in Wrath, and the coolness on my injuries feels fantastic.

"Do you think Vanessa heard me?" I ask.

Charlie shrugs, her lips pursing. That's a bad sign.

"You were loud," she admits. "And you were close to the facility. I'd assume she heard."

That's not good. My presence in Wrath is supposed to be secret, and this will scare Vanessa away. She's doing so well here, and everybody says she enjoys her work. I refuse to be the one who ruins that.

I return to my room, too frustrated to do anything else.

Children scream as they run past my closed bedroom door, but even the happy noises aren't enough to calm me. Their giggles and laughter usually help. My bear loves children, and I'd be destroyed if I ever did anything to hurt them. Being around them isn't enough to settle my racing thoughts, though.

Uncontrollable rumbles continue to pour from my chest, the noise growing louder as the hours pass. It's not the mating call I made yesterday while watching Vanessa through her bedroom window, but it's a low, displeased sound that I'm fearful isn't stopping soon. I knock my fist against my sternum in a sad attempt to silence myself, but there is no change.

The noise reaches its peak when the time comes for Vanessa to leave work and return home, and it takes everything in me not to accompany her. I so badly wish to walk her home, but it's not a good idea after my incident.

I continue pacing the length of my room, my mind and heart in separate places. Vanessa wants space—she's made that abundantly clear—and I should leave Wrath. I was supposed to keep my distance, and I failed today. I got too close, and now she knows I'm here.

I can't bring myself to leave, though. I'm a weak male, and my mate is my everything. I have no reason to exist if Vanessa isn't with me. Now I've gone and made things worse.

I'm sure she heard me. Even if not, it's only a matter of time before the women within the facility begin to talk about the giant bear shifter who broke through the fence this morning. Somebody surely noticed.

Mammon's going to have a field day with this.

It's been hours, and I'm sure my actions are already scattered across the headlines of every news channel. Have they discovered who my mate is? Everybody knows I've found her, but Echo and I have been working hard to keep Vanessa's identity a secret.

It won't take an expert for people to realize I came to the Wrath facility to be near my mate.

I run my hands through my hair, rough with the strands as I force my fingers through the many knots. It's always tangled after shifting between my bear and skin form, and I attempt to smooth it out before giving up and storming out of the room.

I've made up my mind, even if it's a stupid idea. I need to apologize to Vanessa. She undoubtedly knows I'm in Wrath, and I wish to alleviate the fear I'm sure she's currently feeling.

Silas and Gray are lounging by the front door, the two squeezed into a chair only meant for one. They both rise the moment they notice my presence. I ignore them, not in the mood for the distraction they bring.

I need to speak with my mate.

I hope I'm not too late and she hasn't left Wrath, but there's only one way to find out. I think I'd feel through the bond if she'd left, but I can't rely on that. I need to see her with my own eyes, and she should hear my apology directly. She deserves that.

Then I will leave.

"Hey, hey, big guy," Gray says, blocking the front door. "Where do you think you're going?"

I slow, cocking my head to the side before turning toward Silas. I like Gray, so I will give Silas precisely ten seconds to move him out of my way. Silas blinks, and he crosses his arms over his chest as he plants himself beside Gray.

Are they trying to stop me? That's not going to happen.

Aziel is the only one strong enough to do so, and he's upstairs with Charlie. He hasn't yet settled from this morning, and I know Gray and Silas won't go to him for help. They would be stupid to work up the wrath more than he already is, and we all know it.

"Move," I order.

I inch to the side, fully planning to walk around the pair.

Gray copies me, and I suck in a slow breath before stepping forward and going toe-to-toe with him. He grins, and I only have a second to react before his lust fills my lungs. He knows I hate when he does this, and I scrunch my nose in a sad attempt to stop its effects.

I don't have time for this.

"It's not happening," Silas says, drawing my attention. "You can't see her."

I resist the urge to laugh. I'm not a child in need of babysitting. Vanessa is my mate, and these men are in no position to tell me how and when I can communicate with her.

Gray and Silas continue blocking the door. They're not leaving me with many choices, and I sigh as I mentally accept that I'll need to fight them. I feel bad for hurting them earlier, but they make it hard to avoid.

Gray's lust saturates the air around me, the smell just as enticing as it is annoying. I know he's hoping it'll calm me, forcing my body into a state of submission that allows him to persuade me to do what he wants. He doesn't seem to realize its lack of effect on mated shifters.

Our bodies burn for our mates and our mates only. His scent is nothing more than a sweet-smelling annoyance.

The corners of Gray's lips fall when he realizes his lust doesn't have the effect he hoped for. I remain still, surprised when he rolls his shoulders back and prepares for a fight. Incubi don't enjoy violence, but it seems Gray's willing to make an exception for me.

I'm honored.

Silas remains calm, which isn't surprising. He's strong, and he knows it. He's never tried stopping a shifter from seeing his mate, though. I may have bit his arm this morning, but I will tear it cleanly off next time. I've always wondered if demons regenerate limbs.

"Please, Chev," Gray says. "Leave Vanessa alone."

I see red. "She is not your mate. She is mine, and as much as I appreciate your meddling, this is my decision to make."

Silas sighs. "You're not being rational. We're trying to help you." He steps back, and Gray welcomes himself into my personal space. "Vanessa's your mate. Nobody doubts that, but she's frightened and wants to be left alone."

They're not going to make this easy.

"Do you have mate bonds?" I ask. The answer is no. Demons aren't blessed breeds, and they don't have true mates. I turn toward Silas. "Are you so all-knowing that you understand the intricacies of a mate bond?" The answer is also no.

Gray takes my arm, and I brush him off.

"I am leaving."

I push Gray and Silas aside and reach for the door. Gray makes a quiet noise in the back of his throat and reaches for me again, but Silas stops him.

"Let him," he says. "But we *will* be watching, and we *will* intervene if you upset her."

I'd expect nothing less.

I step outside and pull off my clothing. I'm quickest in my bear form, and I shift before taking off into the woods. My muscles burn with how fast I push myself, my paws slamming into the ground with each step. I already know the guards won't let me enter through the front gate as I usually do, so I head toward the hole I made in the fence earlier today.

It hasn't been fixed yet, and I squeeze through before darting toward Vanessa's house.

I shift back and yank on my clothes once it's within my sight, and my heart is beating out of my chest as I approach Vanessa's front door. I'm terrified of what she's going to say and do to me, but I have to do this. My female deserves an explanation and apology, and it needs to come from me directly.

I made a mistake today, and I won't make it again.

The porch creaks underneath my feet, and I stare at her front door for a long minute before knocking. There's a quiet pattering followed by some rustling, and I scramble back several steps so there's ample space between her and me.

Vanessa pulls open the door.

I shrink, making myself small so she doesn't see me as a threat.

She still grows rigid, and I can practically taste her fear. Still, despite it, she doesn't shut the door. Instead, she runs her eyes down my body, traveling from the top of my head to the bottom of my feet.

I remain silent, giving her time to adjust before I begin my apologies.

Vanessa's lips purse as her gaze momentarily lingers near my thighs. I know she finds them attractive, and I wish I were wearing my leathers. The Wrath clothing is modest, and the entirety of my legs are covered.

It's horrible.

I clear my throat as Vanessa licks her lips, softly reminding her of my presence. Her eyes are wide and full of need when she meets my gaze, and I'm faintly aware I'm shaking as she takes another step toward me.

My mate.

Chapter Twelve

VANESSA

THIS IS BAD.

My heart pounds, the pesky muscle refusing to slow. I've been on edge all day, unable to concentrate after I heard that loud commotion from the northwest wall of the facility. I knew immediately it was Chev.

It had to have been Chev.

It's doubtful there are many bear shifters lurking around Wrath, and it's even more doubtful that any of them would be able to make a noise that makes my skin vibrate the way it did this morning. I practically fell to my knees when I heard him, my body burning with emotions I refuse to think too much about.

Not. Good.

I scroll through my phone, desperately searching for anything with my name. Reading about Chev is bad enough, and knowing that soon my name will be included has me breaking out in a cold sweat.

I don't want the attention that will come with that discovery, especially from Chev's admirers. I groan, throwing my phone on the couch when I find an article listing the women residing within the Wrath facility. My name isn't included, but this is only the first iteration.

I need to find out who's leaking the identities of the women inside the facility. This is confidential information, and I'm not going to let the action slide. Somebody's going to lose their job over this article.

A knock on my front door snaps me from my thoughts. It's about time Aziel responds to my messages. I called him this morning, but he didn't answer. I gave him another ring when I got home a few hours ago. I understand he has a family and kingdom to care for, but this is an emergency.

My palms are sweaty, and I wipe them on my pants before opening my front door.

I freeze when I lock eyes with Chev.

He offers a timid smile before awkwardly clasping his hands behind his back. He rocks back on his heels, looking just as uncomfortable as I feel. I instinctively step toward him, the mate bond urging me forward, but I quickly stop myself.

Chev curls in on himself. Is he trying to make himself small? The posture seems unnatural.

His wide, green eyes blink down at me, his expression indecipherable. I'm not nearly as afraid as I was the first time we met, but there's still fear. The mate bond urges my heart to settle, our pesky connection growing stronger despite the distance I've forced between us.

Half of me wants to slam the door in Chev's face, and the other half wants me to launch myself into his arms.

I lower my gaze, scanning his figure in a way I'm sure is noticeable. Chev doesn't move, the man as still as a mountain as I let my eyes wander over his frame. He's wearing Wrath clothing, but they don't fit him. His thighs are about to bust the seams of his pants, and his chest and shoulders pull his shirt taut.

Shifters are large, the men almost always tall and muscular, and Chev is no different.

My gaze lingers on his thigh. After spending weeks staring at images of him, I know precisely where his animal and mate markings are.

Chev clears his throat, prompting me to look back up. His eyelids have lowered, and this time, it's me who's frozen. I feel his warmth, and my pulse races as I realize how close we've gotten.

Was it me who stepped forward, or him?

He raises his arm, and I spend too much time looking at his bicep. Why is he so muscular? How much does he weigh? Bears are heavy, aren't they? I should look that up.

Chev's fingertips touch my cheek. I gasp, my lungs sucking in a sharp intake of breath. My entire body breaks out in goosebumps, and before I can stop and think of what I'm doing, I throw myself against his chest.

Chev's reflexes are quick, and his hand is cupping the back of my head before I've even processed my movements. My mouth is on his, a kiss I think I initiated, and I hold his biceps as I press my front against his.

His body is just as hard as it looks, and his muscles flex against my fingers. I love it.

Chev releases a low noise that has my body trembling, and I slide my hands to his shoulders as he tilts my head back and claims my mouth. His kiss is forceful, full of need and desperation, but I don't find myself nearly as afraid of it as I should be.

It's what I want, which doesn't seem right. It's the bond.

It also helps that the men who abused me never kissed me. Chev's tongue against mine isn't something I've ever experienced before, nor is the hand softly caressing the back of my head. He touches me nowhere else. His other hand hovers beside my waist, like he's afraid to press against the skin.

I rip at his shirt, hating the barrier, and Chev does the rest. His clothing rips as he hurries to free his chest for me. I feel the fabric disappear underneath my hand, and I flinch as my palm lands on his bare shoulders.

My hands move of their own accord, sliding downward. Chev is muscular, and his abs tighten as I drag my fingers through the hair that lives on his chest. It's surprisingly soft. He makes a quiet noise in the back of his throat, and his hands finally land on my hips a second later.

His grip is so light, I barely feel it, but he finally tightens it after a second. I never imagined I'd enjoy a man's touch, but Chev has me desperate for more. I need more of him. It's not long before I'm panting too hard to kiss him back, but Chev hardly seems to mind.

He trails his mouth to my throat, and when he reaches the spot where my shoulder meets my neck, he licks. His tongue is surprisingly rough against my sensitive skin, which makes me imagine it on other parts of my body. It's a dangerous thought, one I know I shouldn't be having.

"Oh," I gasp.

Chev begins to suck on my neck, surely bruising the skin. I've read that shifters like to mark up their mates, but I didn't realize what that meant until now.

I struggle to suck enough oxygen into my lungs, and my mind goes blank as Chev runs his tongue from my collarbone to my ear. The noises seeping from his chest grow louder, continuing until they're all I can hear.

Chev's teeth graze against my neck, the feeling jolting. It's like a bucket of cold water pouring over my head, and I snap back to reality and push Chev away.

He whines, the noise low and throaty as he steps back. His

chest is heaving, and his lips are wet and puffy from their attack on my skin. I hate how much I like it, and I slide my gaze over his exposed chest and down lower.

Chev's straining the fabric of his jeans, the imprint of his erection impossible not to notice. He wordlessly reaches down to cover himself, hiding the view as he takes another step back. I'm faintly aware I'm shaking.

I can't recall the last time a man so visibly aroused didn't force himself on me.

I should be scared. I should be terrified. If it were anybody but Chev, I would be. The bond between us refuses to let me feel the fear. It's like a weighted blanket on my negative emotions, and the blanket has only gotten heavier from our distance.

I refuse to acknowledge Chev's erection, or our frustrating bond, as I cross my arms over my chest and inch back toward my door. I need to be prepared to run inside and lock the door should something go wrong between us. The bond wants me to trust him, but I no longer believe in blind faith.

"I'm sorry," Chev says. He takes another step back, until he's about to fall off the porch. "I didn't mean for that to happen."

He's holding back a smile. It keeps threatening to spread across his lips, and I can tell it's taking everything he has not to let it emerge. Kissing Chev was the absolute worst thing I could've done. I'm sending him the wrong message, giving him hope for something that will never happen.

We will never be together.

"I came here to apologize," he continues. "I'm sure you heard me earlier today."

I nod.

I knew things were too good to be true in Wrath, but the confirmation was a punch to the gut. Despite how hard I try, I'll never truly be free of Chev. He won't leave me alone, not when he has the connections and ability to get everything he wants. I'm just another object for him to own.

Chev clears his throat. "I'm sorry for the trouble I caused today. I've been waiting for you to seek me out, and today's mistakes aren't who I am. I'm a patient man for you, but I was frightened when I felt your pain. I acted without thinking, and I want to apologize."

He straightens up as he speaks, forgetting his purposeful small posture.

Chev is tall, and I tilt my head back to maintain eye contact. It takes every bit of courage I have to hold it, but it quickly becomes too much and I shift my gaze to his sternum. Why did I encourage him to remove his shirt? There are hundreds of pictures of him running around in nothing more than his short, leather skirt, but they do little justice to the real thing.

How many other females have seen him in such little clothing? I'm jealous, and I shake my head to stop that thought from going further. He's not mine, and I'm not his. This bond between us is a mistake, and Chev will soon see that and move on.

Chev shifts his weight from foot to foot, and I realize he's stopped speaking. I look back up, forcing myself to make eye contact.

"What can I do to earn your trust?" he asks.

I'm not ready for this conversation.

A panic I'm all too familiar with begins to fester inside me. It spreads until it consumes me, overwhelming my every thought. Chev cocks his head to the side, his fingers twitching as he visibly fights not to reach out for me.

This is too much.

I open my mouth, but no sound emerges. After another second of fumbling, I hurry back into my home and slam the door shut. My hands shake as I turn the locks. I'm fully aware they're useless in keeping Chev out, but I don't care.

I don't want this. I don't want any of this, and I wipe at my mouth in a desperate attempt to remove our kiss. This was a mistake. I should've never accepted this job.

My cheeks grow wet as my panic rises, and a pain I'm pretty sure is caused by our bond spreads from my chest into every limb of my body. It's an uncomfortable burning sensation, and it continues to grow as I peek out the window beside the front door.

Chev hasn't moved.

He shakes his head and arms before reaching up and touching his lips, his fingers pressing against them as a tiny smile spreads across his face. My heart thumps. I shouldn't care if he enjoyed our kiss and smiles like a giddy schoolboy afterward.

Chev's gaze flashes to the window, and I dart away before he sees me. He's either going to leave or force his way in, and I've spent enough time as a purchased female to know I have no control over his decision. He wouldn't be the first man to force himself into my space and body, and I steel my mind in preparation for it.

Kissing him sent the wrong message, and I shouldn't be surprised if he takes that as an invitation. I've been reading about shifter males these past few weeks, specifically their mating habits, and it's not something I'm interested in. The males always dominate their females, urging them into a submission I will never give.

At least, not willingly.

Minutes pass. Chev doesn't force his way inside my home. Eventually, I work up the courage to peek out the window again.

Chev's still standing on the porch, frowning as he stares at his feet. He's not wearing shoes, which is unsurprising, and he clutches his ripped shirt to his chest in a sad attempt to cover his skin. Is he doing that for me? I know he's comfortable showing skin. All shifters are.

When it becomes clear he isn't leaving, I shove away my fears and unlock the door.

"Will you go on a date with me?" Chev asks the second I open it.

I shake my head, not trusting my voice at the moment. Chev visibly deflates, and I point in the direction of Aziel's home. I can only assume that's where he's been staying.

"Go home," I order. My voice cracks, but it's the best I can do.

Chev flinches as if my words have burned him, his entire body tensing and recoiling. The part of me that recognizes him as my mate screams, but I ignore it. I'm good at ignoring my needs and desires, and this will be no different.

"I understand," he says. *Good.* "I'm going to leave Wrath, and I won't approach you again. I'll keep myself available, though, in case you change your mind."

I nod, already knowing I won't be reaching out.

Chev wavers, clearly hesitating on something, before he dips his head and turns away. He continues to clutch his torn shirt to his chest, holding the fabric like a scared boy.

The sight makes the burning in my chest grow, and I fight the urge to call to him as he disappears into the woods. I'll ask Echo to relocate me, preferably somewhere Chev can't reach me.

That's the only way.

Chapter Thirteen

VANESSA

CHEV HAS RUINED everything.

Once I'm sure he's gone and isn't returning, I shut all the blinds and curtains in my home. Now that I know he's in Wrath, I don't want to risk him peeking in. He's probably been doing it this entire time, and I want to cry as I think about what he might have seen.

Then I go around locking every window and door, ensuring there's no way for him to sneak inside. I don't think he'd actually do that, but it's better to be safe than sorry. My heart pounds as I double-check everything, ensuring it's perfect.

My phone sits on the kitchen counter, teasing me. I told myself I would reach out to Echo, but it's been almost twenty minutes since Chev's visit and I still haven't picked it up. I need to call her before it's too late and she's gone to bed.

I need to do it now.

Instead, I seek out the alcohol I found hidden in the living room my first week here. Nymphs aren't big drinkers—we have that in common with shifters—but desperate times call for desperate measures.

I'm unfamiliar with the type of demon alcohol my home's been stocked with, and I don't bother looking anything up as I pour myself a heaping glass of the first bottle I find. It burns my throat, beyond painful, but it's nothing compared to the searing heat of the bond. It screams for me to seek out and comfort Chev, and it's growing harder and harder to ignore.

Kissing him was a mistake, and it's ruined the progress I've made in the past few weeks. Our bond is working harder than ever to bring us together, making me desperate.

I cringe as I finish my glass, and I immediately pour myself another.

I still don't reach for my phone.

I stare at it, angry with myself for not having the courage to reach out to Echo. She'll help me. I know she will, and a small part of me knows that's why I'm not reaching out.

My phone lights up, and I practically lunge over the kitchen counter. I'm expecting it to be a message about Chev, and I groan when I realize it's just a notification from one of the Chev groups I'm in.

I'm addicted to them, which is equally embarrassing and frustrating. Still, I unlock my phone and read through the most recent messages. Word has gotten out about Chev's entrance into the Wrath facility today, and people are beginning to speculate again who his mate could be.

My name appeared earlier today, but the group members quickly dismissed me. They decided I was too weak to be a real consideration. Their almighty Chev is clearly destined for a strong breed.

Their dismissal hurt more than I'd care to admit, and a small, petty part of me wants to out myself. Especially given how daring they're growing in the chats. The women are discussing the type of sex they think he would have with the different women inside the Wrath facility, and reading it puts a bitter taste in my mouth.

I see these women daily, and I don't want to think about them with my mate. My lip curls at the thought of Chev with any of the females I've come to know these past few weeks.

I hate how much he affects me.

A sharp knock on the door draws my attention, the loud noise cutting through the otherwise-silent room. My pulse races, and I'm careful to remain quiet as I inch forward and peek through the front window. I should've done this when Chev knocked. Opening the door without seeing who it was first was risky, and I paid the price.

It's only Charlie, though. She's standing on my porch, with Aziel directly behind her. I unlock and open the door, eager to hear what they have to say. I assume they're here to discuss Chev.

Charlie smiles and subtly shoves Aziel away as I open the door. Something about him is off, and I step back when the full extent of his power reaches my nose. He's not trying to hold it in as usual, and the crazed look in his eye is concerning.

What's gotten him so worked up?

"Vanessa," Charlie says. She sounds somber. "I should've come over sooner. I'm sorry."

I shrug and gesture for her to come inside. She's got her own things to deal with.

She spins and whispers something to Aziel, and I pretend not to notice how her fingers creep under his shirt and press against his bare chest. His eyebrows furrow as he listens to her, and after a tense few seconds, he bends and kisses her cheek.

I've never seen him show affection before, and I do my best not to look too surprised. Who knew the stoic demon could be so soft? I sure didn't.

Aziel pats Charlie's butt, and she turns away and enters my house a second later. I make brief eye contact with Aziel, not sure if he wants to come inside. He remains on the porch, though, so I shut the door. Through the window, I can see he's still standing on the porch. I have a feeling he'll be here until Charlie returns to his side. Everybody knows of his possessiveness over her.

Charlie and I make idle chitchat as we walk into the kitchen. I know she's here because of Chev, but I don't want to be the one to bring him up first.

Eventually, Charlie clears her throat. "I wanted to apologize for Chev's actions today."

I gulp, tracing the marbling on the countertop with my finger. I'm fully aware she and her mates are close with Chev. It's often joked that he's practically a part of their harem, which bothers me more than I'd care to admit.

Chev has publicly said he's not intimate with them several times.

"Chev is an amazing person, and I know he means well, but he took things too far today," Charlie continues. "I allowed him to enter Wrath and stay in my home, and that was wrong. I'm sorry for putting you in such an uncomfortable situation, Vanessa." She sounds genuine. "He's leaving tomorrow morning after his head heals, and—"

"What happened to his head?"

Charlie blinks, clearly shocked by my outburst. I'm a bit embarrassed, but my concern for Chev outweighs that. I didn't know he was injured. Why didn't he say anything when he came to visit me earlier? He seemed to be okay.

"He fell down our stairs, broke our front door, and busted through the property fence when he felt your shoulder pain this morning," Charlie explains. "The front door was solid wood, and the fence's metal tore up his scalp. It gave him a few bald spots, but the skin should heal soon enough."

I shake my head, my bond burning. Tears fill my eyes, and I

place a hand over my chest as the burning spreads up my throat. Chev is hurt.

Charlie looks frantic. "He's okay. I swear." She quietly curses before hurrying toward the front door. Aziel is still standing on the porch, and she orders him to acquire a photo of Chev's head. Her voice is quiet, but her tone leaves no room for question.

Chev seemed fine earlier, but Charlie's words have me panicked. He tore up his scalp? Does it still hurt? My fingers twitch, my nymph blood urging me to check his injuries for myself.

I wipe at my cheeks, angry and frustrated for crying.

Aziel makes a quick call before handing Charlie his phone. She brings it to me. I don't care if I seem impolite as I snatch it from her hand and bring it to my face. A video call comes through from Gray, and I answer.

The camera faces Chev, and I immediately relax. He's sitting on the ground across from a small child, his legs crossed, as he plays some sort of card game with her. He's not paying the camera any attention, and the person holding the phone walks closer. The video calms my racing thoughts.

"Show me your head," Gray orders from behind the camera.

Chev grumbles something I can't quite make out, his voice low, before he lowers his head. He looks upset. It's written in his poor posture.

Charlie wasn't lying about the bald spots. Several areas are missing hair, but the skin looks almost entirely healed. Gray fingers through Chev's hair, moving the thick strands so he can show all the injuries. Chev remains quiet, but my heart lurches when Gray touches one of the still-healing wounds.

Chev winces. "Don't do that."

He pushes Gray away and resumes his game with the young girl. She must be one of Charlie's children, and she looks content with the shifter. I try not to think too deeply about whether or not Chev is good with children. It shouldn't matter to me.

"Smile at the camera," Gray orders, stepping back.

Chev looks confused. He clearly doesn't realize I'm on the other side of the phone, and he rolls his eyes before lifting his middle finger.

"Fuck off, Echo," he says moments before the video ends.

I laugh. I can't help it.

Everybody knows Chev is close to his sister, and she had nothing but positive things to say about him during my interviews with her. Still, they always seem to be arguing. It makes me wish I had siblings, but the nymph lands were raided before my parents had more children.

I hand Aziel's phone back to Charlie.

"Thank you," I say.

I shouldn't have done this, and I feel foolish for having reacted so violently to hearing Chev hurt his head. He was on my doorstep less than an hour ago. I knew he was fine.

"I can send you another photo of his head before he leaves tomorrow morning," Charlie offers.

I purse my lips, already knowing that's a bad idea. I need to distance myself from anything and everything Chev-related. Still, I can't stop my mouth from opening and my lips from forming a question I so desperately want to know the answer to.

"Where's he going?"

Charlie lowers herself onto the barstool she was sitting on earlier. She holds her belly, gently rubbing the skin. It's mostly flat, and it'll probably be several more months before her pregnancy is truly visible. I've never seen a happily pregnant woman before, and I hope it's a girl.

"I'm not sure," Charlie says. He'll likely return to the shifter lands, but he might stay in his chateau in Lust. Gray gifted it to him as a thank you for participating in the Lust—" Charlie pauses and clears her throat. "He usually goes there to get away from his family and relax."

I nod. I know what she was going to say. It's common knowledge that Chev participated in the Lust ceremony. Gray needed to prove himself to be titled the King of Lust, and Chev let Gray pleasure him.

Many shifters were outraged when they heard, but I think it was noble. Everybody knows how much the shifters value their intimacy, almost all of them saving themselves for their mates. I'm sure it wasn't easy for Chev to so publicly let somebody touch him, and I'm not sure where the females would be if he hadn't done so.

The Lust finances are supporting a significant number of the rehabilitation programs.

Still, my lip curls at the thought of Chev living in some chateau in Lust. I know what happens there, and I hate the idea of my mate being surrounded by such debauchery.

"He can stay in Wrath," I decide.

I blame my rash decision on my earlier panic. Charlie looks shocked as my words register, but I refuse to take them back. Silence stretches between us, and I do my best not to look too alarmed when Charlie darts forward and pulls me into a tight hug.

She's short, and she burrows her face against my shoulder as she squeezes my waist. Nymphs aren't particularly strong or large, but I feel that way when hugging Charlie. Humans are painfully weak, and I could snap her in half with ease.

"Thank you so much, Vanessa." Charlie sniffles before continuing. "Chev has been inconsolable since we told him he has to leave, and this will mean so much to him. I promise he won't bother you again."

I pull out of the hug and offer her a weak smile. I'll have

plenty of time to worry and agonize over my decisions while lying in bed tonight, and I don't intend to panic in front of her. Not again.

Will Chev be watching me sleep? I'll keep my blinds shut, just in case.

Aziel clears his throat and walks into the kitchen, and I watch as he nestles his face into Charlie's hair and hugs her from behind. This domestic side of him is shocking, and I don't think I'll ever get used to seeing him anything other than stone-faced and serious.

Maybe I misjudged his and Charlie's relationship. She seems at ease around him.

"Let's talk more tomorrow morning," Charlie says, leaning against Aziel's chest.

I nod. "Sounds good."

She and Aziel disappear a second later, and I stare at where they once stood before sinking to the ground and lying on the cold floor. What have I gotten myself into?

Chapter Fourteen

VANESSA

I KNOW HE'S out there.

My hands shake as I pull back my living room curtain and peek out the window. I can't see him, but I know he's somewhere out there.

I'm sure my decision to let Chev stay in Wrath sent the wrong message. He's probably taken that as an invitation, which is less than ideal. Still, I can't find it within myself to regret my decision. A small part of me is happy he's here.

Our bond has been vibrating all night, the warmth spreading through my limbs and organs. It feels good, and it's a welcome change from the burn I felt when I rejected him. I knew mate bonds were strong, but I had no idea they could cause physical pain.

I wish I knew more about them. I was taken from the nymph lands when I was a child, and I was never taught about bonds or mates—at least not in detail. I know minimal, and everything I've read online sounds horrible. I suppose I could ask Chev about it, but I fear he'd get too excited. Echo would be the next person I'd go to, but I'd rather die than explain to her how her brother makes me feel.

My hands still shake, and I wipe them on my pants before opening my front door. I'm met with crisp air and the sound of birds, but I ignore it all as I run toward my golf cart. I continually scan the woods for any sign of Chev. I imagine he's too big to hide, but the woods are his specialty.

I know he's out there, and I'd rather be aware of it than be ignorant.

My pulse races, and I set my things in my cart before straightening my spine and looking into the woods. I search them again, still not seeing anything beyond trees and dirt. Maybe he isn't here.

"Chev?" My voice isn't as loud as I want it to be, but shifters have good hearing. If he's out there, he'll hear.

I clasp my hands behind my back and rock on my heels, waiting. For a long moment, there's nothing, just me and the morning air. After a second, though, there's movement. Chev steps out from behind a tree, and he's much closer than I thought he'd be.

How did I miss him? He's twice as wide as the trunk.

His lips curl into a timid smile, but they fall when I don't give one back. I'm too busy panicking, and I wipe my hands on my pants again before gesturing for him to come over. I don't know why I'm doing this or what I want to say, but our bond doesn't care. It urges me to invite him into my space and life, and I'm having difficulty denying it.

It's annoying.

Chev greets me. "Vanessa."

His voice is low, and I force myself to maintain eye contact as he approaches. He stands on the other side of my golf cart, and he plants his hands on the roof before bending to peer through it. I forget how large he is until he's close. It's unnerving.

"Chev," I say.

His shirt is stretched tightly around his shoulders and arms, and it's a wonder the seams haven't ripped. It rides up at the waist, exposing a sharp V leading into his jeans. I refuse to lower my gaze any further.

Silence stretches between us, but Chev doesn't seem to mind. He's grinning at me.

"How's your head?" I eventually ask.

Chev's smile widens, and it takes everything in me not to move when he slowly rounds the vehicle separating us. What's he doing? My throat is dry and scratchy, my nerves at an all-time high as he lowers himself into the driver's seat and dips his head. He seems to sense that I'm too nervous to talk, and he doesn't pressure me with conversation as he shows me the top of his head.

I know precisely where his injuries are thanks to Gray, and I hesitate before bringing my fingers to his scalp. Chev leans into my touch, loud noises emerging from his chest as I timidly move his hair around.

The skin is healed, and the few injuries Gray pointed to last night are gone. Chev has a handful of tiny bald spots from where the fence ripped out his hair, but they're nearly impossible to notice if you aren't looking.

"Does it hurt?" I can't help but ask.

Chev shakes his head, causing his hair to slide through my fingers. It's surprisingly soft, the wavy strands well cared for. Shifters are known for their healthy hair, skin, and nails. Our children will likely have beautiful hair, too.

I rip my hands off his head, shocked and disgusted with my train of thought.

I'll never give Chev children. The only intimacy I've ever encountered has been through force, and the thought of willingly letting a man put his hands on me feels wrong. I'll never want that.

"My mate mark darkened after our kiss yesterday," Chev says.

My eyes, without my permission, travel to his thighs. I take sick pleasure knowing I've caused the damned marking to change. I've spent a long time staring at old photos of him, and I wonder what it looks like now. How dark has it gotten?

I refuse to ask. I should be avoiding Chev, not running my fingers through his hair and discussing his mate mark. This is the exact opposite of what I should be doing. Despite how good the bond feels when I give in, I can't.

I'll never be able to give Chev what he wants, and I'm doing this for him just as much as I'm doing it for myself.

"Do nymphs have mate marks?" Chev asks.

My fingers twitch, and I fight my instinct to reach up and touch my spot. I'm happy it lives on the back of my neck, where it can't easily be seen.

"Yes, we do," I say, purposefully being vague.

Chev frowns. I hate it when he does that, and I blow out a frustrated breath before spinning around. I'm all too aware I'm putting my back to him, leaving myself vulnerable, but I tell myself he isn't going to hurt me as I bundle up my hair.

I can practically feel Chev's excitement as I lift it, exposing the small mark on the back of my neck. The golf cart groans as Chev stands, and a second later, I feel his body heat warming me through my clothing. He's so close that his breath tickles the tiny hairs on the back of my neck.

"I don't see it," he says.

I'm not excited to explain this.

"It looks like a birthmark," I say. "It's dormant, which is why it's so small and light."

That's about all I know. Nymphs are secretive about our marks, and not many outside our kind have information about them. My mother was supposed to tell me about mine when I got older, but the opportunity was stolen from us by the Seekers. I'm one of the last of my kind, so I have nobody to ask now.

I believe the mark will turn dark pink and travel down the length of my spine. I have no idea how to make it do so, though.

Chev hums. "Dormant?"

"I'm not sure," I admit. "That's what my mother once told me. I don't know much about it."

A quiet, low noise begins to pour from Chev. I faintly remember hearing it before, and I clench my thighs together as it travels through me. Chev clears his throat and hits his chest a few times, but the noise doesn't stop.

"Can I touch it?" he begs.

No. I should say *no.* I left the house fully intending to ignore Chev and pretend he doesn't exist, and I'm failing miserably. I didn't get ten feet from my front door before calling out his name, and now he's pleading to touch my neck.

The low noises continue seeping from Chev. He's probably waited his entire life for this. That thought alone has me giving a jerky nod and lowering my chin to my chest.

"Fine," I say.

I can practically smell Chev's excitement. He doesn't move right away, and the wait is excruciating. It's hard not to be consumed by him and the bond, and it becomes especially hard to resist it when he's touching me.

"I'm going to do it now," Chev warns.

I nod.

Just one touch and I'll be on my way. I'm already running late, and letting Chev distract me is irresponsible. I shouldn't have called out to him—that was my first mistake. Hearing about his head injury has me frazzled, and I wish Charlie had never told me about it.

Something soft touches my mark, and I collapse.

My knees buckle, and if it weren't for Chev's quick reflexes, I'd be crumpled on the ground. He wraps his arm around my waist and holds me against his chest, supporting my weight entirely. I clutch at his forearm, unable to focus on anything but his touch against my mark.

Now I understand why the adults were so private about them.

Chev pulls away as he evaluates my reaction, and he loosens the arm around my waist just enough that I know I'm free to pull away at any moment. I don't move. It's probably a mistake. He's giving me an out, a chance to stop this, and I don't take it.

He touches my mark again.

Pleasure radiates down my spine, and I bite back a moan as he brushes his thumb over the small spot. He might as well be touching between my thighs, every sensation on my neck mirrored on my most intimate bits.

It's too good. Am I going to cum?

Chev licks my neck.

Yes.

He licks me again, his rough tongue rubbing hard against me. I reach for him with both hands, desperate to hold the arm wrapped around my waist. I squeeze him as the pleasure grows, a squeaky whine slipping from my lips as my orgasm approaches.

My sex pulsates around nothing, and when Chev begins moaning into my skin, I fall apart. My nails dig into his forearm as I cum, almost drawing blood. Chev holds me through it, and once I've fallen limp, he guides me into my golf cart.

That was by far the most intense orgasm I've ever had, and I can practically feel Chev's pride as he crouches before me and pushes my tangled hair out of my face.

"Vanessa," he whispers. "Are you okay?"

I swallow past the lump in my throat, unsure how I feel. The mere thought of letting somebody between my thighs is revolting, but I don't have the same reservations about the back of my neck. That area has never been defiled, and even though I feel the pleasure in the parts of my body I struggle with, it's different enough.

Am I okay?

There's no crushing disappointment or suffocating fear. I wait for it, thinking it might be delayed, but nothing appears.

"I'm okay," I eventually say.

Chev fucking beams, and despite knowing I shouldn't, I find myself smiling back. This is a dangerous game, one that will most certainly end with me being hurt, but I can't seem to stop. Chev is like a splinter I can't get out, and I'm beginning to worry I don't want to.

Charlie believes in him, and I take her endorsement to heart. Maybe Chev and I can come to some sort of agreement—one that will allow us to be platonic partners. I know he wants children, but if he's willing to forego sex, I'd be willing to be medically inseminated with his seed.

My chest tightens at the mental of image of Chev holding a child—our child. I know he'd be a good father. All shifters are. He would be protective and caring, and our child would need for nothing.

"Can I drive you to work?" Chev asks.

I suck on my teeth, debating. He's already here, and if I'm honest with myself, I don't want to part ways yet. I worry about people at the facility seeing us, but it's only a matter of time before we're discovered. There's no use prolonging the inevitable.

"You can't come inside," I say.

Chev hardly seems to take offense, his head quickly bobbing as I move over and make room for him to sit in the driver's seat. I grab the things I set down earlier and clutch them to my chest as he turns on the golf cart and begins driving us down the long road to the facility.

I'm going to be late for my meeting with Charlie.

I have a feeling she'd be excited if I told her I got held up by Chev, but I won't use him as an excuse. Telling her that would send the wrong message, and I'm not ready to face the questions I'm sure will follow.

My heart continues to pound, the aftereffects of my orgasm lingering. I turn and sneak a peek at Chev, wanting to see if he was affected by our touch. He was—still is. He's hard, his length pressing against the fabric of his pants. It looks painful, but I'm not going to acknowledge it.

"Would it be okay if I drove you to work in the mornings?" Chev asks, drawing my attention. "I can meet you outside your home."

I should say *no*.

"We'll have to leave earlier than this," I say instead. "Because you drive slow."

He drives like an old man, his hands firmly planted on the wheel and his eyes continually darting around, like he's expecting traffic to suddenly appear on this empty, dirt road. I don't have the same reservations, and I get to work in half the amount of time.

"Deal," Chev says. He shoots me a sideways smile. "I'm excited."

I squeeze my eyes shut. Why didn't I say *no*? We finally pull up to the back entrance of the facility, and I practically leap out of the golf cart and sprint toward the doors.

Chev laughs. "Goodbye, Vanessa!"

His voice is full of excitement despite the fact that I'm literally sprinting away from him. I lift my arm, giving an awkward wave, before pushing open the facility doors and hurrying inside.

Charlie's already waiting for me in my office. It's like she knows when I'm in desperate need of advice, and she clasps her hands in her lap as I throw myself into my chair and drop my head onto my desk. It smacks against the surface with a quiet *thud*, but my loud groan quickly drowns it out.

"I told him he can drive me to work in the mornings," I admit. Charlie remains silent, and I let out another loud groan before continuing. "And I let him lick my mark, which turns out to be more pleasurable than it should be." I let out a third loud groan. "And I think I'm excited to see him again."

There's a quiet shuffling as she shifts her position in her chair. I'm desperate for her to say something, anything.

She clears her throat. "You've had a busy morning."

I laugh, even though I think this situation is anything but funny.

"How long has he been watching me?" I ask.

Charlie goes quiet before answering. "He came here about three weeks after you, and he watches you drive to and from work. Sometimes he sticks around while you cook dinner, but he returns to the manor before dark."

I should be disgusted. I should be horrified and angry and putting a stop to it. I know I should. That's the only reasonable response to something like this, but the emotion doesn't come. It's sick and twisted, and I hate myself for it.

It's the damned bond. It's warping my mind, and I have no control over it.

"I don't want him doing that anymore," I say.

Charlie nods. "I'll see to it that he doesn't."

Good. Good. That's good.

"Is there anything else you want to talk about?" Charlie asks.

Yes. No. I don't know where to start.

Chapter Fifteen

VANESSA

I FORCE MYSELF to take a deep, calming breath before peering back through the tiny peephole in my front door. I regret every decision that's led me here.

Chev stands beside my golf cart, his hands clasped behind his back. He promised to be early, and he meant it. In his hand are the keys I typically leave on the dashboard, and I watch with a gaping mouth as he swings them around his finger. He's wearing his leathers, and the large muscles in his thighs flex as he idly wanders around my golf cart.

He wasn't anywhere to be seen when I left work last night, and he didn't come when I called out to him. It left me experiencing an odd sense of loneliness, and I hardly got any sleep.

Was he giving me space? The thought has my heart thumping, and a soft crack emerges in my need to keep him at arm's length. A shifter giving his mate distance? I didn't think that was possible. Charlie said she'd talk to him, but I didn't actually think anything would come from it.

Chev sighs and kicks a rock. How long has he been standing

out there?

I shouldn't keep him waiting, and my hand shakes as I work up the strength to open my front door. Chev's head snaps up as I step outside, his lips curling into a wide grin as I shut the door behind me.

"Good morning, my mate," he says by way of greeting.

The title has me stumbling, my feet tripping over themselves. Chev's hands flex by his sides as he watches me straighten myself out. He's probably fighting against his instinct to run forward and catch me.

This must be Charlie's doing. I confided in her, sharing my fears and issues regarding Chev. She listened to every word, and she promised to talk with him. I assumed it would be a lost cause.

"Did Charlie speak to you?" I ask.

Chev nods. "Yes. She said you felt suffocated and I should give you space." He kicks another rock. "I'll no longer watch you from the woods, and I'll make my presence known when I'm near."

His chest puffs up as he speaks. He looks so proud to tell me this, which makes my heart do backflips. Nobody's ever cared so much about how I feel. My comfort came last when I was a purchased female. The ogres liked it when I was scared, and the cruelest even enjoyed placing bets on who could make me scream the loudest.

"Thank you," I whisper, unsure what else to say. "You shouldn't have been watching me in the first place."

Chev lowers his gaze. "I know. I didn't—" He pauses and shakes his head. "I'm sorry."

I walk down my porch steps. I'm not wearing anything special—jeans and a plain, black shirt—but Chev looks at me like I'm in the most elegant dress he's ever seen. Or naked. He waits until I'm almost to him before speaking again.

"Would you like me to kiss your mark again?"

I trip over my feet, but Chev catches me this time. Our body explodes with warmth whenever we touch, and I instinctively lean against his chest before thinking better of it and pulling away. I need to stop letting him get this close to me. It will only make it hurt more when he inevitably leaves and finds somebody who can give him what he wants.

The thought of him with another fills me with a rage I don't want to think too deeply about. My possessiveness is growing, and I'm beginning to understand why blessed breeds are adamant about saving themselves. I hate violence, but I want to kill every female Chev has ever touched.

"Does my past upset you?" I blurt out.

I wish to swallow up the question the second it emerges.

Chev furrows his brow. "No." His answer is firm.

He hesitates momentarily before cupping my cheeks, his thumbs brushing over my cheekbones and his fingers burying into the hair behind my ears. He's careful not to accidentally touch the mark on the back of my neck.

"Does *my* past upset you?" He repeats my question.

I shake my head.

Chev looks me over, probably trying to see if I'm telling the truth. I am. I know all about his interactions with Gray during the Lust ceremony, and I believe he did what he did out of duty and dedication to the females. Unless something more happened that wasn't discussed in the news.

"Did anything else happen?" I ask. "Anything not reported on?"

"No," Chev says. "The Lust demons were liberal with the details they shared." He shifts his weight from foot to foot. "Can I put my mouth on your mark again?"

His eyelids lower as he waits for my response, a look of need spreading over his features. It does more to me than I'd care to admit. I'm so fucking weak.

"No," I say. "But you can look at it."

I think he's going to be pleased with what he sees.

He runs his thumbs over my cheeks, his touch soft and gentle until I have no choice but to relax. I believe him, which is a dangerous thing to do. Despite knowing that, though, I turn around and drop my head. Chev takes his sweet time bundling up my hair and moving it away from my neck.

"Your marking has darkened," he says.

I hum, pretending I don't already know that. I was in my bathroom looking at it the second I got home last night. The color has transitioned from flesh-toned to a light blush, and the small dot has already begun elongating down my spine.

"It's beautiful," he whispers.

His lips meet the back of my head, but he remains true to his word and leaves my mark alone. I'm not ready for him to touch it again—maybe not ever. I wouldn't have let him do it yesterday if I'd known how it would feel.

I don't regret it, though.

Several long seconds of silence stretch between us. I want to know what Chev's thinking, but I don't ask. I'm afraid of his answer.

He clears his throat and releases my hair. "Thank you for letting me see."

I nod, unsure what else to say, and lower myself into my golf cart. I take the passenger seat, and I do my best to hide my quickened breathing as Chev takes a seat beside me.

The fabric of his leather skirt is lifted as his erection pushes against it, but he ignores it. I stare, unable to look away as he sticks the key in the ignition. Chev begins driving. I continue eyeing his bare thighs and the covered length above them.

Chev breaks the silence. "You're staring," he says. "Would you like to see?"

I lick my lips, knowing this is a stupid idea, before nodding. I *need* to see.

"I'm not going to touch you," I say, needing to make that clear.

Chev nods. "I don't expect you to."

He sucks in a shaky breath before grabbing the edge of his skirt and pulling it up. His animal mark is exposed first, the red bear unchanged. Immediately following it is his mate mark, the skin now a dark gray. It's the skin he exposes last that captures my attention, though.

His cock lies heavy between his thighs, the thick length so hard, it looks painful. It pulsates with every beat of his heart, and the veins running along his shaft are prominent as they fill with blood. It's the first time I've ever voluntarily looked at a penis, and I'm surprised by my lack of disgust.

I thought I'd hate it. Chev seems to enjoy my attention as he groans and shifts in his seat.

"Do you like it?" he asks.

I debate saying *no*, but we'd both know it'd be a lie.

"Yes."

Our bond is working overtime to soothe me, keeping me calm despite being faced with an object that's never brought me anything but pain. The bond is growing stronger each day, making my desperation and desire for Chev to grow along with it.

"It's yours," Chev declares.

I gulp. Hearing him say that does things to me. Things I'm not prepared for. Chev always makes me feel things I don't expect, though, so I suppose I should get used to it.

Despite his clear desire, Chev doesn't push for us to go further. A small part of me expects him to, at a minimum, touch himself, but he keeps his hands planted firmly on the steering wheel. It must be painful to do so.

He eventually releases the steering wheel so he can pull his leathers back down as we near the facility. He's hiding himself from the wandering eyes of the women inside, which I appreciate. I don't want anybody seeing him, and I scan the windows in search of any watchers.

"Would you like to go on a date with me?" Chev asks, breaking the silence.

It's not the first time he's asked that, but it is the first time I debate saying *yes*. Chev's been accommodating to my requests, and I'm coming to accept that our bond isn't going to disappear as I hoped.

I'm nervous to be alone with Chev, but I'm hopeful that if something went wrong, Charlie and her males would be effective in separating us. Charlie's apologies yesterday felt genuine, and my therapist used to say trusting isn't inherently bad.

"If I said *yes*…" I start. "I'd want to stay in Wrath, and I'd want a chaperone."

There's so much we need to discuss, and the short ride to the facility isn't long enough for serious conversations. Chev might call it a date, but I will consider it a meeting. A meeting with a chaperone who can step in should anything get out of hand.

Chev beams. "Deal."

His skirt is still tented around his erection, and I continually glance at it as he pulls up to the back doors of the facility. We sit beside one another in silence. I ran inside yesterday, but today, I'm hesitant to leave. Several seconds pass until I give in and spin to hug him.

I hate how much I want to feel his arms around me.

Chev immediately returns the hug, and his bear begins making noises as I bury my face against his chest. It's more endearing than it should be. This is the first time we've ever truly hugged, even if we're doing it while sitting side by side, and it's nice.

I breathe in his scent before pulling away. Chev quickly releases me, which I appreciate. I hate when men make me feel trapped.

"Does tonight work for you?" Chev asks. I nod, and he quickly continues. "Then I will secure us a chaperone."

He looks excited—too excited—which makes me nervous. I've never been on a date before, and I have no idea what to expect. His hands find mine, and I gulp as he raises them between us and kisses my knuckles. His lips are soft, and they rob me of coherent thought.

Are mates supposed to turn your mind into a jumbled, confusing mess?

"I will see you tonight," he promises.

I nod, still dazed as I fumble to grab all my things and hurry inside the facility.

Chapter Sixteen

VANESSA

TONIGHT COMES TOO quickly.

I try to distract myself with work, desperate to think of anything other than Chev. I continually catch myself daydreaming about him, which startles and unnerves me every time. I don't think anybody has noticed, but I fear my obsession is becoming obvious.

I sneak my phone everywhere I go, and I scour through the several Chev-focused groups I've joined to see if there's any new news about him. There rarely is. He's been staying out of the public eye these past several weeks, and the topic of his mate is dying down. People are losing interest, which is a relief.

I'm afraid it will resume once people discover who I am, though. I can feel it already beginning. Charlie can barely contain her giggles whenever he's brought up in a meeting, and the women inside the facility are starting to put two and two together. I think somebody saw him driving me to work and told others.

My nerves are at an all-time high when I finally go home for the day, and I spend way too long trying to style my hair just the right way. I don't know why I'm trying so hard to look good for this date, but I don't think I could stop if I tried. I try on several outfits before settling on my usual jeans and plain shirt. It's my comfort clothing.

Chev didn't give me a time, and I pace my living room while I wait. Where's he going to take me? I should've asked. I want to know what to expect.

I'm moments away from calling this entire thing off when somebody knocks on my door. I assume it's Chev, and I smooth down my hair before hurrying over and pulling it open. As predicted, Chev stands on my porch.

He's wearing his leathers, and his torso flexes as he clasps his hands behind his back and smiles wildly at me. I clear my throat, too nervous to speak. Agreeing to this date was a mistake, but it's too late to take it back. I'd feel like a monster if I canceled on him now.

Our bond was easy to ignore when I hardly knew Chev, but the more time I spend with him, the stronger it grows. I wonder if he feels the same way, but I'm not sure if I'm ready for his answer. He's not fighting this as I am, and he'd probably jump on the opportunity to tell me just how the bond makes him feel.

Not that I can't already guess.

Chev always looks giddy around me.

"Silas will be our chaperone tonight," he says, gesturing behind him.

The fate stands beside my golf cart, his shoulder leaning against it as he watches Chev and me interact. I wonder what he thinks when he sees us. Does Chev talk about me to them? I'm not sure how I feel about that thought. I don't enjoy being a topic of discussion, but I can't lie and say the idea of Chev bragging about me to his friends doesn't make my blood warm.

Unless he's saying bad things.

Silas's gaze is unnerving. Only a fate could look at somebody with such intensity. I turn back toward Chev.

"Silas doesn't like me much," he says. "But he's agreed to teleport us to the lava pits. The best ones are far from here, so we won't be able to travel by vehicle."

I don't love teleporting. It's how Aziel brought me to Wrath, and it made me nauseous. Plus, I've heard horror stories about demons getting trapped in the in-between, and I'm sure the odds of that are increased when they're bringing others. Chev is large and probably hard to teleport.

Silas is said to be a strong demon, though, and I doubt Chev would let him teleport us if he didn't think the demon was capable. Charlie jokes that her males are older than dirt, and while I know she's being sarcastic, a small part of me wonders just how much truth there is to her statement.

How old is Chev?

"I read that nymphs have affinities to nature," Chev says, drawing my attention.

Can he tell how distracted I am?

"We do," I confirm.

"What do they feel like?"

I suck on my teeth, unsure how to describe how affinities feel. It's like asking somebody how to explain what a color looks like. It just is.

"It's hard to explain," I admit. "I can connect with nature and feel the life force that emanates from it."

Chev hums. "Do you have one toward lava?"

I've never been asked about my affinities before, and my cheeks grow warm as Chev voices his questions. His interest is flattering, and I wish I had better answers. I don't know much about myself, and there are significant gaps of information I never learned.

The nymph lands were almost entirely destroyed when the

Seekers came and kidnapped the fertile women, and what used to be my home is now a wasteland. Most nymph males chose to take their lives after their mates and children were stolen, and the few who remained are no longer friendly. They're shells of their former selves.

Both my parents are dead.

Would Chev take me home if I asked? It's no longer safe, as the area is full of bandits and men in hiding, but I'd love to see it one more time. There's a chance my childhood home is still standing.

"I'm not sure," I admit. "I've never been around lava before."

I've been meaning to go, but I haven't found the time. I've always wanted to visit the lava pits within Wrath. It's home to some of the largest ones, and I've heard they're beautiful.

Chev absolutely beams. "Wonderful!"

He's cute when you get past the fact that he's a wall of muscle who transforms into a literal bear.

Silas steps onto the porch, and Chev immediately clings to his arm. I hesitate, eyeing the demon, before carefully grabbing his other arm. His stoic expression softens.

"Are you ready?" he asks.

"Yes."

The world around me vanishes, and my stomach tightens as it materializes again. The stifling air is the first thing I notice, and I swallow past the lump in my throat as I release Silas and plant my hands on my knees.

I most definitely have an affinity for lava. The air feels incredible, its energy vastly different from anything I've ever encountered. I'm sure I look like a child in the way I stare wide-eyed at the fields.

Massive pools of magma spread out in every direction for as far as the eye can see. It's incredible.

Somebody rubs my back, and I peek to the side to see Chev. Silas is already gone, but I quickly find him leaning against a black tree several feet away. He's watching. Chev continues rubbing my back, and when his bear begins making its noises, I take a calm step away. A meeting. I need to treat this as a meeting.

There have got to be hundreds of lava pits surrounding us. It's stunning, and I struggle to take it all in. I doubt I'd ever be able to see this particular view if it weren't for Silas teleporting us. There's no way we could get this deep into the fields without getting hurt.

The spot they found is perfect, too. It's large enough that I can feel the heat from the lava, but there's little risk of tripping and falling into scalding magma. That would be a sure way to ruin a day.

Chev leads me to a nearby picnic table. There's only one, and it's decorated with candles and food. My heart pounds when I notice it, and I chew at my bottom lip to remain calm. This is romantic.

I wasn't expecting it.

"It's beautiful," I admit.

I sit at the table, and Chev quickly takes the spot opposite me. He's brought quite a spread, and I eye the dishes with excitement. I'm hungry, and Chev even brought foods native to the nymphs' homeland. His thoughtfulness has my heart doing backflips, and I struggle not to tear up as I look at a few dishes I haven't eaten since childhood. Chev put a lot of effort into this.

"I'm happy you like it," he says, a small smile toying at the corners of his lips. "Do you feel connected to the lava?"

"Yes," I say. "It's amazing."

Chev beams. "Do you feel the same way toward forests?"

I have a feeling I know where this question is leading, but I take the bait.

"I do," I admit.

That seems to excite Chev, and he bobs his head before pushing back his hair and reaching for the food. He doesn't say anything further, but I know what he's thinking. The shifter lands are covered in forests. He's thinking about me at his home, in his pack. It's a thought I'm not ready to entertain.

Chev serves me a plate of food, and I find great pleasure in explaining the dishes we're eating. He listens to every word like it's a confession of love, which encourages me to share the few memories I have of each dish.

It's surprisingly enjoyable, but as we finish eating and the conversation dwindles, my nerves emerge with a vengeance. I have a feeling we both know what's coming. We can't prolong the inevitable, and we need to discuss what's happening between us.

I glance at Silas. He's still sitting by the black tree, seemingly not paying attention as he flips the page of the book he's reading. I hope he isn't listening, and I stare a bit longer before turning back to Chev.

The shifter is already looking at me, his head cocked slightly to the side. He's waiting.

"Do you want to sit near the pool?" I ask, gesturing to the large pit of magma to our left.

I really want to get closer.

Chev hesitates, his eyes darting toward it. Is he scared of the lava? I want to ask, but I don't think he'd ever admit to being afraid. After several seconds, he nods and stands. I follow, letting him take my hand and lead me to the spot he's deemed is most safe.

It's a ways away from Silas, and when I cast a nervous glance back at the fate, I'm happy to see he's still reading his book.

The lava is quiet, but occasionally, I'll hear a low, deep gurgling. It serves as good background noise to the uncomfortable air that's grown between Chev and me. We sit beside one another, and Chev wordlessly touches my ankle. I let him rub the bone with the back of his knuckles. It's soothing, and it makes the bond between us happy.

I clear my throat as I work up the courage to speak. "What do you want from me?" I ask. "If we were to give this a try, what would you want our relationship to look like?"

I avoid looking directly at Chev, but I peek at him from the corner of my eye. His chest expands as he sucks in a slow breath, the shifter thinking through my question before answering.

"I want everything," he admits. "But I'm happy with whatever you can give. I know you've had a hard life." Chev clears his throat before continuing. "I just want to be a part of your future."

He continues running his knuckles along my ankle, and I stare at where we connect before prying further.

"And children?" I ask. Chev stills. "If you'd be willing to forego sex, I'd be willing to have your children through artificial insemination," I continue to explain. "I want a family and children, but making one is not something I think I'll ever be comfortable with."

Chev doesn't immediately respond, and the silence is deafening.

"I'd be honored to have a family with you, with or without sex," he eventually says.

Despite Chev's words, I can tell our bond is unhappy. It wants me to give myself entirely to him, but I can't see myself doing that. Maybe we can work our way there over time, but that wouldn't be for a long time. I don't want to suggest it and get his hopes up.

"Where do you draw the line on intimacy?" Chev asks. "You don't seem to mind when I hold your hand or kiss you."

I shrug, not having a good answer. My lines seem to be

continually changing, and I'm having trouble finding where they are.

"I don't mind those things," I say.

I turn to face Chev entirely. He spins to match my position, the lava next to us long forgotten as he stares at me with so much hope. I've given him more than enough opportunity to leave, but he's made it clear he has no intentions to do so. If I'm honest with myself, I think I'd be crushed if he did.

I'd never ask him to stay, but it would ruin me if he left.

"I don't know where my limits are," I admit.

Chev grabs my hands before leaning in and bringing his lips to mine. The kiss is quick, and when he pulls away, he brings my palms to his chest and presses them against it.

"That's okay," he says. "We'll learn what works best for us."

Chapter Seventeen

CHEV

MY PEOPLE ARE clearly surprised to see me back home, their steps faltering and eyes widening when they notice me storming through the woods.

I smile and nod in their direction, but I don't stick around for conversation. I'm in too much of a hurry, and I cast a nervous glare at the sun as I rush toward my cabin. I haven't been home in weeks, all my time spent either in Wrath or at work.

It's time I begin preparing my home for Vanessa, though.

She's agreed to give me another chance, to give our mate bond another chance, and I'm not going to screw it up again. I know she's not ready to live in the shifter lands with me, but my home will be prepared for when she is.

I need to clean. I've grown accustomed to my bachelor lifestyle, and I doubt my mate will be impressed by my home in its current state. It's not terrible, but it sure won't impress her. My linens need to be washed, and I need to begin my kitchen renovation.

I don't cook often, so I mistakenly didn't spend much time on my kitchen when I built my cabin. It's a mistake I regret. Vanessa loves cooking. I watch her do it all the time in the evenings, and she needs more space than what I've given her.

A selfish part of me hopes that if it's good enough, she'll be excited to cook for me. I smell her meals when she cooks with open windows, and I'm desperate for a taste.

I reach my cabin, and I cringe as I push open the front door. The air is stale.

I drag my fingers through my hair, fingering my bald spots before hurrying around and opening all my windows and doors. Some fresh air will be good, and once I've gotten everything open, I begin tidying up. My leathers are strewn about, and I carefully fold and put them away before reorganizing my drawers so there are empty ones for Vanessa.

I do the same to my closet, moving my things to one half so the other is open for her.

The bed is next. My sheets need washing, and I yank them off my mattress before grabbing the spare set I keep in my hallway closet. I sniff to ensure they still smell fresh, and I make my bed with a happy smile.

I used to hate it when my mom forced me to make my bed and clean my room. She insisted it be done every morning, and she'd love to tell me I'd thank her for it someday. I believe that day is rapidly approaching. Vanessa will be very impressed by how tidy I can be.

My new sheets are dark green and made with soft cotton, and I hope Vanessa likes them. I'll buy new ones if she doesn't, but I won't do it happily. These sheets are the best that can be purchased in the shifter realm, and I love them.

I sink my teeth into my bottom lip as I think about the day I can finally bring her here. She'll bring life to this home, adding decorations and filling the space with things that bring her the most comfort. Maybe she'll even fill our home with children.

They'll make a mess and break things, but I'll love every minute of it.

She said she'd be open to artificial insemination, which is more than I expected. I've always wanted a large family, but I'd grown to accept it wouldn't happen after meeting Vanessa. She clearly doesn't want intimacy, and I didn't realize any other options of impregnation were on the table.

I can't stop smiling as I throw my pillows on my bed, and I unconsciously lick my lips as I imagine what Vanessa would look like splayed out on my mattress. I dream of seeing her naked and waiting for me, her body flushed and sex dripping. My mate is the most beautiful woman I've ever encountered, and I'm desperate for her.

She let out the neediest moans when I licked her mark, and it took all of my strength not to rub against her as she wiggled and thrashed in my arms. It was the sexiest thing I've ever seen or heard, and the memory makes me ache.

Aziel's begun teasing me for how often I'm masturbating, but I have no control over it. My body aches for Vanessa, and even the littlest things have me incredibly wound up.

I run a hand over my fresh sheets, feeling their softness, before sliding my other hand underneath my leathers. I'm already hard, and I squeeze myself for some relief. Vanessa has agreed to let me take her to a restaurant for dinner tonight, so I only have a few hours before I'm needed back in Wrath.

Still, my body has other ideas. It doesn't help that I smell like Vanessa. She rubbed her scent into me this morning when I was dropping her off, and I throw my head back as I recall how she so willingly wrapped her arms around me and held me tightly. I kept my arms at my sides, not wanting her to feel trapped, which she seemed to enjoy.

I was tempted to kiss her, but I didn't want to push my luck.

I'm pushing my luck right now. I groan, releasing myself.

My home isn't going to ready itself, and there's no time to waste. Vanessa won't be impressed if I don't finish everything within a reasonable time because I was too busy pawing at my cock. I'd be made the laughingstock of the shifters.

Although maybe she *would* like my distractions.

She seems interested in my body, my female constantly staring. I know she doesn't like a lot of physical touch, but maybe she'd like to see me pleasure myself. Her arousal was practically tangible when I lifted my skirt and showed myself to her the other day, and I know she likes to look at photos of me when she touches herself.

Maybe I'll send her private images for when she's alone. She can grow comfortable seeing my erection without the pressure of me being there.

I gulp, loving the idea of doing just that. I'll discuss it with her this evening while we're eating. I'm most excited about the restaurant I've picked out for us, and I believe it will put her in a good mood. She's most interested in my penis when she's in a good mood.

Forcing my thoughts away from sex, I grab my axe and head outside. I need to remove the exterior wall of my home and set it back almost five feet to make room for the kitchen island I plan to build for Vanessa. It won't be easy work, but it's my fault for not putting more effort into my kitchen when I originally constructed my home.

My parents warned me this would happen, but I was young and cocky and chose not to listen. They'll be pleased to see how I regret my decisions.

"My baby!"

I spin just in time to spot my father's broad grin. He's close, and he throws his arms around me and pulls me into a tight hug.

He's been helping manage the pack while I've been occupied with the females and Vanessa, and he refuses to release me until I drop my axe and return his hug.

"I'm busy, Dad," I say, stepping back and gesturing to my home. "I'm expanding my kitchen."

He laughs, his eyes darting to my axe before returning to me. He knows all about Vanessa, thanks to Echo. She told him everything during our last family dinner night despite my explicit instruction not to.

I don't want them meddling.

"Would you like help?" Dad asks.

I hesitate, scanning his figure, before nodding.

He's supposed to be retired, a forced tradition most older males hate. The last thing we need is a bunch of elderly shifters trying to help during fights and wars, the men convinced they're still strong and valuable. They're a hindrance, and forced retirements encourage them to accept their role as elderly before they actually grow weak.

I shouldn't let Dad help me chop the wood, but I'm desperate to complete my home before Vanessa expresses an interest in moving to the shifter lands. I'd be humiliated to bring her to a half-completed house. It would be dishonorable, and she would probably lose all interest in me.

She'd think I can't provide.

"Let me get my axe!" Dad's already running toward his house. "Your mom has hidden my good one, but I have a spare she doesn't know about."

I watch, hiding a smirk, as I head into the woods. I need thicker trees for my base, and the largest ones are deep in the forest. I've already cut down two by the time Dad finds me, and together, we complete another seventeen before it's time for me to leave.

We're both covered in sweat, and we pile the logs just outside my home. It's not nearly enough, but it's a good start. I'm hoping to complete everything by the end of the month, which is admittedly a lofty goal.

With Dad's help, though, I think it's manageable.

Dad wipes his brow. "Will you be back tomorrow?"

"I'm busy tomorrow," I say, shaking my head. "Maybe the day after."

My day is full of meetings tomorrow, and my few free hours will be spent escorting Vanessa to and from the Wrath facility. I can't give that up.

"You're always busy," Dad points out. "You're our alpha, and we need you here. You're spreading yourself too thin, and we're growing worried."

I huff. "Who's 'we'?"

"Me, your mom, Echo. Everybody in the pack is worried about you, Chev."

Guilt eats at my heart, but there's nothing I can do. I miss my home and family, but I can't leave my mate alone in Wrath. My bear won't let me, and even if he did, I still wouldn't leave her.

"You are my oldest baby," Dad continues. "But now you're a stranger."

At that, I snort and roll my eyes. Now he's being dramatic. He still sees me every week for family dinner, and we spend hours together. Although now that Vanessa is allowing me to escort her home, I might have to stop attending the dinners.

"I need to go," I tell Dad.

He hides his secret axe in my shed before leaving, and I rush to the portal in Charlie's cabin. She doesn't use it as frequently as she once did, but we've all been busy.

I'm a sweaty mess when I return to Wrath, and I hurry to shower and dress for my date. The restaurant I want to go to requires me to wear traditional Wrath clothing, and I frown as I pull up my pants.

I hate these fucking things, and I can't think of one good reason why it's required I wear a shirt, pants, and shoes to eat. They don't help me get food into my mouth, and, if anything, the constricting fabric makes it *harder* to eat.

Demons have a lot to learn from shifters.

"Silas!" I shout, heading toward the front door. He meets me in the foyer. "Are you ready to go?"

He nods, and I grab his arm so he can teleport me to Vanessa's workplace.

Chapter Eighteen

CHEV

MY RANGE OF movement is shit, and I squat to loosen my pants as I wait for Vanessa. I don't have to wait long. I timed her departure well, and I straighten up as the facility doors open and Vanessa comes strolling out.

Her gait changes when she notices Silas lounging in her golf cart, the demon shielding his eyes with one hand while he plays on his phone with the other. He sets the device down when he notices my mate, his lips curling into a kind smile before he stands and greets her.

"Are you ready for our date?" I ask, nudging him to the side so Vanessa puts her eyes on me instead.

She cocks a brow as she scans me, her mouth twitching.

"You're wearing normal clothing today?"

Silas sucks in a laugh. Leathers *are* normal clothing, but I won't scold my mate like I do the Wrath trio. At least, not right away. She doesn't understand because she's never worn leathers and discovered how beneficial they are, but someday, she'll realize.

"The restaurant I've picked out is prejudiced," I say, trying and failing to hide my annoyance. "They don't allow leathers."

Aziel's shirt digs into my armpits, and I grimace and wiggle to try to stretch the fabric. He should bulk up. We're the same height, but his clothing would fit me better if he were wider. I'll have to discuss this with him later tonight.

"Where are we going?" Vanessa asks, glancing at her outfit.

She looks perfect in her bright-blue dress, and my chest puffs up as I realize I'll have the most attractive date there tonight. All the males will be jealous of me and what's mine.

I look to Silas to provide the restaurant's name, the demonic word nearly impossible to pronounce. Vanessa doesn't seem to recognize the place, which is good, and I rock back on my heels as I gesture for her to come closer so Silas can teleport us.

He's not thrilled about being our mode of transportation, but we came up with an agreement that suits both our needs. I'll babysit his children for one weekend if he provides Vanessa and me with two round-trip excursions within Wrath. I used up the first when we went to the lava fields, and this will be the second.

It's a good deal, especially since I would've watched the children for free. Shifters love kids, and the tiny demons have a great time wreaking havoc within my pack. I'll take this time to teach them how to hunt. It's about time the twins learn. They're almost six.

Vanessa approaches, and I place my hand on her waist. She touches the fabric of my shirt, her fingers toying with it before she looks up at me and grins.

"I prefer you in leathers," she says.

I gulp. I want to see her in leathers so badly, but I won't voice my desires. Vanessa wears modest clothing, her fabric lacking shape and covering most of her body. Shifter women show much more skin, and I don't want my mate to feel she needs to dress the same to make me happy.

"Down, Bear," Silas says, grabbing Vanessa's and my shoulders.

I don't enjoy his teasing, but I'm too busy stabilizing Vanessa to comment on it. She wobbles as we're teleported, and I hold her tightly until the world has re-materialized around us. We're standing outside, right next to the large, wooden restaurant doors. The dark-red paint is chipping in the corners, but the cobblestone beneath our feet is new.

"Thanks," Vanessa says, grabbing my arm.

I beam. "Happy to help."

I curl my fingers around hers, interlocking them before leading her inside. Silas follows, and he sits at the bar while Vanessa and I are brought to our table. I requested a booth next to the tree trunk, and I'm happy to see they accommodated.

Vanessa doesn't say anything as we sit. She's too busy staring at the giant tree sprouting out of the center of the restaurant. It's one of the oldest in Wrath, almost ten thousand years old, and this building has been built around its base.

I've heard the food here isn't great, but the ambiance makes up for it. Vanessa feels an affinity to trees, and I hope this one gives her plenty of good feelings.

Her cheeks flush, and my heart pounds as she reaches out and slides her palm down the trunk. Her throat bobs as she swallows, and I find much pleasure in how she shuts her eyes so she can better feel.

"It's beautiful," she whispers.

That's music to my ears.

"I'm glad you like it."

This makes wearing uncomfortable pants more than worth it. Vanessa is so distracted by the tree that she doesn't even look at the menu, and I happily pick out and order food for us both as she pokes and prods at the trunk.

I'm sure people are taking photos of us, but I don't care who sees me admiring my mate. I want everybody to see us together and know we're happy. More importantly, though, I want them to know Vanessa has chosen me.

She's mine.

"The shifter lands are full of trees this old," I say, unable to hold back any longer. "Many are even larger."

That captures Vanessa's attention, and I sit up straighter.

"How old?" she asks. "And how big?"

"Twice as old and twice as big." I'm bragging, but I don't care. "There are forests full of them. Hundreds, thousands of them as far as the eye can see."

Vanessa looks like she's going to jump out of her skin, and I'm sure I look the same as she begins hammering me with questions about my lands. She looks so excited, and I desperately hope she'll be open to visiting soon. I'd love to show her my pack and my home.

"My father is helping me expand my home," I eventually admit. "I'm making my kitchen larger and adding an island."

Vanessa sucks her lips into her mouth, her cheeks reddening. We haven't discussed the possibility of her moving to the shifter realm. There's never been a good opportunity to bring it up, and I don't want her feeling rushed. She's only just agreed to give our relationship a chance, and I won't risk ruining it.

But I can't resist telling her about my home.

"Do you miss your pack?" she asks.

I shrug. "Yes, but I'd rather be with you. My father is overseeing things in my absence."

Vanessa hums. "I've read a lot about your father."

I frown, the reaction automatic, before forcing my face into a softer emotion. People know what happened between my dad and Charlie, and many have condemned him for his desires. The blessed breeds consider him a traitor to matehood, and no explanation from my mother has helped.

I too was angry with my dad for touching a woman who wasn't my mom, but I let it go. My mom's a succubus, and as much as I don't enjoy thinking about it, I understand she has needs and wants that don't necessarily align with shifter beliefs.

I shiver, wishing I didn't know the things I know.

Dad still worships the ground she walks on, and as long as he makes her happy, I'll keep my judgments to myself. My father has never been anything less than a loving parent, and that counts for something.

"What have you heard?" I ask.

Vanessa cocks her head to the side. She's trying to read me just as much as I'm trying to read her. It's a dance I enjoy.

"I read that he was the bear alpha before you, and he helped with the female rescue before you stepped in," she says.

I nod, and Vanessa leans against the back cushion of the booth.

"I've read much about you, too," she continues.

Oh? This interests me greatly, and I prop my elbows onto the table and lean closer. My female has researched me, and I'm eager to hear her thoughts. Most people like me. I don't make women uncomfortable, and I'm friendly to almost everybody I meet. I hope that means she's read good things.

There was a brief period of negative press when word got out that I met and frightened away my mate, but interest in my wrongdoings has diminished. People no longer care, which I personally think is ideal. I hate when people think poorly of me.

"What have you read?" I ask.

Vanessa shoots me a coy smile. She's growing comfortable around me, and I decide not to bring up the images of my penis. I don't want to make our conversation sexual.

I want to learn everything there is to know about my mate, and sex will only distract from that.

Vanessa lowers her gaze to the table, her cheeks turning pink. I continue to stare at her, desperate to know her thoughts. What has she read about me? I need to know, especially when I see how it's making her flush.

"Tell me what you've read, my mate," I tease her.

I'm flirting with her, and I'm enjoying every second of it.

Vanessa clears her throat, meeting my eye. "I read that you're scared of birds."

I stiffen. "Most shifters don't like flying animals," I say. "We cannot easily fight something attacking us from the sky."

Vanessa laughs, the noise high-pitched and light as the server brings over our food. My mate thinks she's so funny, but if she keeps it up, I'll be forced to do something she doesn't like. I'm unsure how to frustrate her without causing fear or stress, but I have some ideas.

She likes seeing my erections, and I'm not above hiding mine until she apologizes. Yes. I think that's exactly what I'll do.

We eat our food in comfortable silence, and I admire Vanessa admiring the tree. I have a feeling she would sit here for days if she could, and I'm so happy she's pleased with my choice of restaurant.

Hours pass, and tables around us fill and empty. Eventually, a server brings over a check and politely urges us to leave. Vanessa pouts. I love it, and I can't stop smiling as I pay our bill and guide her toward Silas. He's still sitting at the bar.

"I hope this was a good date," I admit. "I'm new to this."

Vanessa grabs my arm, her hand resting in the crook of my elbow.

"I had a good time." She gives me a tight squeeze. "Thank you, Chev."

Silas stands as we near, capturing my attention. I pull Vanessa away from him a second later, my nose crinkling. He smells like alcohol.

"Are you two finished?" he asks. "Long meal."

"Absolutely not." I grunt, reaching for my phone.

Aziel picks up on the third ring, and he's here a minute later to bring Vanessa and me back to the facility. Silas is clearly annoyed, but he's a fool if he thinks I'd let him teleport us when he's been drinking.

Vanessa finds the entire thing humorous. She laughs and labels me a drama queen. She also calls me a tattletale, but I don't know what that means, and I don't care. Her insults don't bother me.

I will always protect her from getting teleported by a drunken fool.

Aziel brings us to Vanessa's house, and he disappears a second later. I walk Vanessa up her porch, my hands clasped behind my back. Would it be inappropriate to kiss her? I've been wanting to do it all day.

Vanessa unlocks her door before spinning to face me. Her lips are so close to mine.

"You know," she starts, "I trust you, and I don't think it's necessary for you to bring a chaperone to our dates anymore."

Those words are music to my ears, and I excitedly pull her against my chest before pressing my lips against hers. She squeals, and as realization washes over me, I panic and release her. *Fuck.* I shouldn't grab my female.

Vanessa peers up at me, but she doesn't look upset. I feel horrible, and I remain rigid as she presses herself against me.

"It's okay, Chev," she whispers.

I think I'm going to puke, and I hold my breath as she wraps her arms around me. Then she kisses me, letting her hands wander underneath my shirt. She's not scared.

"I love you," I blurt out.

Vanessa pinches my forearm, but I don't mind.

Someday she'll say it back.

Chapter Nineteen

CHEV

VANESSA IS LATE to leave her house the next morning, so we hardly have any time to talk before I drive her to work. She runs inside the second we arrive, too.

I try not to let it get to me, but it's all I can think about during the day. I attend meeting after meeting, which makes the first half of the day pass quickly. I haven't been to the headquarters in weeks, and with so many people eager to touch base with me, it shows.

Over lunch, I return to the shifter lands and continue working on my home. My dad quickly joins in, and we get a good amount completed before I need to return to work.

Echo finds me after lunch, and she immediately launches into several lectures. I can tell she's been waiting to see me in person to unload, and I putter around on my computer while she vents her feelings. She needs this.

"Have you considered stepping down?"

Her question pulls me from my thoughts. I don't know how to answer it, so I don't. It's not the first time I've been asked, and I know I'm running myself ragged between my work with the females and now trying to build my relationship with Vanessa.

It's not sustainable.

By the time I finish work and return to Wrath, I'm exhausted. Aziel's house is suspiciously quiet, and I listen for signs of life as I shut off the portal and begin heading down the hallway that will bring me to the front door.

Vanessa should be getting out of work any minute now, and I don't want to be late. She tends to leave work at varying times, and I want to get there early so she doesn't have to wait for me. Not that she would. I have a feeling my mate would hop right into her golf cart and drive herself home. She doesn't wait for a man, even if he's me.

"Chev!"

I ignore Aziel, but he shouts my name again.

I resist the urge to groan as I step back into the open doorway I just walked past. It's Aziel's office. He's sitting behind his desk, and he waves me in the second we lock eyes. What does he want?

"What?" I ask.

"Good evening to you, too," he says, spinning his computer in my direction. "Word's gotten out about you and Vanessa."

I step closer to better see his screen. There's an image of Vanessa and me sitting in her golf cart outside the Wrath facility. This must have been taken a few days ago. She has her arms wrapped around me, and I'm staring at her with a stupid smile toying at the corners of my lips. Her face is tucked against my shoulder, but the reporters don't need a clear view of it to figure out who she is.

"What are people saying?" I ask.

Aziel hesitates, which is all the answer I need.

"Schedule me a public interview tomorrow," I order, glaring at the screen before reaching out and touching it. "And send me this image. I like it."

I knew this was a possibility. Nymphs are a weaker breed, and I feared people would have negative things to say about it. I refuse to hear it, and I'll correct the lies being spread about my mate.

I have enough physical strength for both of us, and she carries the emotional strength of our pairing. Vanessa is perfect for me in every way, and I won't let sexist men or jealous women say otherwise.

"I'm not your assistant, Chev," Aziel says.

I'm too angry to respond, and I wave away his words before storming out of his office. Either he'll do it himself or he'll tell his assistant to do it. Either way, I know it will be done. Aziel can be an idiot at times, but he's reliable.

Vanessa's golf cart is still parked where I left it this morning, and I let out a sigh of relief before plopping down in the driver's seat. I don't want to be in a sour mood when I see her, but I can't stop myself from pulling out my phone and checking to see what people are saying. It's only a matter of time before she sees this, and I need to know just how bad things are.

She's insecure about our relationship and what she can offer me, and this is going to make things worse. People will know she was once a purchased female, and they'll accurately assume there's no physical intimacy between us. Men will say they'd never want a woman who won't let them fuck, and women will openly discuss the things they'd let me do to their bodies.

It will crush Vanessa.

I read through the articles, my anger spiking as my assumptions are proven correct. People are cruel, and I curse when I accidentally break my phone. It crunches in my hand, and I let out a quiet groan as I slam it onto the seat beside me.

Then I swipe it off the golf cart altogether, letting it tumble to the ground.

Vanessa is mine, and I want her.

I'll righten things during my interview tomorrow. Then I'll have the news reporters saying these vile things fired. They'll lose their jobs and their livelihood, and if they continue to badmouth my mate, they will also lose their lives.

I do not care.

Vanessa exits the building, and I plaster a smile on my lips as I wave her over. I don't want to frighten her with my anger. She offers a timid wave as she approaches, her arms full of paperwork.

"How was your day?"

She shrugs, and I can tell she hasn't seen the articles. That's good. I need her to stay far away from them. I will break her phone if need be.

She begins telling me about her day, and I do my best to remain focused. My heart pounds as we near her house, and I grab her hand as I park. Vanessa pauses, staring down at where we connect. I think she can tell something is off with me, and I take a moment to collect my thoughts before speaking.

"There's something I need to tell you," I say.

Her pulse begins to race, and she worries her bottom lip between her teeth as she stares up at me. She looks nervous, but I'm sure my expression matches. Still, I want her to hear this news from me.

"A photo of us was leaked," I say. "People know you're my mate."

Silence. It's long and painful as it stretches between us.

Vanessa shuts her eyes. I wait, running my thumb over the back of her hand. Several minutes pass, and my desperation grows. I need to know what she's thinking. When Vanessa finally opens her eyes again, her expression is unreadable. She's hidden her emotion behind a blank face.

She's shut down.

"What are they saying?"

Chapter Twenty

CHEV

I DON'T KNOW how to answer Vanessa. I refuse to repeat the words.

She stares up at me, waiting. I'm beginning to panic. I'm not going to repeat the lies and assumptions. They will do no good.

Her phone is sitting on her lap, and without thinking, I snatch it up and crumple it in my fist.

I'm mildly aware this might scare her, but instead of fear, I see only defeat in her reaction. She knows why I did that, and her chest expands with breath before she slowly lets it out.

"I see." Her voice is quiet. "Would you like to come inside?"

"Yes."

Vanessa climbs out of her golf cart, and I quickly follow. This is the first time my mate has invited me inside her house, but I feel only dread. She's inviting me inside because she thinks I need more time to tell her what's being said. I have no intention of doing so.

It doesn't matter what people are saying.

Vanessa unlocks her front door and steps inside.

"Sorry about the mess," she says, moving to the side and

gesturing for me to enter.

I'm still in disbelief that she's invited me into her home, and a tiny thread of excitement weaves through me as I step inside and look around. This place smells so strongly of her, and I fight with my bear when he threatens to make his mating noises again.

Now is not the time.

"I see no mess," I say.

The place is spotless, and I find the few items lying about endearing. Her breakfast dishes are scattered around the kitchen, and a smile spreads over my lips as I imagine her rushing around cooking something delicious to eat. Sometimes she dances when she cooks, and I wonder if she did so this morning.

Vanessa shuts her front door, but she doesn't lock it as she usually does. She doesn't fully trust me, not yet, and she probably wants to keep an easy escape from me. I try not to let it hurt my feelings, and I stick close to the wall and try to make myself small. This is her home, her space of comfort and safety, and I don't want to ruin it.

She brushes past me, her pace fast as she grabs and throws her dirty dishes into the sink. I want to help her, but I don't think she'd appreciate me drawing attention to the small mess. She's clearly embarrassed.

Instead, I take a seat on her couch.

I can't tell if she's genuinely anxious about the slightly dirty state of her home or if she's trying to prolong our conversation, but I remain patient either way. I still don't know what to say to her, and I use this time to find the most delicate words. I won't go into detail. I refuse, and I will destroy every device in her home if I need to.

After several minutes, Vanessa finally meanders to the couch. Her hands are clasped tightly behind her back, and she scans me head to toe before taking a seat on my left. I'm not too fond of the distance between us, and I stare at the gap between our thighs before turning my upper body toward her. She copies me, and I take her hands.

"Is this okay?" I ask.

I can't tell if her thundering heart is due to discomfort with our touching or just general anxiety. Vanessa glances at our connected hands before giving a jerky nod.

"What are they saying, Chev?" she asks.

I will not lie to her, but I won't give details. They're saying we're not a good match because she's not physically strong, and they assume I'm devastated by the fact that she's my mate. They're talking about how important physical intimacy is for shifters, and how disappointed I must be to have a mate who's been taken before. I read one article that said I probably regret saving myself. It's not true.

Their words make me sick.

"People are not being kind," I admit.

Vanessa's hands shake.

"But they're wrong," I assure her. "I'm so grateful for you, and I'm proud to be your mate. I'm happy with you, Vanessa. You're enough. You're always going to be enough—more than enough."

Vanessa's eyes grow wet. Why is she crying? I slide my hand down her arm, wanting to comfort her but unsure how. I usually wait for her to initiate our contact, but when tears begin to streak down her cheeks, I wrap my arms around her waist and pull her against my chest.

She folds into me, her cheek resting against my skin as she returns my hug. I slide my hand up and down her back, beyond pleased she's letting this happen.

"Is there anything else?" she asks.

I hate this.

"They're making assumptions about our level of intimacy," I say.

Vanessa stiffens, but I'm not surprised. I had a feeling this was going to be the thing that hurt her most—mainly because the rumors are true. She and I are not intimate, and there are no plans for that to change.

I release Vanessa and kneel on the ground between her thighs. I want to hug her tightly, and I think that will be better done when I'm below her. She peers down at me as I wrap my arms around her torso. This position brings my face close to her breasts, but I pretend I don't notice as she buries her face into the hair on top of my head.

Her body relaxes as my scent fills her lungs, which pleases my bear. Loud noises begin to pour from my chest, and Vanessa giggles when she hears them. It's not the mating call my bear usually makes, this one deeper and slower. He's trying to comfort her the only way he knows how, and it seems to be working as Vanessa turns to putty in my arms.

It's lulling her to sleep.

I'm lulling my mate to sleep.

It's the best feeling that exists, and I continue running a soothing hand up and down her back as she gradually goes limp. The mate bond hums between us, beyond content. It's making me sleepy, too, but I force myself to remain awake.

I want to enjoy every second of this.

I hold Vanessa until long after the sky has grown dark. This is the best day of my life, and I bury my face in her hair and smell her for hours. My back aches from being in the same position for so long, and I grimace as I finally work up the strength to pull away and stretch my spine. The movement doesn't wake Vanessa, but I'm sure that has to do with our bond. My scent has surrounded her, and she unconsciously feels safe.

I stare at her sleeping form, hesitating, before lifting her into my arms and carrying her upstairs.

Her bedroom smells so strongly of her, and I allow myself to enjoy it as I pull back her sheets and lay her down. I love how her nose scrunches when I finally pull away, and I hurry back as she cracks open an eye and peers up at me.

I don't want her to be scared of me, and I slouch my shoulders as she looks around the room. It was a bad idea to bring her up here. This is her private space, and I shouldn't have intruded.

To my complete surprise, though, Vanessa blows out a tuft of air and rolls away. I don't think I've ever felt more relief, and despite how badly I want to stay here and watch, I remember Charlie's advice and leave.

My mate likes privacy, and I need to give her space.

I don't want to go, and I make sure to lock all of Vanessa's doors and windows before shifting into my bear and returning to Aziel's home. Silas is waiting for me.

"Where were you?" he asks.

I don't answer. I am an adult, and the time I spend with my mate is of no concern to him.

"You have an interview tomorrow morning. The crew will be at your office at six sharp," Silas continues, following me through the house. "Aziel said you wish to discuss the rumors of you and Vanessa, but you'll have to tell the reporters what topics are off-limits."

"Nothing is off-limits," I say.

I wish to clear every rumor spreading about Vanessa and me.

Silas clears his throat. "Are you sure? They're going to—"

"I'm sure." I turn into my bedroom and shut the door in his face.

Vanessa is sure to find a way to look herself up tomorrow morning, and I want my interview to be the first thing she sees.

Everybody will be talking about it, and I want to clutter the feeds so Vanessa can't find the cruel articles already written about her.

If I could, I'd have Silas scrub the articles from the internet, but I fear upsetting the balance. Things are working well for us right now, and I don't want to give Mammon a reason to speak out against us. Controlling the media is a sure way to do that.

I go to bed, and I wake up and dress before the sun rises. My interview isn't for several more hours, and I sit at the kitchen island and prepare myself for every possible question that will be thrown at me.

The house gradually begins to stir, and when I hear tiny feet pattering in my direction, I get up and begin pulling food out of Aziel's fridge. The shadows typically cook all our meals, but the children wake early—and hungry.

"Uncle Chev!"

I hum and turn toward the tiny demon standing at my feet. Valeria holds the stuffed bear I gave her for her birthday last year, her sticky fingers curled around its throat as she drags it behind her. It's a very ominous hold, but I suppose I should be complimented by how much she likes my gift.

It looks just like me.

Gray says she sleeps with it every night, and I smile before picking her up and setting her on the kitchen counter.

"Are you hungry?" I ask. I already know the answer.

Valeria nods, and I listen to see if any of her parents are awake before pouring her a bowl of cereal and milk. I should make her something nutritious, but I lack patience this morning. Plus, her parents don't let her eat sugary foods for breakfast, and I'm not above breaking the rules to win her affection.

I want the tiny fate to like me.

"Are you excited to start school next week?" I ask, leading her to the table.

She beams, and I resist the urge to laugh when she sets her stuffed bear on the seat beside her. I put the cereal in front of her, beyond proud of myself as she begins to scarf it down.

"Daddy A's taking me shopping for new dresses today," she says, her chin held high. "He said I can pick out five."

I sit across from her and steal one of the marshmallow bits from her bowl.

"Do you know how many Cassia is getting?" she continues.

I shake my head. "How many?"

"None, because she's not going to school because she's still a baby."

I can't contain my laughter, and I press a hand to my lips to stifle it. Cassia hates being called a "baby," and the young wrath resorts to screaming whenever the word is uttered in her direction.

Valeria rambles about all the things Aziel has promised to buy her for school, her voice growing louder as the man in question wanders into the room. He rubs his eyes and nods in my direction before plopping down at the head of the table.

"You look like shit," he says.

He purses his lips and glances at Valeria, clear nervousness written across his features. He's not supposed to swear in front of her. She repeats everything he says.

He turns back to me. "Did you sleep?"

"No."

It's about time for me to leave, and I pat Valeria on the head and make my way to the portal before I get scolded for feeding her sugar. I haven't been to the headquarters in weeks, and I mentally prepare for it before turning on the portal and stepping through.

Noise assaults my ears, and I linger by the portal for a moment before heading toward my office. Echo is already waiting inside, her eyes narrowed on the three men setting up interview equipment—cameras, lighting, everything I hate.

I greet her. "Good morning."

I'm not in the mood to hear her lecture, and I'm relieved when she doesn't give one.

"Can I sit in on your interview?"

I nod, and she takes a seat along the right wall. I settle in at my desk, unused to being here. My office is familiar, but it no longer brings me the comfort it once did. I'm only comfortable with Vanessa.

The three men shoot me continual nervous glances as they prepare for the interview. I openly stare at them. It's no secret that shifter males are protective of their mates, and these men work for an organization that publicly insulted mine. They should be nervous.

Another man enters the room. I recognize him. He's a reporter, one I often see in front of the camera. He himself insulted my mate. I read the transcript of his broadcast last night. I read every fucking word of it.

I'm surprised Aziel organized my interview with him.

My office door opens again, and I bite back a smile as Charlie, Aziel, Gray, and Silas step inside. The children are nowhere to be seen, but I assume they're wreaking havoc somewhere in the building. My heart soars. My friends are here to support me.

"It's time," I say, glancing at my computer.

Vanessa will be awake in one hour and thirty minutes, and I fully intend to be at her house when she does.

My interviewer clears his throat and glances at his notes. He's a tiny man. Easy to crush.

"Yes," he mumbles. "I suppose it is."

His voice shakes, and I share a look with Aziel. He sucks his cheeks into his mouth, visibly holding back laughter. This interviewer spoke quite bluntly when he could hide behind his screen, but he's afraid to talk to me directly. It's humorous.

There's a moment of silence as the man operating the camera finishes some last-minute touches, getting the angle perfect. The man interviewing me takes a seat opposite my desk. His hands are shaking. I love to see it.

We begin.

"Is it true that your mate is Vanessa Bryne?"

I resist the urge to sigh. This is going to be a long hour.

"Yes."

"And is it true she's a nymph?"

His eyes narrow, and I know he's trying to read my reaction. He's hoping to see me flinch or show embarrassment, but I won't. I'm not embarrassed by my mate. I never will be.

"She is," I confirm.

The interviewer's cheeks turn pink, and I glance at Gray.

His lust fills the room. Why is he doing this? The man stumbles over his next question, and I bite the inside of my cheek as he glances at Echo. He's giving her eyes. Why? Echo smiles, and I fight not to react when she presses her elbows together and leans forward.

That whore.

They've planned this.

"My mate is Vanessa Byrne," I repeat. "And I would like to clear up some things."

The interviewer is too distracted by Echo to lead our conversation, and I happily take advantage of this as I talk about my mate.

"Several rumors are going around about us, most of which are untrue. Echo hired Vanessa several months ago as a facility manager, and we didn't discover we were mates until her second week here. She was hired on her own merit, and she's made several improvements within the Wrath facility. I will tell you them all now."

I discuss the classes she's encouraged the women inside the facility to partake in and the impressive successes they've been. I'm practically beaming with pride while I talk, and I have to pause several times to calm before continuing.

"Vanessa is passionate about her work," I continue, "and her resilience is something I greatly admire."

Her history with the ogres remains private, and the information is safely stored in our protected files. I will never share her personal business with others.

My heart pounds, and I clear my throat before beginning to discuss my next topic. This will ruin my career.

I share my wrongdoings. I admit to the mistakes I made when we met, going into detail so people understand why she ran from me. I'm not the good man they think I am, and I want them to know that. They once defended Vanessa, but enough time has passed that they've forgotten what I did to her. I make sure they remember.

The small man interviewing me continues to stare at my sister. He does this for the entire hour, hardly getting a question in. I don't mind. I have a lot to say.

"We are finished now," I say when the hour ends.

The man puts the camera down, and the lights blinding me are turned off.

Gray's lust gradually dissipates, and he shivers before grabbing Silas and Charlie and disappearing from the room. I'm hardly paying them any attention, though. My sister is still pushing her breasts out, and I glare at the side of her head as she stands and saunters out of the room. She's proud of herself. I'm going to smack her with a stick later, and then I'm going to tell Dad what she did.

I don't need her fighting my battles.

My interviewer turns back to me, and he puffs up his cheeks as he shifts his attention to his notes. I'm sure there were plenty of questions he wanted to get to, but he was too distracted by Echo to ask them. I did a lot of speaking, but not a lot of answering.

He'll likely be fired for this. I never give interviews, and this was a good opportunity.

Aziel approaches my desk.

"Would you like me to take you to Vanessa's?" he asks.

Of course. I stand and hold out my arm, waving it in his direction. He snorts, and I'm staring at my mate's front door a second later.

Chapter Twenty-One

CHEV

I WAIT OUTSIDE, sitting on Vanessa's porch.

She should be awake any minute now. I broke her phone so she can't use the alarm, but the sun should be shining through her bedroom window by now. I want her to wake up, and I tap my fingers against the ground while I wait.

Eventually, I hear stomping inside, and I stand just as Vanessa storms out of her front door. She must have changed into a nightgown sometime during the night, and she looks at me with crazy eyes and messy hair. I don't think I've ever seen her move so fast this early in the morning, and I try not to panic.

Is she angry?

She storms toward me, and I hold my breath as she throws her arms around my waist. I want to enjoy it, but I find I'm too nervous to. I didn't tell her about my interview, and maybe that was a mistake. I don't think she knows about it, though. I broke her phone, so there's no way for her to have seen anything.

"Are you okay?" I ask.

It doesn't appear she's been crying. She buries her face against my neck and breathes me in. Despite my panic, I enjoy feeling our bodies pressed firmly together. Vanessa is tiny in my arms, and she smells good. I wrap my arms back around her. I will hold her for as long as she wants me to.

Several seconds pass before she pulls away.

I can't help but notice how thin her nightgown is. I've seen her wear it before when I was watching from the woods, but now I'm close enough to see detail. There is a lot of detail—particularly of the skin underneath. I can see the shape of her nipples and every curve of her body.

Has she realized she's wearing this in front of me? It seems unlike her.

"Did you mean it?" she asks.

I blink, struggling to follow along.

"Your interview this morning," she clarifies. "Did you mean it?"

I nod. I meant every word I said. Vanessa is everything I've ever wanted, and I'm honored to be her mate.

"I meant every word," I promise her.

Vanessa pulls me back into her arms, and I'm more than happy to return the hold. She buries her head against my chest, and I rock us side to side. I am obsessed with this woman.

"How did you see it?" I ask. "I broke your phone."

"I still have a TV. Every channel was broadcasting it."

Of course.

Vanessa pulls away, and I push a strand of hair behind her ear. I enjoy seeing her face unobstructed, and it's a good distraction from the breasts that threaten to steal my attention.

"Are you hungry?" Vanessa asks, a light flush spreading over her cheeks. "I'm making breakfast."

She's offering to cook for me? I've been waiting for this, and I swallow past the lump in my throat as I nod. I want to kiss her, but I refrain as she wraps her hand around mine and leads me inside.

What did I say that made her so happy? I can't think of anything especially noteworthy or sappy. All I did was tell the truth. If this is how she reacts when I do the bare minimum, I can't wait to see what she does when I go out of my way to please her.

I slide into a seat at the kitchen island before she sees my body's reaction to her. Her innocent touches are arousing me, and I need to get away before I make her uncomfortable.

She must have cleaned since I was here last night, as her kitchen now spotless. I immensely enjoyed the look of her home lived-in, but I suppose this is nice, too. It's clear Charlie decorated the place, but I see touches of Vanessa throughout. There's a stack of cookbooks resting on the kitchen counter, and there are several short vases full of sprouting plants.

My body gradually softens, and only once I'm sure my arousal isn't noticeable do I stand and approach one of the vases. Aziel warned me that Vanessa doesn't like cut flowers, and she's growing these from seed. Their tiny roots are visible, and I trace them with my eyes before turning back to my mate.

She's pretending to be busy working, but her heart is racing. I distract her.

"Do you feel an affinity for these?" I ask, gesturing to the flowers.

Vanessa shakes her head, her lips curling down in the corners. "No," she says. "I don't feel anything for flowers. I just like the look of them."

I'm going to remember that. I don't have any flowers decorating my home, but that will be easy to change. I'll plant some the next time I'm home, and I'll make sure to do it from seed. Hopefully, they'll be sprouting by the time Vanessa decides to come home with me.

Vanessa begins pulling food out of the fridge.

"How'd you sleep?" I ask.

The question is selfish, but I don't care. She spent most of the night in my arms, and I'm eager to hear how that made her feel. I think I'll throw myself into a volcano if she says she didn't enjoy it, but I'm hopeful it doesn't come to that.

"I had a good night," Vanessa admits.

Her cheeks redden before she turns toward the stove. Her back is to me, and I quietly join her in the kitchen. I'm careful to move slowly and keep my steps noisy, not wanting to come across as frightening. I hate that Vanessa fears me, and if I could make myself a smaller man, I would.

"Did you enjoy me holding you?" I ask.

Vanessa's grip on her spatula tightens as I approach, but it's the only reaction she gives. She's nervous, but I hope in a good way. She makes me nervous, too.

I continue toward her, but I stop when I smell her arousal. My bear immediately perks up and begins making noises, but I don't blame him. Why is Vanessa aroused? I'm not sure what's gotten into her today, from her enthusiastic hug and cooking me breakfast to her arousal, but I'm not complaining. Vanessa is opening up to me, and I love every second of it.

I come up behind her, and her addicting scent grows. I fight against my bear when he tries to make his mating noises, but it doesn't work and they come pouring out, anyway.

"Did you enjoy me holding you?" I repeat.

Vanessa clears her throat before giving a jerky nod.

I hum, hiding a smile as I stare at the back of her head. I'm growing hard, and I'm relieved she's facing away from me. There's no hiding the way my leathers are tenting.

I want to tease her, but I'm scared to go too far and ruin the delicate balance we've found. Vanessa doesn't know what she wants, which I understand entirely, but she also doesn't like initiating. She prefers me to do it, but it's hard when the line between arousal and fear is so thin.

"I can smell you," I whisper.

Vanessa sucks in a shaky breath. Her arousal is so thick, and I so badly want to taste it. I want to put my mouth between her soft thighs, and once she's cummed on my tongue, I want to replace my lips with my cock. I'm a dirty male.

"Chev…" Vanessa says. "What're you thinking?"

"You know what I'm thinking."

She turns off the stove and sets her spatula down, but she still doesn't turn around to face me.

"Are you…?" She pauses and clears her throat. "Is your…?"

"Yes." I answer her unspoken question. "My cock is hard."

She gasps. "Are you touching it?"

"Should I be?"

There's a long pause, and I hold my breath. I'd never dream of touching myself in her presence. I feel dirty enough when I do it alone, but to do it in front of her is not a thought I've ever entertained. It's not something I thought she'd be comfortable with.

Vanessa's arousal continues to saturate the air, my scent mixing in. I slide my hand up my thigh, but I won't touch myself until I have her explicit permission. I need her to tell me she wants it.

"Yes," Vanessa says.

I shut my eyes, squeezing them tightly in the desperate hope this isn't a dream. I might die if I wake up and discover none of this is real.

My length twitches, and I sink my teeth into my bottom lip as I curl a hand around myself. My hips instantly jerk forward, seeking friction, and I tighten my grip before sliding my fist from base to tip. I let myself moan, wanting Vanessa to hear it.

"I'm touching myself," I admit.

Vanessa grabs the counter in front of her, curling her fingers around the edge before moving her hair off the back of her neck. She's showing me her mate mark.

I'm so fucking hard.

Her mark has grown darker and longer, extending into the neckline of her silk nightgown. I carefully pull the fabric away from her back so I can see where it ends. The line is thin, no thicker than a stem on a fallen leaf, and it ends between her shoulder blades.

Vanessa shivers, but I don't touch her. I can tell she wants me to, but I refuse. I do curl my fist around myself, though. The temptation is too great not to.

"I won't make assumptions," I say. "You need to tell me explicitly what you want."

She's shaking.

"Touch my mark, Chev."

My hips jerk forward, my cock sliding through my fist.

I use my other hand to touch Vanessa's mark. It teases me, and I happily trail my fingers down the length of it. She's so fucking soft. Someday, if she lets me, I'd love to rub myself against her mark. I want my cock to be the reason she cums.

I slide my thumb from the base of her mark to the very top. Vanessa moans, the noise quiet and full of need.

"Do my fingers feel good?" I ask.

I place my palm against her shoulder and rub my thumb up and down. I know it makes her cum, but I want to learn more. I want to know everything about it.

"Yes," Vanessa gasps. "But it feels better when you put your mouth on it."

I release myself, afraid to cum. I wasn't expecting that, and I'm getting too excited.

I release her neck, too, and I plant both my hands on the counter before sucking in a slow, calming breath. I need to calm down before I embarrass myself.

Vanessa touches the back of my hands, her fingers tracing the visible veins before she spins in my arms. Her eyes meet mine for a brief second before dropping down. There's no point hiding my erection—it's impossible—and I remain still while my mate eyes me. My leathers cover me, but barely.

"You're always hard when you touch me," she says. "Do you take care of yourself after?"

I nod. "I can taste you on my tongue for hours," I admit.

It only takes one or two strokes for me to reach completion, but that's a minor detail I'm not going to tell Vanessa. I never want to lie to my mate, but if she asks, this will be one I tell.

Vanessa reaches for the tie on my side, the only thing holding my leathers together. It's a loose knot, and my heart pounds as she loosens it and lets the fabric fall to the floor. She's removing my clothing.

She's looking at me.

My erection hangs heavily between my thighs, and I hope she's not disappointed by what she sees. Vanessa continues to stare, but her expression is unreadable. Our bond hums, which I take as a good sign, and I clasp my hands behind my back as I wait for further instruction.

I've always fantasized about being rough with my mate. Most shifter males are, but I don't feel that urge with Vanessa. For once, I'm thankful to have incubus blood in me. While I don't share most of their desires, my need to please my mate is one I *have* picked up on. I want to make Vanessa happy more than I want to dominate her, and my bear makes no complaints as I lower my chin and wait for her to tell me what to do.

My female has been through so much, and I will never be a

male who takes from her.

My mark is almost black by now, and I resist the urge to shiver when she ghosts her finger over the skin. She's so close to my cock. One slight movement, and she would be touching it.

Vanessa clears her throat, her eyes still lingering on my shaft. "I'm okay with you pleasuring yourself while you lick my mark."

My bear begins his annoying fucking rumbling, but Vanessa only smiles as I punch my chest to try to make it stop. That smile turns into a laugh as she spins and moves her hair out of the way again. She wants me to lick her, and she wants me to touch myself while I do so.

I punch my chest, desperate for the embarrassing noises to stop.

"Let him." Vanessa chuckles. "I like it."

I drop my fist, and the noises grow louder.

"Can I cum?" I ask.

"I should hope so."

Vanessa laughs, proud of her little joke, but it's cut short when I dart forward and drag my tongue up the length of her mark. She plants her hands on the countertop, stabilizing herself as I curl my fist around myself and stroke. My Vanessa curses, encouraging me to continue.

This is the best day of my life.

I fuck my fist at the same pace I lick her, my hips twitching as I pant against her warm skin. It feels so fucking good, and heat coils in my lower belly. I'm going to cum so quickly, and I squeeze my eyes shut as it builds.

Vanessa's moaning grows louder, and I cry against her as my cock begins to leak. It wants to be inside her, and I tighten my grip on myself as I begin to cum. Vanessa shivers, and I quickly catch her when her knees give out.

She pants as she orgasms, and for a long moment, the sound

of our heavy breathing is the only thing filling the room. Then it's replaced with giggles, and I let out a relieved sigh as I drop my head onto her shoulder. The sound of Vanessa's laughter makes my heart soar, and I hide my grin in her hair as her shoulders shake against my chest.

My mate is happy.

"I love you," I say.

Vanessa's fingers find mine, and she doesn't seem disgusted when she accidentally touches the cum on my palm. She doesn't necessarily seem pleased about it, but she's only grossed out in a way I assume most people would be.

There's no fear when she interacts with my fluids.

"It's too soon for that, Chev," Vanessa says.

"Okay." I don't care. I'm only conceding to please her.

I will continue to love my mate, even if she thinks it's too soon. Vanessa may be able to shape most of my emotions and decisions, but she has no control over this. I love her, and nobody will make me change my mind.

"I think I've worked up an appetite," I say, finally releasing her.

I need to wash my hands and redress.

Vanessa chuckles at my subtle request for her to continue cooking, and I shift my weight from foot to foot before playfully tapping my fingers against her butt. Vanessa swats me away. It's the first time I've touched her butt, and I feel awfully proud of myself as I head toward the sink.

I'm a very sneaky male.

Chapter Twenty-Two

VANESSA

CHEV PULLS UP to the back door of the facility, and I debate asking him to take me home as I stare up at the building.

I'm sure everybody inside knows about Chev and me, and they've probably seen the interview, too. Thanks to Chev destroying my phone, I don't know what people online are saying about me, but I can make guesses.

They aren't going to be happy.

I'm terrified.

"Are you okay?" Chev asks, no doubt sensing my worry. "Do you want me to take you home? I can call Aziel and Echo and tell them you aren't feeling well."

I shake my head, silently rejecting the idea. As much as I'd love to do precisely that, it's not the right decision. I refuse to hide away in shame over my mate bond. It's an action I'll live to regret, and I know it would upset Chev. He's outwardly proud to be my mate, and while I don't need to go screaming my excitement from the rooftops, I don't need to cower, either.

"I'm fine," I lie.

I turn and wrap my arms around Chev, pulling him in for a

hug. I wonder how many women are watching us from the windows, and I fight the urge to look as I pull away. Chev tucks a strand of hair behind my ear, his fingertips just barely grazing against my skin.

I don't want to leave him.

"Would you like to come over for dinner?" I ask. I've been enjoying his company, and I'm growing to trust him. He won't do anything to me. "Just me and you."

Chev visibly straightens up, seemingly excited about the reminder that he doesn't need to bring a chaperone. He hasn't made a fuss about my requirement, but I'm sure he doesn't love it. My lips twitch as a smile flickers across his face.

"I'd love to," Chev says. He brushes his knuckles down my cheek. "It's about time you asked me on a date. I'll wear my finest leathers."

He's trying to lighten the mood, and it works. Despite my pounding heart and racing thoughts, I laugh. It's genuine, too, which I didn't think would be possible today. Seconds pass before I pull away from Chev and climb out of the golf cart. I'm already teetering on the edge of being late, and I can't avoid going inside any longer.

I smooth my hands down my plain work dress before heading inside. Only two guards are standing near the back entrance, and they offer me their usual friendly smiles as I approach.

"Morning," the one on the left says.

He pulls open the door for me, and I hurry through. I look over my shoulder one final time, locking eyes with Chev before the doors close. He hasn't moved, and he wears a worried expression as he watches me walk into work. It's not a good sign.

I head immediately to my office.

He may have broken my phone, but I have a computer. I need to know what people are saying about me, and I find myself holding my breath as I lock my office door and sit at my desk. I mentally prepare for the worst as I start my computer and navigate to the most popular news channels.

What I see shocks me.

There's definitely hatred, but it's not spewed toward me. It's spewed toward Chev. People are picking apart his interview, specifically the part where he shares the start of our relationship. He discusses in detail how he showed himself to me and locked me in my office, and he even took things a step further and detailed how he followed me to Wrath and stalked me.

He painted himself in the worst light possible, and people have latched on to it.

Tears fill my eyes and stream down my cheeks as I read, and I'm horrified by the cruel words. Chev must have known this would happen. He's not foolish. Even I saw how he painted himself during his interview, but I never anticipated it would cause this much backlash.

He ruined his reputation to spare mine.

I find a few articles from yesterday, ones where I'm painted as a disappointment, but they're far and few between. I doubt people like me any more now than they did yesterday, but they hate Chev more.

I navigate to the smaller, Chev-centered online forums next. The women who write here think Chev can do no wrong, and I'm relieved to see they haven't changed. They still hate me and worship Chev.

I never thought I'd be so relieved to read such horrible things about myself. The women speak all my worst fears and insecurities into existence. They say I'm too weak and damaged to ever truly make Chev happy. They accurately guess that we don't have sex and never will, and they hypothesize how long it will take him to grow sick of me and leave.

Chev has always been vocal about his excitement to find his mate, and he's spoken occasionally about how much he's looking forward to having children and sharing a bed with another. He never said anything explicitly about sex, but it was implied. Chev's always been a horny male, and he's not very good at hiding it.

One woman in the community made a video montage of Chev saying these things. I can only stomach about half of it before slamming my computer shut.

Chev will have his children. We won't have sex, but I can give him his family. We aren't ready for kids now, but I'll be happy to do it when we are. He'll be an amazing father, and I have to trust that will be enough for him.

I have to trust. I have no other options.

Chapter Twenty-Three

CHEV

CHARLIE STEPS INTO the bathroom, a laugh already on the cusp of emerging.

"You look very handsome," she compliments me.

I know she doesn't mean it. She's laughing at me. It's written clear as day on her face. She leans against the door frame, resting her shoulder against the wood as she watches Gray wash my fur. I barely fit in the tub in my bear form, but I need to be cleaned.

Cassia directs the shower spray at my face, the tiny wrath full of giggles. I swipe at her, and I'm impressed by her lack of fear as my bear's claws come only inches from her face. Instead, she giggles harder and swings her head back and forth, letting her heavy, wet hair slap around her head. She and Gray are soaking wet, but that tends to be what happens when you stick a full-grown bear in a bathtub.

Vanessa has invited me to her home for an unsupervised dinner, and I want to look my best for her.

I can count on one hand the number of times I've been cleaned in my bear form—particularly as an adult—but the humiliation of having Gray and his child assist is well worth it. Grooming is typically only done among immediate family and mates, but I don't have the patience to deal with the questions my dad is sure to spout when I ask for help bathing.

I doubt Vanessa will request to see my bear, but I want him to look good for her in case she does. First impressions are important.

Gray sits on the tub's edge, working a conditioner-soaked comb through my fur while Cassia rinses the soap off my legs. I liked it better when David was here. He was mindful of the water's temperature and the direction of the spray, but Silas pulled him away to finish his schoolwork and replaced him with the tiny wrath.

My chest vibrates when Gray snags a knot near my spine, and when I try to wiggle away, he grabs my shoulder and forces me to remain still.

"Stop complaining," he huffs. "Do you want your fur to be soft or not?"

I swipe his hand off my shoulder, annoyed, before forcing my limbs to be still. I *do* want my fur to be soft.

Gray smiles. "We're almost done."

He said that twenty minutes ago and twenty minutes before that, so I no longer believe him. Gray's a dirty liar.

Cassia gradually loses interest and wanders away with Charlie, leaving Gray and me alone. I'm happy for them to leave. It's embarrassing having to be washed like a small child, and the fewer people who see it, the better.

Gray clears his throat. "Do you want me to get your front?"

I huff, nodding as I kick out my legs and spread my arms. Well, I spread as much as the small tub will allow. Gray shifts to sit on the ledge in front of me. He leans forward and massages soap into my chest and stomach, his fingers burying in deep as he works it through my fur.

I'm not too fond of his hands on me, but I have to admit he's thorough.

We avoid eye contact as he cleans the area between my thighs.

I loved dirt as a child and had to be cleaned quite often by my mom and dad, but I never remember it being this awkward. Innocence is bliss, and I hardly ever noticed the hands scrubbing my balls and cleaning around my foreskin. I was too busy trying to fight my way out of the bath, angry that the dirt I had worked so hard to cover myself with was being removed.

"How do shifters typically clean themselves?" Gray asks.

I shrug. How's he expecting me to answer him? I can't talk in this form.

Gray seems to realize his mistake as he laughs and grabs the showerhead, and five minutes later, I'm standing and shaking out my fur. About damn time. This was arguably the worst hour of my life, and I'm never doing it again.

In the future, I'll throw myself into a lake or rub against trees, as I've done for most of my adult life.

Gray lingers in the bathroom as I shift back into my skin form, and he grimaces as he notices my raw skin. This usually happens when my fur is scrubbed too hard, both forms agitated and red, but it'll go away soon. I throw a towel around my waist and gesture for Gray to leave, which he does after a few more attempts to start conversation.

I know the incubus wants to be my friend, but I already have one of those and I don't need another. Besides, I don't think my mate would like me hanging around the male who touched me intimately. Aziel sure doesn't like me and Gray being alone together. The wrath is jealous of me, and I'm surprised he wasn't lingering around the bathroom.

I cleaned my best leathers last night, and I put them on before wandering into Aziel's bedroom and finding Silas's cologne. He has one I enjoy, and I spray a bit on my torso. Blessed breeds like the natural scent of their mates, so I'm careful not to cover mine completely.

I find a mirror and evaluate myself one last time before leaving to see Vanessa. I typically run there in my bear form, but I don't want to dirty my freshly cleaned fur. I take Charlie's golf cart instead.

Vanessa's blinds are already closed for the evening, blocking my view of her as I climb her porch and knock on her front door. I can smell the food, and it's incredible. Aziel told me I eat more than anybody would realistically know to prepare and should eat before coming, which I thought was a good idea.

I ate a large meal prior to Gray cleaning me, but my stomach still rumbles when I smell Vanessa's cooking. I'm so excited to eat her food.

My mate pulls open the front door with a smile. She eyes me up and down before stepping to the side and welcoming me in. She's wearing a dress, which isn't anything unusual, but this one shows more skin than I've ever seen before. It ends many inches above her knees, and most of her shoulders are exposed.

Because of our height difference, I know I'll be able to see down the front of her dress if I look. I make a pointed effort not to do so.

"You look beautiful," I compliment her.

Vanessa ducks her head, her cheeks flushing. I try not to look too imposing as I cup her chin and tilt her face upward. She grows only redder, and I absolutely love it as I lean in and press my lips to hers.

Her hands find my chest, the touch causing my bear to begin his noises. It's embarrassing, but Vanessa says she likes the sounds, so I don't try to stop the rumbling. It continues even when I pull away and follow her into the kitchen.

"It smells amazing," I say, peering into the pot on the stove.

"What're you making?"

I don't recognize the red sauce, and I resist the urge to dip my finger in as Vanessa comes up alongside me.

"It's a human dish," she says. "This is a beef and sweet tomato sauce, and I'll mix it with noodles."

Noodles?

Vanessa must see my confusion, and when she explains noodles to be thin wheat strings, I about lose it. That sounds so good.

I do my best to hide my frustration as Vanessa pours three boxes of wheat strings into a pot of boiling water. I shouldn't have listened to Aziel's advice. Vanessa is making more than enough to feed me, and I regret my earlier meal.

"Thank you for cooking for me," I say, taking the initiative to set the table.

Vanessa's too busy to reply, and I take advantage of that as I adjust and light several candles lying about. They smell like cedar and rain, and I smile to myself as I dim the overhead lights. I want our meal to be as romantic as possible.

Vanessa faintly chuckles when she notices what I'm doing, but it doesn't bother me. I'm a romantic.

She sets the meal in a large bowl and carries it to the table, and I bring over the homemade bread she made with it. It smells so good. I'm going to die a happy man. We take our seats, and I immediately reach over and fill Vanessa's plate.

"Tell me about your day," I say.

I serve myself while she talks, and I fight back a moan when I finally try the food. It's just as delicious as I expected, and I once again curse Aziel when I grow full after only my third serving. Vanessa eats half of one serving, and she rolls her eyes when I lean forward and scoop a little more on her plate.

"I want my mate big and strong," I tease, gesturing to her fork.

Her abrupt silence tells me I've said the wrong thing, and I replay the words in my head before realizing where I made my mistake.

"Not like that!" I say. "I meant I want you to be healthy and full. Plump!" Her eyes turn offended. I'm not making things better. "Please don't be angry. I love you just how you are," I continue, frustrated when my bear forces a series of low rumbles from my chest. "I was trying to be funny."

My bear is always getting on my nerves, and I punch my sternum before dragging my fingers through my hair. This evening was supposed to be perfect, and I'm ruining it. I know Vanessa is insecure about her smaller size, and I shouldn't have said anything about it. I don't need her to be tall and muscular like the shifter women I've grown up around.

My heart pounds, and Vanessa pushes her food aside before rising and climbing onto my lap.

I freeze.

"You're okay, Chev," she says. "It's going to take more than that to drive me away."

I hope so.

"Carry me to the couch," she continues. "There's something I want to try."

I'm up in a heartbeat, holding her to me. My hands are underneath her thighs, my fingertips touching the bare skin below her dress. I love it, and I swallow past the lump in my throat as I bring her to the couch. What does she want to try? Is it sexual?

I debate laying her on her back, a move most shifter males would make, before changing course and sitting so she's straddling me. This gives her more control, and I think she appreciates that.

Vanessa plants her hands on my shoulders, and I try my best to remain still as she feels my muscles. She's so soft and warm, and my body betrays me as I begins hardening. There's no way to hide it. She's sitting directly on me, so I know she feels it pressing against her.

We both ignore it.

I can smell her arousal, though. I know she's reacting to me, her body begging for mine. I'm not going to make the first move, and I curl my hands into tight fists as she leans down and presses her lips to mine.

Fuck.

A low groan slips from my throat when she opens her mouth and teases me with her tongue, and after a second, she grabs my wrists and pulls my hands to her waist. I happily hold her hips. I don't have to worry about pushing her too far when she's the one making the decisions.

We kiss for what feels like forever, but it's not nearly long enough. When she pulls away, I'm so hard, I ache.

"Touch my mark," Vanessa whispers.

Those words are music to my ears. I slide my hand up her hip, pausing once I reach the top of her ribcage. Vanessa cocks her head to the side, and I meet her eyes as I inch toward her breasts.

I want to see them so badly, and I can't help but roll my hips as I pull the short sleeve of her dress over her shoulder. I wait for Vanessa to stop me before dragging it down her arm. The fabric is stretchy, thank the heavens, and I moan as the material covering her chest folds over on itself and the top of her nipple comes into view.

I pause again to ensure she's comfortable.

"For fuck's sake, Chev," Vanessa huffs. "Touch them."

She brushes my hand away and yanks down her top.

I moan. "Oh."

The fabric of her dress now rests at her waist, fully exposing her breasts. Vanessa's are the most beautiful ones I've ever seen—

not that I've seen many—and I can't take my eyes away as I cup them.

They fill both my palms completely, and even then, there's more that doesn't fit. I frown, angry I cannot wholly cup her chest. Vanessa laughs as I spread my fingers to try to take more, but that noise is cut short as I sit up straighter and capture her nipple with my mouth.

I lick from the bottom of her breast to her nipple, loving how it hardens against my tongue. I want to bite, but I'll save that for another time. I shift my attention to her other breast, giving it the same love and attention before pulling away.

Vanessa is panting now, her core subtly rocking against me as I reach behind her neck and touch her mark. She spreads her legs and sits more firmly on me, bringing the underwear between her thighs into my line of sight.

This is wonderful. Her underwear is wet, and it forms around her sex in a way that leaves nothing to the imagination.

"Touch yourself," she orders, scooting down my thighs.

I like when she tells me what to do, and I don't hesitate to grab my aching length. I hiss when I finally get a hold of myself, and I stroke quickly as I rub my fingers over her mark. This is better than I ever could've imagined, and it takes everything in me not to cum when Vanessa lowers her hand between her thighs.

She rubs herself as I pleasure her, her fingers stroking her clit over her underwear. I want her to remove the fabric so I can see her bare flesh, and I feel all my prayers have been answered when she lightly nudges her underwear to the side so she can better touch herself. Her sex is slick with arousal, and I stare at the pink skin as she presses her fingers against her clit and rubs.

My hand tightens around my cock, squeezing so tightly, I'm sure to cut off circulation, but I don't care. This female is made for me, and I rub her mark faster to match how she pleasures herself. She grunts when I do so, and I take that as a sign to continue.

When Vanessa's legs begin to shake around my waist, I know she's close, and when she curses and goes still, I know she's cumming. I follow immediately, releasing her neck so I can cup her breast as I spill on myself.

I'm making a mess of my leathers.

Vanessa slumps against my chest, and I happily fold her into my arms. This is the best day of my life.

"You're a horny female," I say.

When Vanessa pulls back, I'm happy to see a smile behind her fake outrage.

"You're no better!"

"I never said I was." I grab her hips and drag her sex up and down my bare abdomen. "And I'll be only hornier now that I have my mate's slick on me."

Vanessa furrows her brows, staring at my now-glistening torso, before clamoring off me and hurrying to her sink. I'm beyond pleased with myself, and I playfully push her away when she tries to clean me. I'll not be doing so until the smell of her arousal is gone, and that could be days.

"Back away!" I scream, jumping over the couch when Vanessa gets too close with the wet towel. "I have been a very good male, and I deserve to wear you."

I love how she continues to chase me, and when I let her corner me and wipe my stomach five minutes later, I'm surprised by how she follows it up by wiping my cum, the back of her hand grazing my soft length.

Chapter Twenty-Four

VANESSA

I LIE BACK in bed and stare at my new phone, unable to stop reading this morning's articles about Chev and me. I'm always so weak when it comes to them, but I'm pleased with the turn they've taken this past week.

Slowly, painfully slowly, public opinion on our relationship seems to be improving.

Chev begs me not to look, but I most definitely read everything being said about us. It's impossible not to, especially after Chev's interview. I can deal with people saying bad things about me. It hurts, but what they're saying is ultimately true. I'm a weak breed, and I'm a damaged, purchased female who struggles with physical intimacy.

It crushes me when people say bad things about Chev. He's a good man who continually goes out of his way to make me comfortable, but the articles paint him as a horrible mate. They're lying.

There are rumors that Chev goes around threatening people who speak poorly of me, but he denies it every time I ask. It's not a good look, and Mammon is starting to publicly accuse him of manipulating the media. Nothing's going right for him.

A cheesy smile spreads over my lips as I look over the most recent photo of us. Chev's always watching me with that corny grin of his, and the more I see it, the more obsessed I grow. He's not what I expected, and I find myself even further tied to him with every interaction. At this point, I don't think I could ever be without him. I want him. I actively crave him.

"Vanessa?"

I drop my phone onto my chest, my heart pounding as I turn in the direction the voice came from. Why is Chev inside my house? He's peering through the crack of my bedroom door, his eye barely visible as he peeks in on me. He stares momentarily before pushing the door open, revealing his wide smile.

"Why are you still in bed?" he asks, stepping inside. "You're going to be late for work."

His eyes dart around, the shifter not at all subtle as he looks at my things. He's been joining me for dinner every evening since I made him spaghetti earlier this week, but he's only been in my bedroom once.

He peers at my dresser, and I resist the urge to laugh when he picks up one of the ceramic birds Charlie put in here for decoration. It's not my style, but I must admit it's a cute blue jay.

Chev glares at it like it's the ugliest thing he's ever seen. He may be unwilling to admit it, but I'm starting to think he genuinely fears birds. It's a common joke that shifters don't like flying animals, but give how he glares at my decoration, I'm beginning to believe it.

Who knew such a large, deadly bear could be so afraid of a tiny bird?

I sit up, and Chev roughly places the bird back on my dresser. He turns to me with a slight frown, but it disappears as my sheets slide to my waist, exposing the top I wore to bed. It's thin and light, and I can tell it's taking all of Chev's strength to keep his eyes above my shoulders.

"It's the weekend," I say. "I don't work today."

Chev knows this, and I eye his thick hair for any signs of injury. Did he hit his head again? The small bald spots from his injury are impossible to see if you're not actively looking, but I can usually find one or two when I get close. They healed nicely, which is good, but I still worry.

"Oh, no…" Chev says, clearing his throat. "I must have forgotten."

He avoids eye contact, but when he finally does make it, I can see his acting clear as day. If there's anything I've learned from my time with Chev, it's that he's a terrible liar.

"Did you miss me that much?" I tease. I was admittedly dreading having to spend an entire day without him.

Chev beams. "Yes, of course I did." He pauses and paces the length of my room. "But I came here for a reason. I have a question. It's been bothering me all week."

I wouldn't say I like the sound of that, and I lean against my headboard while waiting for him to explain. Chev continues to pace, his nervous actions only worsening my worry. Have I upset him? I've tried to be as upfront as possible regarding our relationship and what I can offer, but maybe I misconstrued something.

"Chev?" I urge.

The suspense is killing me.

He scuffs his foot along the ground before sucking in a slow breath and finally meeting my gaze. "Why haven't you asked to see my bear?"

I blink. "What?"

Chev huffs. "I cleaned him for you days ago, but you haven't asked once to see him."

I blink again, and I struggle not to smile when he crosses his arms over his chest. His innocent look turns into a glare when he notices my reaction, but I can't help it. Is he pouting?

I've seen him get frustrated with others several times, but never have I seen what it looks like when that emotion is directed toward me. His expression is a lot softer, and there's an insecurity behind it he's never had with anybody else, at least as far as I'm aware.

Do I make him nervous? Insecure?

The realization is baffling.

"I didn't know I should have asked," I admit. "I'd love to see your bear."

Chev doesn't move, and I crawl to the edge of the bed. He steps forward to meet me halfway, and I ignore the voice in the back of my head telling me to be scared as I rise to my knees and cup his cheeks. He shaved this morning, but his face is already stubbly. The hair tickles my palms, and I give his cheeks a light scratch in the way I know he likes.

Chev continues to pout as he tilts his head, causing my nails to graze the spot on the underside of his chin. I scratch the area before pulling him closer, silently asking for a kiss.

He's happy to oblige.

"Please show me your bear," I whisper against his lips.

When I pull away, all semblance of his frustration is gone.

Chev gestures for me to follow him, and I don't hesitate to do precisely that. I never realized how important it was to see his bear, and while I've thought about it a few times, I feared it would be impolite to ask.

It seems that assumption was wrong.

Chev bounces down the stairs and out my back door, moving around my home like it's his own. I don't mind it. He knows my boundaries, and he's never tried to push them. He's patient and receptive, and he's more attuned to my emotions than even I am at times.

I think he's always paying attention, even when it doesn't look so.

We step outside, and I wrap my arms around my torso. Wrath is unbearably hot, but the air has a surprising chill this morning. It's crisp.

Chev begins removing his leathers, his nimble fingers untying his skirt and tossing it aside in record time. He's facing away from me, and I scan his bare form before snapping my head back up when he turns around.

"You might want to spin around," he warns. "People find this part gross."

I can handle gross. I want to see everything, even the things he doesn't think I'll like. I've seen videos of shifters transforming between their animal and skin forms before, so I have an idea of what to expect. Chev's bones will break and reform into the shape he's taking, and either fur or skin will sprout and cover his body.

"I want to watch," I say.

Chev looks wary, but after a moment, he shrugs and begins.

Oh.

Seeing it online is one thing, but I quickly realize it's entirely different when it's happening before you. Chev's shoulders pop out first, the bones dislocating before his hips shift and he drops to all fours. He releases a quiet groan, but he doesn't seem to be in much pain.

Mild discomfort, yes, but not nearly anything close to the agony I imagine I'd feel if my body were to break like this.

The transformation is quick, his bones rearranging in mere seconds before fur begins to grow. It was practically instantaneous in the videos, and I'm glad Chev is going slow so I can truly see how his body is changing.

It's gross, as he said it would be, but also strangely fascinating. I try not to look too shocked when he's finished and I'm face to face with a giant, brown bear. He's fucking huge, and he walks toward me with heavy footsteps.

I instinctively back away, which makes him whine. Chev plops down on his butt, his legs spread and paws resting on his ankles. He's as tall as I am in this position, but it's better than him towering over me like before.

He doesn't move, my mate as still as a statue as I shove aside my nerves and approach. His eyes follow my every movement, and the noises quietly seeping from his chest burst to life as I reach for him.

I can't help but laugh, finding it endearing.

The noises are much louder in this form, and I can tell he's annoyed by them. It's comforting to see. His body may be different, but the man inside is still Chev. He paws at his chest as I run my hand through the fur on his head.

It's soft, and I let myself feel his pointed ears before trailing down his back. I'm petting him, but he doesn't seem to mind. I've read that shifters don't appreciate being treated like household pets, but it's hard not to make comparisons when he's so docile and limp under my touch.

"You're big," I say.

His head bobs.

"And cute," I continue, my words no louder than a whisper.

Chev huffs and wiggles out from underneath my hand. It seems I've taken the complimenting too far, and I chuckle as I cup his snout. Our mate bond pulsates between us, preventing me from feeling fear as I manhandle the giant shifter who could easily kill me with one swipe of his paw.

"You can stand now," I say, stepping back.

Chev rises, straightening his spine and displaying his

maximum height. The noises emerging from his chest deepen, and I'm confused by them until I realize he's trying to show me how big he is.

I comb my fingers through the fur on his stomach, continually shocked by how soft he is. I expected his fur to be knotty like that of most wild animals, but it isn't. It's coarse but still easy to sift through.

What a surprise.

"Would you like to catch us lunch?" I ask.

I've been reading about shifters, bears specifically, and that seems to be a big thing for them. They pride themselves on catching their food, and they especially enjoy doing it for their loved ones. It's a way to provide.

Chev releases what sounds almost like a bark before spinning and darting into the woods. His body exudes power as he runs, and I watch until he's entirely disappeared from my line of sight.

I press a hand to my forehead.

What has my life turned into? I spent most of my life at the hands of violent, abusive ogres, and today I'm in Wrath with a bear alpha as a mate.

A bear alpha who's currently in the middle of killing an animal for me to eat.

I cup my cheeks and shake my head, still in disbelief, before heading back inside. I'm willing to bet Chev will be hungry when he returns, and I want to have food ready for him. He eats an alarming amount, and I love his excitement whenever I make him meals. I'm providing for him.

Chapter Twenty-Five

VANESSA

I HUM, TAPPING my fingers against my desk as Charlie and I review this week's agenda.

The facility is in much better shape now that she's back, and we've gotten into a good habit of meeting every week. I love it. My proposed changes are approved and implemented within the time it took to get a meeting on Aziel's calendar. The process is smooth, and I'm proud of how much I can get done.

Charlie is quick, and she has much deeper pockets than Aziel. He always had follow-up questions about cost, but she trusts my decisions. It's the first time I've ever been trusted with authority.

I feel useful, and I hope I'm making a difference to the women here.

"Have you had a chance to look over the meal plans for next quarter?" Charlie asks.

I groan, shaking my head. One of the facilities in the elven lands has some serious structural issues, and they want to send their women here until it's fixed.

"Not yet," I say. "The elves have been keeping me busy."

Charlie laughs and bobs her head. "I've seen the messages."

There are dozens of them. The Wrath facility is small, and it will take a lot of navigation to comfortably accommodate the number of women they wish to send over. I don't want the females already here to feel cramped, though.

The managers in charge of the shifter and dragon facilities said they have some room, and I think we'll have to split up the women currently living in the elven facility. It's not ideal, but we don't have many other options.

"I plan to look it over this week," I say.

I scan my desk, looking for the meal plan documents Charlie gave me last week. Creating them falls under my job description, but Charlie enjoys making them and she's pretty good at it. I doubt I'll find any issues. I never do, but I still appreciate her asking me to review it for final approval.

I was worried about what working with her would be like, fearful she'd circumvent me because of her title and standing within the Wrath kingdom, but it hasn't been an issue.

"There's no rush," Charlie says. "I know you're busy."

Too busy.

Charlie glances at her phone, and even before saying anything, I know she has to leave. Her males tend to get antsy when she isn't back when she says she's going to be, and after her incubus came storming in here one afternoon when we'd gotten to chatting, she's been careful about leaving on time.

I think it's overly possessive, but I remind myself it isn't my relationship to judge. Charlie seems happy with her males, and that's all that matters. I'm not the one married to them, so it doesn't matter how I feel.

"I should get going," Charlie says.

I nod. "I'll see you soon."

She makes her way out of my office, and I return to work. I have a few messages I'd like to get out before Chev joins me for lunch. I invited him to come here, which I've never done before. I'm admittedly quite nervous.

I send out three messages before my office door bursts open and my oversized mate comes storming inside. He doesn't bother knocking. I wonder how he gets any work done when he's constantly running between the Wrath manor and the facility, but whenever I ask, he tells me he has it handled before abruptly changing the subject. I think he's struggling to keep up with everything and is lying for my benefit. He doesn't want me to worry.

I'm still worried, though.

Thoughts of moving to the shifter realm have crossed my mind, but I'm yet to voice them. I'd hate to get Chev excited about something I'm still unsure of.

He's been updating his home to my liking, which I appreciate, but the thought of living with him is frightening. The men who owned me covered me in jewelry when we went out in public, but in private, I slept on a wooden pallet in a mouse-infested basement most nights. Men are different in public than they are behind closed doors.

I know Chev isn't like the ogres. I know that to my very bones, but something still holds me back.

"Can I see your breasts?" Chev asks, kicking my office door shut.

I snort. "*What*?"

Is he serious?

Chev smirks and toys with his leathers, messing with them just enough that I can see the bottom of his mate mark. He's always trying to tease me with it, the man acting like a sultry whore whenever we're alone and he's in his leathers.

His mark is entirely black now, the thick ring around his thigh fully darkened. I love the look of it, and I find myself leaning forward as it enters my line of sight.

"Your breasts," Chev says, refusing to lift his skirt any higher.

A part of me wants to play coy and see what he'll do if I refuse, but the larger part that wants to see his mated mark wins. I reach for the bottom of my shirt. I don't mind showing him my chest, and Chev rocks back on his heels as I pull the fabric up.

I lock eyes with him as I do the same with my bra, fully exposing myself.

Chev's attention quickly lowers to my chest, and he stares as if this is the most exciting thing he's ever seen. It feels good knowing I'm the only female he'll ever lust after like this. I'm his mate.

Chev finally exposes his mate marking. I scan the black skin, beyond happy with how dark it's gotten these past few weeks. Mine has grown, too, the thin line now trailing all the way down my spine.

"You're beautiful," Chev compliments me.

His cock twitches, his body reacting to me, but he drops his skirt and turns away before we get carried away. He already came in his fist while licking my mark this morning.

I put my bra and shirt back on, and only once my breasts are covered does Chev begin readying the food he brought for lunch. I was so distracted, I didn't even notice he was carrying a bag. It's large, and he seems eager as he sets a giant container of cooked meat on my desk. I wait for him to pull out more, and I fight back a laugh as I realize the meat is the entire meal.

Chev beams as he opens the container, showcasing his work.

There doesn't seem to be much, if any, seasoning on it, but I don't mind. Given how Chev grins and nudges the container in my direction, I know he caught and cooked this himself. That excitement overshadows any hesitance I might have over eating bland meat.

I'd eat it every day of the week if it made Chev happy.

I peel off a piece and slip it between my lips.

"Do you like it?" Chev asks.

He doesn't give me time to taste the food, and my lips twitch as I chew. Chev waits impatiently, tapping his foot against the ground until I swallow. The meat indeed doesn't have any seasoning, but it's cooked perfectly and is incredibly tender. I like it.

"It's good," I say. "I assume you caught it."

Chev nods. "Just this morning."

He waits for me to eat several more bites before taking one himself. It's polite, but I have a feeling the man snuck several bites while catching and cooking the animal. He can eat meat raw, and I'm sure he took advantage of that.

"How's your day going?" I ask, gesturing for him to sit opposite my desk.

Chev glances nervously at my chairs before taking a seat. The wicker creaks as he lowers himself into it, the material struggling to hold his weight. I should invest in sturdier furniture if he's going to make a habit of coming here. The items I selected are cute and can easily support the weight of myself and the other women in the facility, but Chev is too big.

Now I understand why the shifters make everything out of sturdy wood.

"It's good, but busy," Chev says. "I'm going to the office after lunch to meet with Echo and several others on the leadership team, but I'll be here in time to take you home."

I'm not worried about him being late to pick me up. Chev is punctual.

"A meeting in the office…" I say. "Must be important."

From what I hear, Chev hardly goes to the office. He's been working out of Wrath for months, probably so he can remain close to me. I imagine it must make things complicated, but he hasn't complained.

Chev takes another bite of food. "It is. I'm stepping down, and we're deciding who's to take my place."

He speaks so casually, it takes me several seconds to truly understand the weight of his words. He's stepping down? Since when? I know he's been stretched thin, but I never imagined it would lead to this.

I shake my head and set my hands in my lap.

"What?" I ask, eager for him to clarify. "Why?"

Is this because of me?

"I'm so sorry," I blurt out.

Chev shakes his head, immediately shutting down my apology.

"This is expected," he says. "My role was only ever meant to be temporary. I have an entire pack to manage, and now that I have my mate, I need my time back. I don't enjoy having to work so much."

Is he just saying this so I don't feel guilty? Mammon has been dedicating a lot of time calling Chev's integrity into question, and I fear that could be impacting his decision. Chev's been the head of the Seekers' organization for years, and it's excelled under his leadership.

He's done so much good.

"I'm excited to leave," he continues. "My people need me, and Echo has been training to take my position. She will do good, and I will have time to focus on you and my pack."

I wipe my palms on my pants, drying the sweat.

"They aren't firing you?" I ask.

Chev shakes his head. "No. I've requested to leave. My father hurt his back while chopping wood for me last week, and I realized it's unfair of me to continue pushing my alpha responsibilities aside."

Does this mean he's going to be returning to the shifter lands? I can't blame him for wanting to return home, but I've selfishly grown accustomed to having him nearby. I'd never ask him to stay, but I'll be devastated if he leaves. I don't want to be apart from Chev. There are several portals he can use to visit me, but there's a comfort in knowing he's in Wrath.

"Tell me about your day," he says, changing the subject.

I want to ask more about his decision and what it means for us moving forward, but I want to organize my thoughts before I do. My heart pounds, and I shake my head before giving him a recap of my day.

Chev hangs on to my every word, and my cheeks turn a bright shade of red. The remainder of my lunch passes in a blur, and before I know it, Chev's getting ready to leave. He doesn't seem pleased to return to work, and he lingers for as long as possible before making his way to the door.

I drop my head onto my desk the moment he's gone, already knowing I won't be getting any more work done today.

Chapter Twenty-Six

VANESSA

MY HEART POUNDS, and I clutch my papers to my desk as I step through the portal.

Chev has given his notice at work, and in less than one month, he'll no longer be working here. I still don't know how I feel about it, especially since his last month will be spent at the headquarters.

The council practically demanded it. They're angry with Chev's continued absence, and they requested he spend his last month in a place where he's more readily accessible to Echo and the others.

I'm playing it cool, but I miss him. He didn't have time to drive me to the Wrath facility this morning, and despite the ever-growing pile of work I need to get through, I'm finding myself heading to the headquarters for the first time in months.

The last time I was in this building was when I met Chev, and it takes me a moment to adjust after stepping through the portal. I forgot how loud and busy this place is. Several people hurry around, and I notice many throwing sly glances in my direction.

It won't take Chev long to hear I'm here, and I hide a smile as I head toward my office.

The room is untouched, and I get to work while I wait. It takes less than an hour before my office door bursts open, and my smile grows as a glowing Chev enters the room.

"Can I help you?" I tease.

Chev crosses his arms over his chest, causing the muscles to bulge and steal my attention. I'm sure he's doing it on purpose. I'd bet money that Chev has a praise kink. The moment that thought filters through my mind, I clear my throat and shake my head. Those are dangerous thoughts.

"I'm offended you waited until I quit to come into the office," Chev says. He raises a brow and leans against the door frame. "I'm even more offended you haven't come to see me."

I shrug. I wanted to see how long it would take him to come to me, and I'm not disappointed. I also wasn't sure he'd want me here. I know he's been busy, and he's gotten further behind on his work than he initially let on.

He's been trying to do everything out of Wrath, but I assume it's hard to work when surrounded by the Wrath trio and their children. I've heard stories of Chev having to cut a meeting short because one of the toddlers came to him crying after their parents told them *no*.

The children seem to have a soft spot for Chev. I like it. Hearing people talk about how good Chev is with children is comforting, and it has very inappropriate feelings stirring within me.

Our mate bond doesn't have the same reservations toward men that I do, and it's doing a surprisingly good job calming my fears whenever Chev and I are together. We've already done much more than I ever thought possible, but the bond is greedy. It wants intimacy, and it wants sex and children.

"Do you want to get lunch with me?" Chev asks.

I purse my lips and glance at the clock. "It's still early."

"Would you like to work from my office, then?" Chev pushes off the doorway. "I can bring in a desk for you, and we can share the room."

He trails his fingertips across my desk, his movements smooth. A small part of me always expects him to be clunky, but he seldom is. Despite how awkward his words can be, the way he physically moves never is. He's a predator through and through.

"I don't think we'd get much work done if we shared an office," I say.

Chev's lips twitch, and only once I repeat the words in my head do I realize how they can be taken. I'm sure he knows I didn't mean it sexually, and I don't bother trying to correct myself. Either way, what I say is true.

If Chev's not trying to start a conversation, I am, and the few times we aren't talking, it's only because we're staring at one another. We won't get any work done.

"Do you think the pull of our bond will ever lessen?" I ask.

Chev physically recoils. "Why would you ask that?" He steps back. "Do you want it to?"

I shake my head. "Of course not."

I like our bond—a sentence I never thought I'd say—but I don't know much about it. I've not spent much time with mated pairs, and I don't know what to expect. I know our bond will always exist, but will I always be so distracted by Chev? Will it always be so consuming?

"You grew up in the shifter lands surrounded by mates," I say, "but I hardly know anything about them. I'm just curious." I clear my throat before continuing. "I was taken from my parents when I was a child, and ogres don't have mates."

Chev relaxes, his tense muscles softening. "The bond will never become less intense. We'll learn to grow comfortable with it, though…" He trails off, his eyes narrowing. "But I'll make sure you never become too complacent. I'll keep you aching for the rest of our lives."

My lips twitch. *The rest of our lives*. I have a mate I'm going to spend the rest of my life with. What a peculiar thought.

"I'll always ache for you, Chev," I promise him.

I rise and walk around my desk, eager for physical contact. Chev doesn't hesitate to open his arms and pull me into a hug, and I bury my face against his neck the way we both like. Despite how complicated I sometimes feel he is, he's easy at his core.

He just wants to be loved.

So do I.

Chev squeezes me, and his fingers trail over the back of my bra. He lingers on the spot where the skin indents around the elastic.

I'll never understand the male desire for breasts, and I hold in a laugh as Chev pulls back and stares down at my chest. His smile as he does so is infectious, and he makes brief eye contact with me before cupping one.

"If you'd like, *I* can be your bra."

He looks at me with earnest, wide eyes, and I feel only slightly bad for how I swat away his hand. He immediately steps back and puts space between us. He's always doing that, physically removing the entirety of himself whenever I ask him to stop. I appreciate it more than he knows.

I see the effort Chev puts into ensuring I always feel comfortable around him. The more time I spend with him, the more I've noticed it, and he's slowly chipping away at the protective barrier I've built around my heart.

I've been the only person I can rely on for as long as I can remember, the only person I knew had my best interests at heart, but Chev's worming his way in. I have a feeling this man would die for me if it came down to it.

"Is that a *yes* to moving into my office?" Chev asks, returning to our earlier conversation.

I hum, debating it.

"We really shouldn't," I say.

"I won't bother you," Chev pleads, lifting his skirt to show his mated mark.

He gives me a sly look as he teases the black line, once again trying to tempt me. I don't have the heart to tell him that, while I love seeing his mark, it's not nearly as alluring as he seems to think. It's the easiest way to tell when he truly wants me to do something, though. I've grown to live by the rule that if Chev tries to seduce me with his mark, he really wants me to say *yes*.

"I'll do it under one condition," I decide.

Chev nods so fast, I'm surprised he doesn't give himself a headache. "Anything," he promises.

My smile grows. "I'd like to see your home."

Chev stares, his eyes wide with shock. I've never asked to see the shifter lands before, but he's always bragging about the large trees and changes he's been making to his home. I know he's eager for me to visit.

He's been keeping me updated on the progress of his kitchen renovation, and he's just about finished. The exterior walls are completed, and all that's left to do is build in the center island and put up cabinets.

Chev steps forward, swooping me into his arms. "I would be honored, my mate," he says. My feet dangle off the ground, and Chev twists me side to side before setting me back down. "I'll carry your desk."

I didn't realize he intended to move me into his office *right now*. He doesn't even bother emptying the drawers before picking up the entire piece of furniture. *Fuck.* Chev is strong.

He easily lifts my desk above his head before storming out of my office and down the busy hallways. I follow, too embarrassed to make eye contact with the people who stop and stare. I'm sure we're a sight to see. Chev is carrying a desk half his size and I'm following behind with my computer clutched tightly to my chest.

Echo is one of the ones who stares, and she doesn't bother stifling her cackles.

Chev grunts and kicks a foot in her direction. "You are an ugly, hairless bear."

Echo gasps and storms away. Chev smiles at her retreating figure, and I roll my eyes. Those two are constantly arguing, and I feel bad for their parents. They must've been a handful growing up.

When we enter Chev's office, I realize he already arranged the space so my desk easily fits inside. He cleared space for me before even asking if I wanted to share.

"A bit presumptuous, don't you think?" I ask.

Chev only shrugs, clearly not feeling the least bit embarrassed as he sets down my desk and fiddles to get it into the perfect position.

"I gave you the good side," he says, gesturing to the large window to the left of my desk.

What have I just agreed to?

Chapter Twenty-Seven

VANESSA

AGREEING TO SHARE an office with Chev is the worst decision I've ever made.

He doesn't bother pretending he's not staring at me, and he's getting unnecessarily aggressive whenever somebody uses the portal outside his office. He can hear it, and he abruptly stands and stares every time somebody tries to use it. If he doesn't stop, people will begin exclusively using the one outside Echo's office, and she'll sure make a fuss.

The loud squeak of Chev's chair reaches my ears, causing me to lose focus.

"That's enough!" I snap.

Chev spins toward me. "No."

I don't think Chev has ever told me *no* before, and I don't know how to react. He doesn't back down, either, and he ignores me entirely as he stalks toward the door to see who just entered.

I'm going to fucking scream.

When he sees that it's just a random employee—as it is every single time—he relaxes and returns to his desk. I watch the entire thing, my anger continuing to build. I appreciate his concern and desire to protect me, but this is getting out of hand.

"I think it might be better for me to return to my office," I say.

Chev doesn't even look in my direction. "No."

He's on a roll with that word today.

"Excuse me?" I ask.

If I want to return to my office, I very well have the right to do so. Chev can't force me to work out of his office, especially if he's going to be this possessive. I'm busy trying to solve problems caused by the elven facility, and Chev is busy transitioning his work to Echo.

We have a responsibility to the females, and I take that seriously.

"You will work here," Chev continues, doubling down.

I close my laptop screen and suck in a slow breath. *Stay calm, Vanessa. Stay calm.* We've never argued before, and I'm not mentally prepared for it. I knew better than to engage with an angry ogre, but I don't want to cower from Chev. If this is going to work between us, I need to be his equal.

"I don't think you're in a place to decide that," I say.

Chev huffs. "Yes, I am."

I don't know if he woke up on the wrong side of the bed, but Chev's in a fucking mood today. We made plans to go to the shifter realm together over lunch, and maybe that's making him antsy. I know he's excited about it.

"No, you're not," I push.

My palms are sweating, and my heart is pounding, but I don't back down. I'm standing my ground.

Chev shuts his laptop and turns entirely to face me. He cocks his head slightly to the side as he scans me, his angry expression not evoking any of the fear it once did. Despite how mad he gets, I know he won't hurt me.

"You can't carry your desk yourself," he says. "And I'm not

putting it back."

I resist the urge to throw something at him. "There are plenty of other offices I can go to and plenty of strong men who I'm sure would be more than happy to carry my desk back for me."

I know saying this will make Chev jealous. Maybe I'm in a bit of a mood today, too.

Chev's eyes grow comically wide before narrowing. "I'll crush any male you try to bring into our space."

"Oh, I'll crush *you*," I threaten him.

There's a moment of silence before Chev begins laughing. I take great offense to it and throw a pencil across the room. It bounces off his forehead. Violence is never the answer, but it admittedly makes me feel better. I don't appreciate Chev's attitude.

He plucks the pencil off his desk, his laughter quieting.

"Please don't leave," he says. "I'll be calm."

I press my lips together, thinking it over. I honestly don't want to leave. As annoying as Chev is, I enjoy working with him. His presence is comforting, and I'm surprisingly productive. I don't waste time worrying about what he's doing or where he is, and my compulsive need to look him up and read through news articles or community posts isn't nearly as strong.

I nod. "I'll stay."

His tense muscles relax, and I return to work. The calm only lasts a few minutes before I hear the portal whirring to life. I glance at Chev, but he's already watching the door. The muscle in his jaw twitches, and I can tell it's killing him to remain seated.

I can't hide my smile, and after several seconds, Chev returns to work.

Several hours pass in comfortable silence. Chev manages to refrain from checking the portal a little more than half the time, but he's careful not to be so distracting when he does get up. It only helps a little, but it's more than I thought he'd be able to do, so I don't complain.

I count down the minutes until our agreed-upon lunchtime, my nerves growing with every quiet tick of the clock above the door. I'm going to visit the shifter realm with Chev. I'm trusting him to take me to his domain. I've never been so nervous.

"Are you ready?" Chev asks as the time nears.

I hope he can't see my fear. It will make him feel bad.

"Yes," I say. "I am."

I'm scared of his demeanor changing once I'm trapped in his lands, but I shove that fear aside. Chev has been good to me, and I know he won't hurt me. I rise from my desk and follow him to the portal, and I wring my hands together as he turns it on and sets the destination.

It lights up, the blackness shifting into a blue haze.

"Are you sure about this?" Chev asks. He must sense my nerves. "We don't have to go."

Yes, we do. I agreed to it, and behind all my anxiety is excitement. I want to see Chev's lands and his home. I want to see how my mate lives.

"I'm sure," I say.

I squeeze my eyes shut and step through the portal, and Chev quickly follows. It makes me dizzy—it always does—but the slight discomfort is quickly overshadowed by the feel of the forest. The energy that seeps from the trees is more than I've ever encountered, and I find myself holding my breath as I walk out of the cabin where the shifter portal is located.

Chev wasn't lying about his lands having giant trees. They tower above me, casting a large shadow that blocks out the sun's heat. It's warm here, but not nearly as sweltering as Wrath. I quite enjoy it.

The nearest tree calls to me, and I press my forehead against the bark before sliding my hands down the trunk. This is overwhelming, and I let myself fill up on the energy surrounding me as I try to settle my feelings.

Chev follows me out of the cabin, his bear already making its low, rumbling noises. The bear and I have become quite acquainted with one another, especially now that he brings me a dead animal almost every morning. It's as endearing as it is gross.

At least he skins them for me.

I pull away from the tree and turn toward Chev, unable to stop smiling as I look around. I didn't expect to have this strong of a reaction to his home. The area resembles the faint memories I have of the nymph lands.

Chev takes my hands. "Let me show you around."

He leads me through the trees and onto a small, worn path. Everything here is so green and lush, and I can already feel myself getting attached to it. I assumed I would like Chev's lands, but I didn't imagine my feelings would be so immediate or intense. It's probably the bond.

"It's beautiful here," I say.

Chev looks down, hiding a smile. "Thank you."

He holds my hand tightly, not letting go. We walk along the small path for several minutes, which I find curious. I thought the portal would be closer to his home.

"Why did the portal lead to that cabin?" I ask.

"The portal was originally installed so Charlie could come back and forth," Chev admits. "That was the cabin she lived in during her time here."

Oh, interesting. I faintly remember hearing that Charlie lived in the shifter lands before mating with her males. She'd gotten into some trouble with Mammon, and Chev and his father took her in and offered protection.

We walk for another few minutes before finally reaching a

building. It's nestled within the trees, and my mind races with questions as we approach. Is this Chev's home? The wooden house is larger than I expected, and hundreds of tiny flowers bloom along the walkway leading to the small porch.

They're colorful and delicate. This is Chev's home.

It's a cumulation of things that give it away, ranging from how he quickens his steps to the odd feeling of comfort that pulsates through our bond. Plus, I haven't read a thing about shifters enjoying flowers. They leave their land as it is, and while it isn't unheard of, it's not typical for them to decorate their lawns.

Chev did this for me.

"It's beautiful," I say. My voice is barely above a whisper.

Chev squeezes my hand. "Would you like to see inside?"

My cheeks turn red. Would I like that? I'm desperate to know what the rest of his home looks like, but I'm afraid I won't want to leave if I see what's inside. I'm already feeling a stronger connection to this place than I should. I'm fantasizing about a life here, which is dangerous.

Plus, I know Chev hopes this visit will lead to my agreeing to move in with him, even if he hasn't said it outright. He can't live in Wrath forever, and he needs to move back to the shifter lands eventually.

"We can eat outside," Chev suggests, noticing my hesitance.

I shake my head. "I want to see it."

I know I've made the right decision when Chev's lips curl into a giddy smile. He's so excited, and I can't bring it within myself to ruin that. I want to see his pride. I want to love his home.

Chev leads me up the two steps of his porch before pushing open his front door. I notice it's unlocked, and when I eye the wooden door, I realize there's no lock installed. Does Chev not fear intruders? Especially during his extended absence?

A small entryway leads almost immediately into the living

room, and I hesitate before stepping inside and kicking off my shoes. Chev copies me, and he shuts the door before placing a hand on the small of my back and urging me to enter further.

"I originally built this when I was seventeen, but I've made several changes over the years," he says. "The living room is the one room I haven't updated."

The floors are made of cherry-colored hardwood, and it's surprisingly smooth under my feet. They lead to intricate baseboards, which I assume were crafted by Chev. I look around. Everything I see is detailed and quality, showcasing just how much time, energy, and pride Chev put into his home.

This must have taken him years to build.

I step into the living room. A leather couch is pushed up against the far wall, and across from it is probably the largest fireplace and chimney I've ever seen. Two floor-to-ceiling bookcases surround it, both of which are already filled.

"I'm not much of a reader," Chev admits, noticing my gaze. "These are generational books. We'll add a few to the collection over the years, and then it will be passed to our eldest once they've completed their home."

Our eldest. We're going to have children someday, and we'll raise them in this home. I wrap my arms around myself, trying to imagine myself living here with a family. Little feet will be loud against the hardwood, and so much of Chev's hard craftsmanship will be destroyed over the years.

I think the house will look better with the inevitable scuff marks and holes children always leave scattered about.

The living room opens on the right, leading to a kitchen and dining area. The kitchen is spacious, and I feel my chest warming as I notice all the tiny seedlings he's decorated the rooms with. He listens.

The dining room is smaller. There's a rectangular, wooden

table in the center and a cabinet built into the far wall. I can't see what's inside, but I assume it's full of dishes.

Chev walks into the kitchen and stands a few feet in front of the stove. "The island is going to go here." He gestures around. "And then I'll paint and decorate."

I follow him into the room, a cheesy smile working its way to my lips as I take everything in. The kitchen is large, and on the ground sits about fifteen different paint swatches and a small handful of backsplash tiles. Chev rocks back on his heels as he watches my reaction.

"I love it," I admit.

His shoulders soften, and with a happy nod, he leads me down the small hallway connected to the living room. His steps slow as we pass the first closed door, but he ignores it and continues forward.

I pause, curious about his reaction.

I turn and open the door before I overthink and change my mind. It leads to a bedroom, and I peer inside to discover why he was weird about it. A neatly made bed is in the center of the room, the dark-green sheets matching the earthy feel of the rest of the home. Across from the bed is a dresser and two double doors that I assume lead to a closet.

"This is my room," Chev says, walking up behind me.

His chest presses against my back and his hands land on my hips, and I lean against him with a content sigh. Our bond hums, always happy when my mate is holding me.

"You weren't going to show me?" I ask.

I feel him shrug. "I didn't want you to think I was putting the moves on you."

My face warms. That's considerate of him, even if it's unnecessary. Chev isn't exactly sneaky when trying to be intimate. Even when he tries to be sly, his intentions are transparent.

"I want to show you the bathroom," he continues. "I've filled it with everything you could possibly need."

He's filled it? With what? My excitement grows, and I hurry down the hallway to where I'm guessing the bathroom is. The door is open, and I'm faintly aware of Chev's laughter as I step inside. To the left is a walk-in shower, and I stare in awe at the glass doors as Chev pulls open the floor-to-ceiling shelving on the right.

I stare for a long moment before gulping.

That's a lot of items.

The entire cabinet is full, with products covering every shelf inside. It's more than I could ever use, and I flush as I realize Chev has even organized them. There are several cute bins below the shelves of containers, and upon closer inspection, I realize they're filled with different types of hair accessories.

Chev happily walks me through everything he's bought, clearly proud of his collection.

I can't bring myself to do anything more than stare, and once he's finished, I rush forward and wrap my arms around his waist. He quickly returns the hug, his lips grazing my forehead before I tilt my chin and kiss him properly.

What have I done to deserve this man? I never imagined this was how my life would turn out. I never thought a relationship and love were on the table.

My heart pounds as I grab Chev's biceps and lightly push him against the doorway. He grunts, but he doesn't try to stop me. I know shifters like to be dominant, but Chev happily lets me take charge.

It's what I need to feel comfortable.

A low moan pours from his throat when I slide my fingers down his torso, but he keeps his arms pressed firmly against his sides. I appreciate it, and I take my time feeling the muscles lining his torso. They flex underneath my hands, and his leathers shift as his body reacts to my touch.

"Would you like to put your mouth on me?" I ask.

Chev nods and reaches for my neck. I move away.

"Not on my neck." I clarify. I clear my throat before continuing. "I mean, on *me*."

It's not something the ogres did. They didn't care about female pleasure, and I want to try with Chev.

"I can't promise I'll like it, but I want to try," I say.

I stare at Chev's chest, too embarrassed to make eye contact, but I don't fight him when he places a finger under my chin and tilts my head back. He runs his thumb over my lip, his touch light, before urging me to look him in the eye.

I do, and I chew at my bottom lip as I take in his soft expression. His eyes dart all along my face as he searches for some sign of hesitance from me, but I don't give one. I want to enjoy the closeness of physical intimacy with him, and I want to try. Besides, I trust that if I don't like it, Chev will stop.

He won't make me feel guilty or bad, and he won't push me to do more than I've already agreed to.

Chev gulps. "I would be honored, my mate."

He holds eye contact with me as he picks me up, and I wrap my legs around his waist as he carries me into his bedroom. He sets me on the bed, his movements slow, before he abruptly throws himself onto his back on the mattress.

"You'll be in charge," he explains. "I'll lie on my back and keep my hands to myself, and you'll sit on top and use my mouth."

Chapter Twenty-Eight

VANESSA

CHEV'S EXCITED. HE licks his lips as he stares up at me, his chest heaving. His hair is sprawled out underneath his head, the brown curls messy. I eye them as I work up the courage to move.

It takes a minute or two, but Chev is patient. He fills the time by playing with my fingers, his movements slow and gentle. My hand feels small within his, especially when he holds and squeezes my palm between his thumb and pointer finger.

My pulse is racing at least a million miles a minute. Some of it is due to fear, but most is excitement. What if I put myself on his tongue and find that I don't like it? What if Chev doesn't like it? He's kind, and I know he'd lie to save me from embarrassment.

I pull my hand out of Chev's, and I hesitate before pressing my palm against his stomach. His skin is warm, and I hold back a shiver as his muscles flex underneath my fingers.

If I look down further, I know I'll find his leathers tented. If there's anything I'm sure of, it's Chev's desire for me. He's not shy in his eagerness.

All signs of the happy, laid-back man I've grown accustomed to are gone when I finally meet Chev's heated gaze. His lips are pulled tight, and his eyes are narrowed in at where my fingers linger on his lower abdomen. The column of his throat bobs, and I hold back a smile as I trail my fingertips over his hip.

I'm surprising myself with my confidence, and I suck in a slow breath before untying and pulling open his leathers. Even if Chev finds my taste off-putting, I think he'll still find pleasure in making me feel good.

His cock lies heavily on his stomach, the hard length twitching. He's large in all ways, and I let the side of my pinky graze his shaft as I trail my hand back up his abdomen.

Chev moans, but he otherwise remains still.

My male is beautiful, and I take pride in knowing he's all mine. His heart is mine, his soul is mine, and his body is mine. Mine.

I continue to admire his bare form before removing my clothes. Chev's breathing is rougher now, the man practically panting as I strip. He lets a curse slip from his lips when I'm entirely naked, and I give him a second to look before throwing my leg over his torso and sitting on his chest.

"You smell so fucking good." He moans, craning his neck to try to peer between my thighs. "I can't wait to have my tongue on you. I can't wait to taste you."

I curl my fingers into his shoulders and squeeze my thighs around his torso. His words are low and throaty, and I can practically feel his desire for me through them. I want this, too, and I push my nerves aside as I lift to my knees and shuffle toward his head.

Chev grabs my hips once I'm above him, stopping me. He glances between me and my sex before speaking. "I love you, Vanessa," he starts. "If you decide you don't like this, I'll still be honored you were willing to try. Please don't force yourself to do something you don't enjoy because you think I want it."

His words are solemn, but he fixes the mood with a teasing pinch on my hips.

"Okay?" he asks.

I give a jerky nod. "Okay."

Chev releases me and shoves his hands underneath his butt, pinning them down so he doesn't accidentally touch me. I can't even begin to express how much it means to me.

I've never done anything like this before, and I scoot forward until my knees are on either side of his head. Chev giggles, his lips pulling into a broad smile. I have a feeling if I were to look behind me, I'd see his toes wiggling.

I grab his headboard and use it for stability as I begin to lower over his mouth. I freeze the moment I feel his lips on me, my body rigid, before the bond urges me to relax and I lower a bit more.

Chev doesn't move, holding his lips still as I press myself against them.

This isn't bad. I shut my eyes and spread my thighs further, and I curl my fingers over the wooden headboard as his mouth begins to open and his hot breath hits me.

I don't know what to think. I expect to be disgusted, maybe bombarded with painful memories, but neither happens. All I can think about is Chev below me. Chev touching me. Chev licking me.

He consumes my every thought, leaving room for nothing else.

He doesn't touch me, though. He only breathes, his patience reaching levels even I don't think I possess.

"Chev," I eventually whine. He smiles, and I groan as I realize he's waiting for me. "You can lick me now."

His pupils expand, and his eyes roll back slightly before he finally lets his tongue out from behind his teeth. I jolt when it makes contact with me, the warm, wet feeling shocking. He eases his tongue between my folds, licking the entirety of my slit.

It feels incredible, even better than when he licks my mark, and I groan when Chev finds my clit and flicks the tip of his tongue over it. He's teasing me, and I lower myself further so he doesn't have to crane his neck to reach.

Chev looks filthy between my thighs, his lips and face wet as he licks roughly at my sex. His eyes lock with mine as he pleasures me, the sight too much. *Fuck.* I rock against him as the fire in my abdomen grows. Our bond loves this, and I'm pretty sure my chest will explode if I don't cum soon.

"Put a finger inside," I blurt out, needing more.

Chev's hands find my hips a second later. He keeps his touch feather-light, and he trails his fingers up and down the outside of my thighs before wrapping one arm around my waist and the other between my legs.

I stiffen when he touches me, and Chev stills until I tell him to continue. I'm determined to let him. I want to feel my mate's hands and body on me. I deserve that. My heart pounds as I bob my head, silently telling him to do it.

"Fuck," Chev whines. "You're so soft."

He turns his head to the side and playfully bites the inside of my thigh. It doesn't hurt, but I still give a little jolt of surprise.

"Look at me," he orders.

I peer down at him as he runs his thumb along the length of my slit, and he holds eye contact before slowly easing his middle finger into me. I clench around him, the reaction instinctual. Penetration always meant pain, but this doesn't hurt. It takes me several seconds to relax, and Chev rocks his finger into me once I do.

"Does it feel good?" he asks. "Do you like being filled by your mate?"

I shut my eyes, unable to continue watching.

"Yes," I admit.

Chev eases his finger in and out of me before pulling me back to his mouth. I jerk as his lips make contact with me again, his tongue licking every bit of skin he can reach. He lets me control everything, and I lean forward so my clit gets most of the attention from his tongue.

Then I snatch the hand resting on my hip and drag it to my chest.

Chev doesn't hesitate to cup my breast, his fingers playing with my nipple. He knows I like that, and I arch my back as the pleasure builds.

"Chev," I gasp. "I'm going to cum."

He moans, continuing to pleasure me until my thighs are shaking and I'm thrusting against his tongue and finger. It feels so good, and I cry into the headboard as my orgasm overtakes me. It's like nothing I've ever felt before, and I let out a quiet whine when Chev gives my clit one last lick and pulls his finger out.

I remain still, needing a moment to breathe. Chev takes advantage of that as he presses his tongue against my entrance, trying to push in. He so badly wants to be inside me. I let him lick at me before lifting and moving back down his chest. His mouth and jaw are soaked.

Chev props himself up on his elbows. "That was amazing."

He's hard, his tip already covered in precum. It must be painful. Chev moves to sit up, but I place a hand on his chest and push him back down. He falls back without hesitation.

"Touch yourself," I say.

I want to see it.

Chev slides his hand down his torso, and before I change my mind, I place mine on top. He slows, hesitating, before continuing. I let him lead, and I hold my hand against his as he curls his fist around himself.

"I'm already there," he admits.

He doesn't pleasure himself right away, too busy staring at my hand. He's technically the one touching himself, but I'm there. I let one of my fingers fall between his, resting on his bare skin.

His shaft is soft and warm, and I love the noise he makes as I brush my finger over it. He continues to hold himself, and I make eye contact with him as I let the remainder of my fingers fall between his.

"Vanessa," Chev gasps. "What're you doing?"

I squeeze his length, and when I give a timid nod, he slowly works his fist up and down. I follow his lead, and we stroke him together.

"I want to make you cum," I say.

Chev grunts. "You're about to, my mate. I'm going to cum so fucking hard for you."

He speeds up his movements, his eyes darting to my chest. I know he likes my breasts, and I lean forward so they hang.

I can tell he enjoys the sight by the loud moan he lets out, and a second later, he stops moving his hand and begins fucking our fists instead. The tip of him continues to leak, and I watch him disappear and reappear behind our fingers.

"I'm about to cum," he warns.

I don't remove my hand. I want to feel it.

"Van—"

Chev's voice abruptly ends with a moan, and his cum splatters across his chest. It almost reaches his chin, and I jolt. Still, I continue to hold him, refusing to let myself feel bad as his cum seeps between our fingers.

This is my mate. Chev is my mate.

He covers himself and my hand, and only once he stops leaking do I release him. He grunts, but he otherwise remains silent as I climb off the bed.

"I'll be right back," I say.

I head into the kitchen, needing to clean my hand and take a moment for myself. Chev follows, his footsteps heavy as he walks behind me, but he doesn't try to speak. He watches silently as I wash my hands, scrubbing his cum off me.

I don't like the feeling of it.

Chev's warmth surrounds me, and I avoid leaning against his cum-covered chest as he takes over scrubbing my fingers and palms.

"Are you okay?" he asks.

I nod.

Chev kisses the side of my head. "Please use your words. I need to hear it."

"I'm okay," I admit. "I like touching you. I like making you feel good."

He relaxes around me, and I pull my hands out of the sink before turning to look around the kitchen. He's reconstructed this entire room for me. He's planted a hundred little flowers outside and filled his bathroom with every product I could ever want. He agreed, without hesitation, to a life without intimacy and has never once pushed me for more.

We're alone on his lands, in his home, but he still never pushed me. It would've been easy for him to pressure me into doing more, but he only takes what I explicitly ask for and offer.

"Do you like living in Wrath?" I ask.

Chev clears his throat and steps in front of me. He looks concerned, his nose scrunched as he scans me from head to toe. After a moment, he shrugs.

"I don't mind it," he says. "I miss my home, but I would miss you more if I left."

At this point, it's apparent that fighting our bond is useless. I can't imagine a future without Chev, and I doubt he can, either.

He's waited his entire life for me, and we're only prolonging the inevitable.

These lands are Chev's home, and despite how little time I've spent here, I feel comfortable. I can see myself sleeping in his bed with him and cooking in the kitchen, and I can imagine our children wreaking havoc in the woods outside.

Our bond hums, and I place a hand over my heart as Chev nervously grabs a towel and wipes the dripping cum off his chest and stomach.

"What're you feeling?" he asks.

I hear the fear behind his words, and I instinctively step forward to comfort him. Chev is my mate, and that's grown to mean something to me.

"How long would it take to move my things here?"

Chapter Twenty-Nine

CHEV

VANESSA'S LAUGHTER IS loud, and I stop speaking so I can better listen to it.

She's upstairs packing her belongings with Charlie, and it seems the two are having much fun. I've overheard them saying my name several times, which I love. Charlie enjoys talking poorly about her males, but Vanessa only says good things about me.

She must love me more than Charlie loves hers.

I grin and shove a couch pillow into a box. I'm unsure what belongs to my mate and what came with the house, but Aziel doesn't seem to care either way. He's keen to get rid of all the tiny decorative pillows, but I like them. They're soft, and I'm happy to take them off Aziel's hands.

"Vanessa has been taking advantage of her paychecks," Aziel mutters, holding up a ring.

It's a red one she purchased a few days after visiting the lava pits, and it must have slipped off her finger while she was lying on the couch. It makes me happy to imagine my mate purchasing herself little trinkets. I'll buy her thousands of them.

Gray and Silas teleport into the room, the two all over one another. The incubus curls his body around the fate, and I roll my eyes when I notice him sliding a hand up his shirt. It's annoying, and I toss a box toward them to stop the flirting.

They promised to be efficient, but Aziel and I are packing things faster than they're teleporting them to my home. My people don't like when demons are on our land unsupervised, and I promised them I'd have everything completed within an hour.

We're running out of time, and the horny incubus is to blame. His mates should've fed him before bringing him out today.

"Enough," Aziel snaps.

Silas straightens up, but Gray lingers. I watch with mild interest as he turns and grins at Aziel, his eyes shining as he slides his hand further up Silas's chest. I turn away and begin wrapping the stupid bird figurines Vanessa insists on bringing with her.

I hate them, and I hate that she's insisting they come with us, but I won't argue it.

At least, not right now. I'll wait until she's settled before slowly transitioning them out of our home. I'll first put them in a drawer, hidden from the eye, and bring them to Echo's after a few months. She'll keep them in case Vanessa notices their departure and grows angry. If she doesn't, I'll have Echo throw them away after six months.

If Vanessa happens to notice afterward, I'll lie and say I don't know what happened before offering to buy bear ones as replacements. It's the only lie I'll ever tell my mate, but it must be done. These atrocities cannot possibly live in our home around our babies. They'll be frightened of them.

A smile spreads over my face as I think about our future children. Vanessa and I haven't discussed when we'd like them, and I don't imagine it will be for a while. She's busy with work, and I don't think she's eager for the distraction a pregnancy will bring. Maybe in a few years when she feels more established at work. She'll probably be in a larger facility then. Hopefully, the one in the shifter lands.

Still, I can't wait to fill our home with tiny footsteps.

"This one is ready to go," I say, spinning around.

Silas is gone, as are two boxes he must've taken with him, but Aziel and Gray are now the ones wasting time. Aziel has his hand curled around Gray's neck, forcing his head into a submissive tilt, and I watch the two before huffing and carrying my box over.

Aziel doesn't let up as I approach, and I physically place my body between them until he has no choice but to release the incubus.

"You can do that later," I say, shoving the box against Aziel's chest. "You're in charge of transporting, and Gray will help me pack."

Gray's too slow, probably lingering around my home whenever he's there. I have a feeling my things will be moved when Vanessa and I return, and I hope Gray hasn't made my home smell of him. I also hope he isn't terrorizing my people.

He's been obsessed with my lands since we invited him to give a sex demonstration several years ago, and I know he takes great pride in the large number of shifter women who are attracted to him.

I think the women are being inappropriate.

I don't lust for the succubus who took us males into a private room and spread her legs. We were nothing but polite, and there was no scent of arousal to be found as she explained her body and demonstrated how most women enjoy being pleasured.

It was educational, and I don't know what Gray did, but he left a lasting impression on the women. It bothers many of the shifter males.

Aziel grabs two boxes and disappears, and I direct Gray to the bathroom.

"All the products under the sink need to be packed," I say. "You can help Vanessa and Charlie once you've finished."

Gray nods, his eyes lighting up when I say Charlie's name. I'm happy the tiny human found peace with her males.

"I heard you promised to catch Vanessa an ucka as a moving-in present," Gray says.

I set down the objects in my hands. I already know where he's heading with this.

"And there's going to be much more meat than you two can eat by yourselves," Gray continues. He shoots me a lopsided grin. "We have three small mouths that would love to spend the weekend helping you work through it."

Oh. That's not what I was expecting. I thought he was going to ask me to share some with him, and I was already preparing my rejection. I don't mind sharing with his children, though, and I did promise to babysit them as payment for using Silas as a vehicle.

"That sounds nice," Vanessa says, rounding the corner of the stairwell.

I trip over my feet rushing to her, and I only feel slightly embarrassed by the laughs I receive as I grab the box she's carrying. Gray does the same with Charlie, and we make brief eye contact before bringing the boxes to the pile with the others.

"You say that until you're waking up to a tiny fate standing in the corner of your bedroom staring straight into your soul," I tease Vanessa.

It's a joke, but I shiver at the thought. Valeria is a kind child, but she can be quite frightening. Shifters don't love fates, and I'm not too fond of her trying to sneak into my head when I'm weakened by sleep. She's done it before, but my future is mine only.

My pride swells when Vanessa walks around the couch to join

me near the boxes. She steps confidently and without thought as she brings herself into my personal space. I hurry to finish what I'm doing and wrap my arms around her, eager to hold her.

"Did you finish everything upstairs?" I ask.

Vanessa nods and leans against my chest. I kiss the top of her head. We're going to sleep together under the same roof tonight, and I've never been more excited. I will have hours to spend with my mate curled up against my chest, and I hope she sleeps well with me.

Gray grabs a box and teleports away just as Aziel and Silas return for more. I continue to hold Vanessa, and I subtly bury my face in her hair when I think she's not paying attention. Her smile tells me she's noticed.

"Are you ready to go home?" I ask. She nods, and I slide my hand down her back. "I'm going to use the portal, but Aziel can teleport you if you'd like."

I know all this teleporting is tiring for the demons, and I won't ask them to bring me, too. Aziel and Silas are probably the only ones strong enough to do it, but I don't want to hurt them. I'm too heavy, and they like to complain.

"I'll go with you," Vanessa says.

That's what I was hoping she'd say.

I turn to Charlie. "Do you want to come?"

I don't want her to, but it's polite to offer. I want to return with my mate alone, and I want Vanessa and me to unpack and make up our home together. I'd like to be private.

I had to beg my parents to stay away and give Vanessa time to decompress. They agreed, but they aren't pleased about it. They're excited to meet my mate.

"No, but thank you," Charlie says.

Vanessa smiles, and I smell her again before leading her outside. Her golf cart is parked in front of the house, and I make my way to the driver's seat.

"Let me drive," Vanessa says.

I hesitate.

My mate is dangerous with this, and I don't trust her driving—I never have. Despite my reservations, though, I nod and make my way to the passenger's seat. Only a few seconds into the ride, I find myself gripping the handle, and it takes everything in me not to shove my foot into the dirt and slow down the cart.

I take her hand and hold it close as she whips into a parking spot just outside the facility doors.

"There's no need to look so frightened, Chev."

I clear my throat. "I'm not frightened."

It's a lie, but Vanessa doesn't push it. It's her I'm frightened for. She could drive the cart full-speed into a tree and I'd be fine within a few hours, but she doesn't heal quite as quickly as I do. The thought horrifies me.

Vanessa leads me inside the facility, and I do my best to ignore the women who give me eyes. I don't think Vanessa realizes how many females look at me, and I'd like to keep it that way. She'd be upset.

"I need to stop by my office," Vanessa says.

I pretend to be shocked. She loves her work, and I knew she wouldn't be able to take an entire day off.

"I'll be in the kitchen," I say.

Vanessa disappears down the hallway leading to her office, and I rush to the kitchen and grab a handful of the fruit packets the pantry is frequently stocked with. They're one of my favorite snacks, and I shove as many as I can into the waistband of my leathers before grabbing two more fistfuls and heading to Vanessa's office.

She's on the phone, so I sit in one of the tiny chairs outside and wait. Ten minutes pass before she emerges, looking guilty.

"I'm not upset," I promise her.

Her guilty look doesn't diminish, and I pull her in for a kiss until she's smiling again. I much prefer this, and I run my hand down the mating marking on her back as we finally head to the portal. I'm eager to bring her home.

"Did you finish everything you needed to do?" I ask.

Vanessa nods. "Yes. Did you clear the kitchen of snacks?"

I'm sure she can see the packets sticking out of my waistband, so I don't bother denying it. I know she orders extra for me.

Aziel and Silas are standing around my kitchen counter when we finally arrive home.

"It looks good in here," Aziel says.

I love having my home complimented, and I beam as I look around the space. Aziel's the only person who's spent considerable time here before the construction, so he can see the improvement more than anybody else.

"Thank you," I say, glancing between him and Silas. "You may go now."

Vanessa pinches the back of my arm, but I ignore it. I want to spend alone time with my mate, and I won't apologize for it.

We need to unpack and fill our home with her belongings. I also need to know what side of the bed she wants to sleep on and whether or not she likes to fold or hang her shirts. There are so many things for us to learn about one another.

Silas gives me a rare smile before disappearing, and Aziel is quick to do the same. I wait until they're gone before spinning Vanessa around.

"Welcome home," I whisper. My voice is rougher than I'd like, and I clear my throat before continuing. "I love you."

I've been waiting to say it again, not wanting to rush her, and now is the perfect moment. Vanessa's eyes grow moist, and when she rubs her thumbs over my cheekbones and cups my face, I know she feels the same way.

"I love you, too."

Her words are quiet and full of insecurity, but I don't care. I know this is scary and new for her, and I'm beyond honored she's willing to make this leap.

"Should we start unpacking?" she asks.

I nod. It's like she read my mind.

Chapter Thirty

CHEV

THIS IS THE best day of my life.

I force myself to remain still as Vanessa pulls back the sheets and climbs into bed. It's been a long time since I've slept on a mattress that fits me, and the fact that I now get to do so with my mate is better than I ever could've imagined.

Vanessa clears her throat as her leg brushes against mine.

"Are you wearing underwear?" she asks.

I huff. "Of course I am."

And I hate it, too. The damn fabric is constricting, and it's prohibiting my thighs from breathing. I won't be surprised if I wake up needing an amputation. My limbs have no blood flow, but I'll suffer if it keeps Vanessa comfortable.

"I thought you hated normal clothing?" Vanessa asks.

She's smirking, and I roll my eyes as I realize she's making fun of me. She knows I hate when she refers to the clothing worn by the other breeds as "normal." My leathers are normal, and they're by far the most comfortable.

I have room for movement in them.

"My legs are shriveling up as we speak," I say.

My smile grows when Vanessa lets out a proper laugh and snuggles against my chest. She's everything, and I wrap my arm around her head and urge her to come closer. I want every inch of my body pressed against hers.

The pajamas she wears are soft, and I'm happy she decided not to wear the ones with lace. They're my favorite to look at, but they're itchy. I don't want them rubbing against me in the middle of the night.

Vanessa tangles her leg with mine, and I stiffen when she hooks her finger into the waistband of my underwear. What's she doing? She gives the elastic a gentle tug, her heart pounding so loud, I can hear it from here.

"Take them off," she whispers.

A small part of me knows I should question her statement and confirm she's okay with me being naked beside her, but my desperation to free my limbs has me yanking the offending fabric down and kicking it off my feet without a second thought.

I sprawl out the second I'm freed.

"Do you feel better?" Vanessa asks.

I nod. "So much."

Vanessa seems pleased, and I remain painfully still as she lifts the covers and peers underneath. She's in a good mood tonight, but I'm sure not going to complain. I stare at the side of her head as she looks over my bare body. I'm neither shy nor insecure, but I can't say I'm not nervous. If she doesn't like how I look, I might die.

She purses her lips and cocks her head to the side. I have no idea what it means.

"I don't think I've ever seen you completely soft before," she eventually says.

I tuck my chin into my chest and stare down at myself. I'm not in my most impressive state right now, but I was under the impression it wasn't needed. Our cuddling isn't sexual, but that can be changed if she requests it.

"I can fix that," I say, directing my gaze to Vanessa's breasts.

It's the quickest way to make me hard.

Vanessa shakes her head, her eyes widening as she watches me stiffen.

"Oh, no, it's not a bad thing," she says. I don't believe her, not one bit, and I lick my lips as I watch her nipples stiffen through her shirt. "I was just making an observation."

An observation she'll never make again. I will remain hard for my mate—every minute of every second of every day.

Vanessa drops the sheet, hiding me from her view.

"Chev," she scolds.

I shrug.

"I enjoy it when you're soft," she says. My female is a very skilled liar.

I gesture toward the blankets.

"But you like it better when it's hard," I say.

Vanessa sighs. "I like it both ways for very different reasons. Now, will you fix it?"

I suck my cheeks into my mouth. *Fix it?* My erection is not some broken object to be *fixed*. I love my mate, but sometimes, I don't think she respects my penis as much as I do.

"I worship your breasts and slit, but all you've done tonight is insult my manhood," I say.

I'm teasing her, and I smile so she knows I'm not being serious. Vanessa wrinkles her nose, an action she loves to do when she's annoyed with me, and my smile grows when she reaches out and flicks my forehead.

"My mate is unsatisfied with my body and my offerings…" I sigh, throwing an arm over my face. "I am a worthless male, undeserving of love and—"

My dramatics are cut short when Vanessa launches herself at me. She forces my arm away from my face and leans so far over me that her hair tickles my cheeks. I love it, and she glares down at me before flopping back onto her side.

I look forward to annoying her for the rest of our lives.

After a few seconds, Vanessa peers underneath the sheets once more. I knew it was coming, and I fight a smile as she looks over my softened length. She's interested in my body in all its different states, just as I am in hers.

Our bond hums, and I hope she enjoys the quiet noises my bear forces out of me as I relax into the sheets. The bed smells like her, and it's comforting. She must feel the same way about me, as it only takes her minutes to fall asleep.

The second I hear her first snore, I turn and kiss the top of her head. I love her, even if it means I never experience a night of blissful sleep again.

It's hard to fall into a deep rest when she's near, my body on high alert, but I'm hoping that lessens over time. This is new to me, and the unknown upsets my bear. Eventually, I give in and drag Vanessa on top of me, finding the most comfort when her body is sprawled entirely over mine.

The action wakes her slightly, and she lifts her head with a quiet groan. There's a bit of drool on her chin, and she wipes it with the back of her hand before dropping her head back onto my shoulder.

So fucking adorable.

I'm pretty sure I've only gotten an hour of proper rest when the sun begins to shine through my window, but I've spent many hours staring at my mate, so I'd say it's well worth it.

"Good morning," I say the moment Vanessa stirs.

She grunts and rolls off me. The action shoves her knee into my balls, but I manage to hide my pain as she rubs her eyes and drags a pillow over her face.

"I think I love you most when you're sleepy," I say.

Vanessa ignores me, so I throw my leg over her waist and sit atop her stomach. Her eyes creak open and briefly fall to my abs, and I flex them until her cheeks grow red. This is the attention I was looking for.

"What time is it?" she asks.

I shrug. "Early."

"How early?"

"You don't need to be up for another thirty minutes."

Vanessa drops her hands to my thighs, her fingers dangerously close to my exposed manhood. I do my best to ignore it as she rubs her thumbs back and forth over my upper thighs, not wanting to ruin the moment.

She's doing it out of instinct, and my bear seems to like it, if his annoying purring is anything to go by. Vanessa's lips twitch as the noises pour from my chest, my female always finding humor in my bear.

Despite how much the noises bother me, I no longer hold them back.

Several minutes pass before I work up the strength to get up. Vanessa rolls her head to the side, lazily watching me stand and dress. My best pair of leathers is dirty, and I dig through my drawers before finding my second-best pair.

"Would you ever consider wearing leathers?" I ask.

I busy myself with the ties so Vanessa doesn't feel too much pressure to answer, but I'm sure she can tell I'm eager to hear her response. I'll understand if her answer is *no*, but I hope she considers it.

Vanessa throws her legs over the side of the bed and stands.

"I'm not comfortable showing that much skin," she says.

She steps forward and peers into the drawer where I keep

mine.

I already had a pair made for her, and I duck my head as she reaches in and pulls them out. She fingers the fabric, and I clear my throat as I take them from her and put them back in the drawer. I'm embarrassed, and I want to hide them away. She wasn't supposed to see them.

"Are those for me?" she asks.

I shrug.

"I'm not upset you don't want to wear them," I say. "I just thought it would be nice to have a pair ready in case you ever do."

Vanessa rests her cheek against my shoulder. "I wouldn't mind wearing them for you in our home, but not outside in public."

Our bond pulsates. I love that, and I find my hands are shaking as I yank open the drawer and grab the pair of female leathers I just hid from her. I want to see them on her…urgently.

"May I?" I ask.

Vanessa giggles, her eyes wide as I lift her sleep dress up and over her head. I don't think she minds me seeing her bare, but I still keep my gaze averted as I wrap the leather top around her chest. It pushes her breasts together, drawing attention to them, and I tie it just tight enough to stay up.

The skirt is next. I wrap it around her waist before tying the overlapping ends together.

Fuck.

Vanessa tugs at the bottom of the skirt before turning and looking in the mirror. Her cheeks are flushed, and she runs her hands over her exposed midsection before skimming them over her chest.

"I'm happy I'm the only male who will ever see you in these," I admit.

Leathers fit differently on shifter women. They don't have nearly as much curvature to their bodies as Vanessa, so the leathers cover more. Vanessa is spilling out of the top and bottom. This is for my eyes only.

Vanessa fights back a smile as she looks at herself, and I do the same. She looks good, and I think she knows it.

"I'll wear them for you this morning," she says.

I've never heard better words, and I happily follow her into the kitchen. She doesn't have to be at work for another hour, and I'm looking forward to spending the morning with her.

"Are you hungry?" Vanessa asks.

What a silly question. "I'm always hungry."

It's the truth, too. I've always had a large appetite, and when it comes to Vanessa's cooking, I fear it has no limits. I'd eat anything she made, and I'd do so happily. Everything is so good, and it makes my kitchen skills feel inadequate.

Vanessa looks in the pantry, her eyebrows furrowed. I stocked it before her arrival, so it should be full of everything she needs. I took the liberty of searching her kitchen back in Wrath so I knew what kinds of ingredients and products she enjoys.

"I'm going to hunt you an ucka," I say. "Soon."

It's this week's number-one priority. Finding an ucka large enough to honor my mate may take days, so I need to begin tracking as soon as possible. It's tradition, and I won't disappoint. I'll get her one twice as large as the one my father brought my mother when they first mated.

"I'm excited," Vanessa says. "I've never tried it before, but I've read it's a shifter favorite."

It's *the* shifter favorite, and it's incredibly hard to get. Only the strongest shifters are big and fast enough to take down an adult ucka. Several men in my pack choose to hunt in groups, but as alpha, it's expected I go on my own.

It's one way I prove my strength to my people.

I sit at the kitchen island while Vanessa pulls two wooden

bowls out of my cabinet.

"I might be working late tonight," she says. "I have a lot to catch up on after taking most of yesterday off. Would you mind meeting me at the portal so I don't have to walk through the shifter lands alone? I don't think I'm quite ready for that."

I purse my lips. Meet her at the portal?

"Aren't you going to be working with me?" I ask. I was under the impression we would be sharing my office until I fully transitioned my work to Echo. I only have a few weeks left before I'm officially done. Vanessa and I should enjoy it while we can.

Vanessa shakes her head. "Not today. I need to work out of Wrath."

I hum, and Vanessa pats my hand before turning away and pulling open my fridge. I'm displeased.

"So, will you meet me at the portal?" she repeats.

"Of course," I say. She doesn't need to ask. "But tomorrow, you'll come to work with me?"

Vanessa nods. "Yes. I'll work with you tomorrow."

Good.

Chapter Thirty-One

VANESSA

I DRAG MY fingertips across my desk, unsure how to voice my thoughts.

Charlie sits across from me, her eyebrows furrowed as she looks over my proposed events plan. The women here have been enjoying the fitness classes, and they're almost always full. I want to add a few more, particularly stretching and another self-defense class.

"We should cut the painting class," Charlie mumbles. "Nobody attends."

I agree. The art classes were the most popular in my facility, but nobody here seems to particularly enjoy them. I'll be sad to see them go, but there's no point in spending money on something that isn't being used. We need the budget, and it will offset some of the costs of taking in a few women from the elven facility.

"What is sex like with your mates?" I blurt out the question before I change my mind.

Charlie freezes, and her gaze darts toward me before she sets down her paperwork and gives me her undivided attention. I'm sweating, and I avoid eye contact. I could make an appointment with my therapist to discuss this, but I don't want his diplomatic answers. I want real answers from real experience.

"It's hard to say," Charlie says. She's fighting a smile. Her twitching lips give it away. "It changes a lot. Sometimes, they're aggressive, and sometimes, they're gentle. It depends on the day and mood, but I always enjoy it."

I'm relieved she doesn't ask why I want to know. I assume it's pretty obvious. Chev and I are growing closer, and I want to try for more. I trust him more than I ever thought possible, and I'm comfortable with him. He makes me feel safe.

Charlie clears her throat. "Sometimes, they let *me* be in charge."

"How?" I need to know.

"I'll go on top and set the pace. Silas likes it when I tie him up."

Silas likes being tied up? I never would've guessed. I hate the idea of ever being tied up again. The mere thought of feeling ties on my wrists or ankles makes me want to scream and claw at my skin, but it could be interesting to try with Chev. He sat on his hands last time, and it was helpful.

He didn't touch me until I gave him permission, which made it significantly easier to relax. Would Chev be open to it? I don't even know how I'd go about having that conversation.

"What do you tie him up with?" I ask.

I can't think of a single fabric that Silas wouldn't be able to easily break out of. Demons are absurdly strong, and so is Chev. Even giant, wooden doors and thick, metal fences aren't enough to stop my mate. He still has the bald spots to prove it.

Charlie shrugs. "Silas has some special ties we use. They're enchanted or something. I've honestly never asked."

I wonder where he bought them. I could ask Charlie if she'd ask Silas, but she's not necessarily known for being discreet and her mates are clever. It wouldn't take them long to realize she's asking for me. Maybe I can do some research later and see what I can find online.

"You can borrow a pair if you'd like," Charlie says. I press my lips together, not immediately answering. Charlie continues. "Silas has tons, and he won't notice."

It wouldn't hurt to try. I'm pretty sure Chev is up for anything. He's horny, and he's more than happy to take whatever I'm willing to give. I want to give sex to him. I want to give sex to me. I want to feel that closeness and connection with him.

"I'd love that," I say.

Charlie beams, and I stare at my desk while waiting for the blood to leave my cheeks. I'm sure they're impossibly red. This has been one of the most uncomfortable conversations I've had in a while, even if Charlie seemed more than happy with it.

She finishes looking over my proposed event plan before heading out for the day, and I putter around before getting sucked into some more work caused by the elven facility. It makes the day go by quickly, and before I know it, I'm heading to the portal and returning to the shifter lands.

Chev meets me at the cabin, as promised, and he holds my hand tightly as we return to his home. I know his family and friends live here, but Chev's decided to keep them distanced for the time being. He says it's because he wants to spend time with me alone, but I secretly think he's doing it for my benefit. He doesn't want to overwhelm me.

I brush my thumb along his wrist as we step inside our home, silently wondering what they'll feel and look like with those ties around them. I should bring up the idea with him, but I struggle to find the courage.

I won't worry about it until Charlie's gotten the ties from Silas. It's a problem for future Vanessa.

Chapter Thirty-Two

CHEV

I STRUGGLE TO slow my limbs and remain calm as I notice the time. I'm running late, and that knowledge is making me sporadic.

Vanessa moved in two weeks ago, but we haven't truly been able to enjoy one another's company. She's been so busy with work, but the elven facility she's been struggling with has finally resolved its issues. I want to celebrate.

Vanessa was quite offended when I told her I wouldn't be available to walk her home from work this evening, which I thought was worth it because I was going to surprise her with a delicious meal. A delicious meal I'm fucking up in every possible way.

I thought I'd remember the recipe for the wheat sticks better than this.

She made it look easy.

My mate will be here any minute now, and all I've got to show for it are burnt strings and a messy counter. At least the sauce I made is good. It wasn't always that way, but I added salt until it was delicious.

Shifters don't typically cook with salt, but requests for it have spread since Vanessa made our lands her home. She's quickly creating a friend group, and even though I find her friends annoying when they're constantly in my home stealing my mate's attention, I'm glad she's finding happiness.

I slam my fist against the counter before grabbing the pot on the stove and throwing the charred remains outside the back door. I forgot I needed water to cook the wheat strings, a mistake I won't make again.

This is my favorite meal, mainly because it's the first one my mate ever made for me, and now it will be the first one I've made for her. That's romance if I've ever seen it.

I make sure to put a large amount of water into the pot before setting it back on the stove. This time, I won't mess up. I also throw in a handful of salt before peering into the oven. Vanessa didn't tell me how to make this, but I found a recipe online.

My cheese-covered bread looks crispy, and I crack the oven door open to smell it. The heat hits me in the face, but it's worth it. It smells amazing. I love human food.

The water is just beginning to boil when the doorknob twists and my mate comes walking inside. She looks fantastic in her jeans and sweater, and I lean against the counter as she enters the kitchen. I'm playing it cool.

"What's all this?" Vanessa asks.

She approaches, and I find myself holding my breath as she peers at the pots of boiling water and tomato sauce. Her cheeks turn red, and I watch the change before ducking and pressing my lips to hers. She's gotten comfortable with my kisses, and I squeeze her tightly as I tease her with my tongue.

When I pull away, she's breathless. *Good.*

"I made dinner," I say.

The room is smoky from my first failed attempt, and Vanessa's nostrils flare as she dips her finger into the sauce. Her eyebrows raise as she tastes it, and I rock back on my heels as I wait for her approval.

"It's very salty," she says.

I nod. "Yes, it is. Just like you."

The way her nose scrunches tells me she's not happy with my compliment, which I don't bother trying to understand. My mate's skin is very salty after a long day in the heat. It's in her sweat, and I love it. Maybe that's why I enjoy the table salt she's stocked our home with so much. It tastes like her.

I step behind Vanessa and wrap my arms around her waist, eager to have her in my arms. I spent most of my day trying to catch up on the pack work I've missed during the last few years I've been prioritizing the females, which made the day go quickly. Not quick enough, though.

I still missed my mate.

Vanessa leans into my arms, still looking down at the stove. The action exposes her neck to me, and I quietly brush her hair aside before licking the dark-pink mark. Vanessa shivers, and I do it again.

"Chev!" She gasps, throwing an elbow into my side.

I groan and back away, pretending her elbow has wounded me, before returning my focus to the wheat sticks. The water is finally boiling, and I grab our last four boxes and pour them in. Vanessa watches from the side, and I take it as a good sign when she doesn't step in to correct me.

"I'll be right back," she says, squeezing my bicep.

I nod, too busy checking the cheesy bread to inquire why she's trying to run away from me so soon. I usually get two to three hours from her before she deems me annoying and insists I give her space.

Vanessa's footsteps are light as she putters away, and I listen as she enters our bedroom and shuts the door. What's she doing?

I want to know, but she doesn't like when I follow her around.

The strings are just beginning to grow soft when I hear the door open, and I about knock over the entire pot of boiling water when she enters the room in her leathers. I've only seen her in them once, and I take one look at her exposed breasts before groaning and spinning away.

I face the counter to hide my reaction. I don't want Vanessa to feel like the leathers are a sexual thing, and I want her to be comfortable in them. That's not going to happen when I'm running around with an erection the size of my forearm every time I see her in them.

Vanessa walks up behind me and wraps her arms around my waist, and I resist the urge to cry at the feeling of her barely covered breasts pressing against my bare back. This is not good.

I grab Vanessa's wrists and hold them against my abs, preventing her from wandering. She giggles, her soft body rubbing against mine as I shuffle to the side and continue cooking with one hand.

"What are you doing?" Vanessa asks, kissing between my shoulder blades. Why does she do this to me? "Turn around and look at me."

I shake my head. I can't do that. The second I do, she'll see my erection and it'll ruin the innocence of the leathers. Vanessa huffs when I don't obey, and she pinches one of my abs between her pointy fingers.

I don't relent. I want to see her so badly, but I can't. I need time for my erection to soften, which is damn near impossible when she's pressed against me like this. I'm going to die.

"Look at me, Chev," Vanessa says. She sounds upset.

I squeeze my eyes shut before releasing her wrists and turning around. I can't bring myself to look her in the eye, but after a long second, I give in to her orders and lower my gaze.

Vanessa is trying to kill me.

The leathers are dark, and she tied the top so tight, it pushes her breasts up. She holds my waist as I eye her belly and, eventually, her skirt. Her thighs look so soft. Are leather shirts always this short? I've never noticed. I don't look at the thighs of other women.

"Come to the bedroom," she says.

I swallow and point to the oven. "Dinner."

My Vanessa smells of nerves as she leans around my torso and turns off the heat. I'm nervous too, but I don't argue as she takes my hand and leads me to the bedroom. I think my heart is going to explode.

When she pushes open the bedroom door, I freeze. What is this?

I take three steps back, struggling to understand. There are two black silk ties on the bed, neither belonging to me. I'm not stupid, though. I learned a lot while living in the Wrath manor with Gray.

I once wandered into his bedroom and found Silas tied up with silk ties that looked exactly like this. It was a scary sight, one I wish I could remove from my memory. Does Vanessa want me to tie her up? I will not.

I've never asked about her past with the ogres, but they have specialized interests and I've drawn assumptions. They liked to tie up their females, and I will not do the same to my mate.

My heart pounds as I pick up one of the ties and bring it to my nose. It smells like the Wrath trio. I'm not sure which one of them gave these to Vanessa, probably Gray, but I'm sure as fuck going to figure it out. The bond between us burns as my anger grows.

"I will not do this," I say.

Vanessa frowns and glances between the bed and me.

"Oh…" There's a long silence. "You sat on your hands last time, so I thought you'd be comfortable… I'm sorry."

I gulp. *What?*

"You want to tie *me* up?" I ask.

Shifters don't enjoy being restrained. My bear is on edge at the mere thought, the male angry and pacing inside my brain. I'd do it for Vanessa, but I don't want to. I'd much rather sit on my hands or hold the headboard. Something I can easily break from.

Vanessa clears her throat and nods.

"I was talking with Charlie, and she said this might be a helpful way for us to be together," she explains. "I liked it when you licked me because I was in control, and I thought maybe if I tied you up, I would be more comfortable."

I drop the tie onto the bed. "Were you not comfortable that time?"

My chest grows tight with fear that she didn't enjoy what we did. I've asked a million times, and she always assures me she liked it.

Vanessa frowns. "Of course I was."

"If you were comfortable, why do you want to tie me up?"

I struggle to keep my voice low and calm as I ask my questions. Have I done something since then to make her uncomfortable? I sleep naked most nights, but she very explicitly told me it was okay. Maybe it's because I wake every morning with an erection. It goes down quickly, but I can't control my dreams.

I cross my arms over my chest.

Vanessa runs her hands through her hair.

"I want to do more than just oral, Chev," she says.

Every muscle in my body stiffens. More than oral? Is she referring to sex? I was under the impression it wasn't on the table. I'll happily let her tie me up if it means sex. I'll shove my body into a metal tube if it means I can feel my mate on my cock.

I glance between her and the ties before climbing on the bed and bringing my wrists to the headboard. Vanessa looks shocked by my sudden change of heart, and I wiggle my eyebrows before grabbing the ties and holding them out for her.

Knowing they're for sex changes everything. I'll do anything for sex.

Vanessa worries her bottom lip between her teeth as she takes the ties and kneels on the bed. She looks petrified, and I wince before sitting up and pulling her onto my lap. This isn't right. I don't want my mate having to talk herself into sex with me. I'd rather never have sex than do it when she isn't entirely sure.

"It's okay, my mate," I say, wrapping my arms around her waist. "There'll be no sex today."

I want it, but I refuse to do anything when she's nervous and unsure. My earlier confusion has ruined the mood, and I want everything to be perfect when she decides to take me.

"I'm sorry," Vanessa says.

She clears her throat and moves to say more, but I bring my lips to hers to stop the words. She has nothing to apologize for. A conversation about the ties would've been better than a surprise, but Vanessa isn't to blame. She probably thought I'd like the spontaneity.

Vanessa relaxes as I kiss her, and I run my hands over her exposed sides before sliding them to her butt. She giggles as I cup and squeeze, carefully touching her over the leather skirt.

"You're perfect," I whisper. "And I'm happy with what we have. I don't need more."

She relaxes further into me, and I lean against the bed's headboard. Vanessa is still in my lap, her knees on either side of my hips. The position is dangerous, considering we're both wearing leather skirts with nothing underneath, but neither of us comments on it.

My bear begins to purr when we smell Vanessa's arousal, and

I trail my lips down the side of her neck. She weaves her fingers into my hair, and her hands quickly travel to my abs. I love it when she touches my muscles.

"Put yourself inside me."

I stiffen. What?

Vanessa pulls back and stares down at me, her cheeks flushed and chest heaving. I can't tell if she's doing this because she feels guilty, so I shake my head. She's pushing herself too much, and it isn't necessary. I don't need sex.

It's safe to say Vanessa doesn't look pleased with my rejection.

"I love you, Chev, and I want to feel you," she promises. "I'm not scared, and I'm sure this is what I want."

Chapter Thirty-Three

CHEV

I THINK I'M dying.

Vanessa smiles when she sees the shock in my expression, and with a slow exhale, she rises and reaches underneath my leathers. *Oh.* Her fingers wrap around my length, and I shut my eyes and try not to embarrass myself.

"I want this, Chev," she whispers. "I want you."

She unties my leathers, and I lift my hips as Vanessa pulls them out from underneath me and tosses them aside. They land on the ground with a quiet *thump*. I fist the sheets, curling my fingers into the soft fabric as I fight the urge to reach for Vanessa.

My eyes are still shut, and I squeeze them harder as something wet and warm envelops the tip of my cock. It's tight, and I slam my head against the headboard.

If I open my eyes, I will cum, and I blindly reach for her thighs before sliding my hands around the back of them and finding my way in between. I find myself quickly enough, and I inch my fingers upward. I'm between Vanessa's thighs, and I moan as I feel where her warm sex stretches around my length.

I'm inside her.

Vanessa sinks lower before releasing the base of my shaft and grabbing my shoulders. I continue to feel where I'm entering her, in complete disbelief. Is this truly happening? My mate pants as she lowers herself, and I only pull my hand away when she's seated completely. Her walls are so tight, and when she clenches, I groan and slam my hands over my face.

This is the best thing I've ever felt.

I'm going to sit here like a good mate and let Vanessa use me for her pleasure. She's riding me, letting me fill her warm body, and I'm going to cum deep inside it. Mine.

My breaths are choppy when I finally work up the strength to open my eyes. Vanessa's face and neck are a dark red, and her lips are swollen from her teeth sinking into them. I don't look at where we connect, already knowing that will be too much. I don't want this to be over too soon.

Vanessa uses my shoulders for leverage as she rises, and a low moan emerges from her throat as she drops back down. It takes everything I have not to embarrass myself and finish too soon. Females like it when their males last longer than thirty seconds. That's what the succubus said when she came to our lands and taught us how to please our mates. She stressed that it was essential.

I listened.

I lower my gaze to Vanessa's chest. She's still wearing her leathers, which is probably for the best. The sight of her bare breasts bouncing as she takes me would be too much.

"Take it off," Vanessa says, noticing my gaze.

I shake my head. "I can't."

"Why?"

"Because I'll cum."

Cold air hits my shaft as Vanessa rises, but I'm immediately plunged back into her warmth as she drops back down. She's so tight around me, and I bend my knees as I bring a hand to the back of her neck. I know reaching between her thighs would be too much, so I stroke her mark instead.

The way Vanessa moans and drops her head tells me she likes it.

She begins fiddling with the ties holding her top in place, and I groan.

"My mate," I warn her. "Don't do that."

Vanessa only shoots me a devilish smile. My mate is an evil, evil woman.

Her leather top is removed, exposing her bouncing breasts. They're so inviting, and I get one glance at her pebbled nipples before cursing.

"Fuck," I gasp, pressing harder against her mark. "I'm sorry, baby, I'm so sorry."

I sit up straight and wrap my arms around her as I cum. A good mate would've lasted longer, and Vanessa was cruel to show me her breasts and overwhelm my eyes. She knows how much I love them.

I accidentally squeeze so hard, she can't move, but I'm quick to release her the second I realize. Vanessa grabs my biceps and holds them down as I spill inside her, and I curl my fists into the bedsheets as she continues riding.

I'm still inside my mate, and I love how she continues to use me. She knows what she wants, and she's going to take it.

Vanessa's moans grow louder as she reaches down and begins rubbing herself, and I finally give in and look at where our bodies connect. *Oh, fuck.* I'm covered in her arousal, and her sex stretches around my thickness as she eases herself up and down. I stare, wholly entranced as she bucks, writhes, and wiggles on me.

I continue to stare as she cums, her body clamping down around me. It's the best thing I've ever felt, and when she finally pulls off and sits on my thighs, I could die a happy man.

My cum pours out of her.

Mine.

I grab her hips and nudge her off my legs, continuing until she's flat on her back. Vanessa looks confused, but I'm not in a state of mind to explain what I'm doing as I bundle up her ankles and lift them in the air.

"Chev!" she squeals.

I don't let go.

My bear is so loud, I can barely hear anything over his purring. He's just as pleased as I am, and he's making it known. Vanessa is flushed and soft from her orgasm, and I lift her legs higher until her butt is no longer on the bed.

"What are you doing?" she asks.

I wiggle her side to side.

"Gravity will bury my cum in you," I explain.

I know all about gravity, and this will help ensure she grows pregnant with my babies. Vanessa's on birth control, but I know my seed will overcome that.

"Aren't you going to ask if I'm okay?" she asks.

I blink, loosening my grip before changing my mind and lifting her even higher. Then I think better of it and peer at Vanessa over her toes. The bond tells me she's perfectly fine, elated even, and after a moment's hesitation, I drop her legs and scoop her in my arms.

I hide against her chest so she doesn't see how my eyes grow wet and my bottom lip wobbles, but I'm sure she can taste the tears as she pulls me in for a kiss. Vanessa's my everything, and her trust in me is beyond words.

"I'm so honored you're my mate," I whisper.

Vanessa rubs my back, comforting me, before squeezing my shoulders in the silent command to let go. I don't want to, but I do. She stares into my eyes with a look I've never seen before, and I hope it means something good. I didn't anticipate this happening, not in a million years, and I slam my fist against my chest when my damned bear refuses to shut up. He's too loud.

"Did you enjoy it?" I ask, needing to know.

Vanessa nods, and I look down. She drips my cum, just how I like it.

"Are you going to go off your birth control?" I ask.

Vanessa's hesitation is all the answer I need. She doesn't want my babies, at least not now. I force a smile on my face. I won't make my mate feel guilty for not being ready to have my children. It's her body and her decision—even if I'm excited.

If I could carry babies, I would've put hers inside me months ago. I would've begged for her eggs and shoved them into my belly the day we met. My stomach would already be rounding, and I'd have their bedroom and crib built weeks ago.

Maybe that's why she doesn't want my babies. I haven't built a room for them, and I have no furniture. She doesn't think I can provide.

"Chev, Chev," Vanessa says, grabbing my cheeks and forcing my attention back to her. "I just want to enjoy you before we bring children into the mix."

I glance back down at where she's dripping. I suppose having sex without worrying about poking the baby is nice. Plus, pregnant females are fawned over in my pack. I love my Vanessa, and I might lose my mind if I have to endure my people trying to visit and watch her grow. Everybody will bring her meals, and the males will build her objects if they feel I'm not doing it quickly enough. The fact that I don't already have a nursery is shameful.

I will beat any males who bring my mate infant furniture and offer their assistance in helping me prepare. She's mine, and caring for the baby is my responsibility.

"This is maybe for the best," I admit. "I'm not prepared, but I'll get started on the room and furniture now."

Vanessa laughs, and I trail my finger down the swell of her breast with a low hum.

"You should leave these out always," I say.

Vanessa swats me away, but our bond tells me she likes my obsession with her body. I love how her flesh caves under the pressure of my fingers, leaving tiny indents. Someday, I'll lay her down and touch every inch of her. There'll be no part of her body I haven't felt.

I lean in and smell her neck, double-checking that she's not pregnant.

She's not, her scent unchanged, and I tap her belly before climbing off the bed and holding out my hand. Our dinner will be ruined, but I'll destroy a thousand dinners if it means I get to have sex with my mate.

"We should clean up," I say.

I'd like her to wear my cum for the remainder of the night, but I know better than to ask. I can see the way she fidgets. She doesn't like having it inside her, so I'll never tell her how much I enjoy it.

Shifters don't use condoms, but I'll secure some from Gray for future sex. When the time comes for Vanessa and me to create children, I'll prepare towels and water and help her clean as quickly as possible. That's assuming she allows us to create children in the way that's most natural to my people.

Vanessa practically jumps out of bed at the mention of cleaning up, and I swoop her bridal style in my arms so gravity doesn't make more drip out and smear against her thighs.

"I'll be careful next time," I whisper, kissing her forehead.

For a long moment, there's silence, and when I turn to look at Vanessa, I notice her eyes are wet. Our bond is uncomfortable, and I feel horrible despite knowing she's not angry with me. I didn't know she wouldn't like me finishing inside, but I do now.

We get in the shower, and I hold her gaze as I trail my hand up her thighs and clean them. Her sex is next, but I don't touch it. She doesn't like that, so I pull away and let her do it herself. Vanessa grimaces as she wipes her folds, and she wiggles as she tries to push the remainder of my cum out.

"It's because you forced your breasts into my face," I tease, trying to lighten the mood. "You know how much I like them."

Vanessa snorts, and I take great pride in how her mood improves. I'm distracting her, and I continue to do so until she's clean and free of my cum.

"I'm excited to eat your spaghetti," she eventually says.

Good. I'm proud of my wheat strings.

"I think turning off the flame ruined the food," I admit.

Vanessa doesn't respond, probably because it's true, but she's the one who turned it off, so I'm going to blame her.

"It's your fault if it's not delicious," I say.

Vanessa gasps. "*Chev!*"

I jump away when she moves to strike my shoulder, and I'm only slightly horrified by the non-masculine giggle that slips from my throat as I hurry out of the shower to escape her attack. Vanessa lands a good hit on my side before I can get away, and I notice that her attack is precisely the same as Echo's.

My monstrous sister has been training with my mate.

This means Vanessa has likely taken a thousand hits of a stick. Her nymph blood allows her to heal quickly, so the bruises would be gone before I see them, but I don't like the thought of them having been there in the first place.

Echo has a very particular teaching manner, and the next time I see her, I will whack her hard with a stick. I don't care if it causes Dad to come at me. He's an old man, and I will whack him too.

I don't care.

Chapter Thirty-Four

CHEV

VANESSA HATES IT when I do this.

I stare at her face, ensuring she's in a deep sleep before gently pulling back the covers and crawling out from under her. She gets scared when she wakes to me getting out of bed, my large body sending her brain into a momentary spiral, and I do my best not to disturb her as I place my feet on the floor.

Moving as slowly as my muscles can, I inch off the bed and pull the covers back up her body.

That was smooth.

Vanessa's still asleep, my beautiful mate none the wiser as I tie up my leathers and head into the living room where the Wrath children are sleeping. I agreed to watch them for one weekend in exchange for using Silas as a vehicle, but that was months ago and now it feels like they're always here.

I don't mind, especially since it allows me to teach them the skills their parents have failed to do.

Valeria is already awake and staring at the ceiling, and I whistle to get her attention before jerking my head toward the door. The mini fate frightens me, but I'm reminded she's just a child as she grins and scampers outside.

Cassia is hard to wake, and I poke at her with my toe until her eyes blink open. She looks at me with pure hatred, the young wrath not happy about being woken up, but she doesn't make a fuss as I help her to her feet.

She tried to bite me the last time she spent the night here, so I'll count this as progress.

"Go outside," I whisper, keeping my voice low so we don't disturb Vanessa.

She drags her feet across the ground, but she listens nonetheless as she joins her sister outside.

David is the easiest to wake, clinging to my leg within seconds. He still likes being carried, and I hold him on my hip as I lead all three kids to my back shed.

Vanessa thinks this is unnecessary, but I disagree. These children may not be shifters, but I'm still their uncle. I have to teach them these essential life skills. Aziel sure isn't going to do it. He's a useless father, and I make sure to tell him that every time I see him. He's lucky I'm here to help.

I keep three child-sized axes in the back of my shed. Cassia and Valeria squeal when they see them. David wiggles in my arms, and I set him down so he can grab his axe and join his sisters.

"It's time you learn how to chop down trees," I say. "We'll begin building your first home today."

Cassia lets out a war cry, and I laugh. She's Aziel's biological child, and it shows. David is clingy like Gray, and Valeria is weird like Silas.

I grab the lunch I packed yesterday evening and lead the three into the woods. This is good practice for when Vanessa decides she's ready to give me a child. She's been living with me for exactly four months and seventeen days, and I think she's getting comfortable with the idea.

We've had penetrative sex six more times since our first, and I can tell she's enjoying it more and more. She lets me lick her whenever I want now, and I can't even count the number of times I've gotten to feel her warm cunt on my tongue.

"Come on," I say, leading the tiny demons to a small cluster of young trees.

It will break Vanessa's heart to learn I've encouraged the kids to chop down nature, but it must be done. They need to learn how to build a home for their future mates, and most shifter children are taught at this age.

"Cassia's wandering off!"

I can always count on David to keep his siblings in line.

Valeria begins lecturing David about squealing while I look for the disappearing wrath. My heart skips a beat when I spot her, and I let out a loud huff before running after her. She's on her hands and knees peering into a hole, and I wrap an arm around her waist and snatch her up before the snake that lives in it grows angry.

Stupid child.

She screams and kicks, and I grab her axe with my free hand before carrying her back to her siblings. David laughs at her, only furthering her anger.

"Down!" she shouts, kicking at my stomach. "Down!"

The trees here are young, planted with the sole purpose of being cut by children, and I put Cassia in front of the one I want her to take her aggression out on.

"Have any of you swung an axe before?" I ask.

Cassia throws herself onto the ground, but I ignore her. Her parents always run to her when she throws her tantrums, but she'll quickly learn she won't get the same reaction from me.

"No," Valeria says, spinning around with her axe.

She's going to lose a limb.

David sits on the ground and plays with the blade of his, dragging his finger along the sharp edge. It takes about half a second for him to cut himself, and his eyes fill with tears as he stares at the blood.

"Ow," he whispers.

He doesn't come to me for comfort, and I wait patiently for his finger to heal before continuing.

"I'll show you," I say.

Cassia's tantrum stops as I begin demonstrating how to use an axe, and within minutes, the three children are all copying me. They aren't very good, but most children aren't. It'll take years for them to learn, which is why we like to start young.

David figures it out quickly. He has good aim, and he follows my directions perfectly. Valeria struggles to swing, but she's getting the hang of it. Cassia isn't making much progress. I gave her a smaller axe because she's younger than David and Valeria, and I suck my cheeks into my mouth to prevent myself from laughing as she storms up to David and steals his. He doesn't seem to care, and he happily switches with his younger sister before moving to his next tree.

Valeria's hard at work, hacking away at the base of her chosen tree.

Their demon blood makes them stronger than most shifter children, and once they learn the motion and technique, they begin making good progress. I'll bring them to larger trees next time.

"Try not to swing so wildly," I say when Valeria misses her trunk. "An intentional hit is better than a hard one."

She misses again, and I help adjust her stance. I keep an eye on Cassia and David while I work with Valeria, ensuring they don't hurt themselves. I'm a good instructor.

David is next to get help, but he needs the opposite instruction. "You need to swing harder," I say, crouching to his left. "Put your muscles into it."

He turns and shoots me one of his rare dirty looks before widening his legs and swinging again. It's much better. I shift my attention to Cassia. David's axe is clearly too heavy for her, but I let her have a few minutes before switching her back to her smaller one. Immediately, both she and David improve.

Having a good axe—one appropriately weighted and sized—is key.

"You're doing great," I say, continuing to make my rounds between the three children.

I'll have each one chop down four trees before showing them how to remove the branches. Then, they'll pick where they want to build their home. I'm very excited.

David screams as a tree falls and almost lands on him, and I bark out a laugh before showing him how to direct the direction of the fall. Silas will kill me if I let one of his children get crushed. They'll live, and I personally think it will teach them a valuable lesson on safety, but I doubt Silas will see it that way.

Useless male.

Two hours pass before each child has their four trees, and I pull out the food I packed for lunch. The bloodhounds smell it and come running over, their axes swinging dangerously around their legs. Valeria and David set down their axes to eat, but Cassia holds on to hers. I fear it will be hard to get it back from her at the end of the day.

"I packed ucka and juice," I say, pulling the food out of my backpack.

All three little demons dive in, sticking their fingers into the ucka meat and ripping off large chunks. They eat like wild animals, and I love it.

I originally planned to eat with them, but as I watch Valeria practically pounce over David to get an especially juicy-looking piece of meat, I realize I underestimated their appetites. I lie on my back and listen to them eat instead, specifically Cassia.

She chokes sometimes.

Twenty minutes pass before they collapse next to me, their faces covered in grease and their eyes sleepy. There's not much ucka left, but I pick apart the few chunks of meat they didn't get to and eat while they nap. I often fall asleep after a big meal, so I know exactly how they feel.

It's not long before they're up and moving around again, and I show them how to clean their trees. I've already picked out and cleared the general area where they'll build their house, and I hold their axes while they work together to carry their logs to the spot.

The shifter children around their age have been building homes closer to the pack's center, but I chose a spot on the outskirts of the pack, closer to my house. Shifters love kids, but I know the demon blood makes them wary.

"Here we are," I say as we reach the area I cleared for them. "Look around and decide where you want your home to go. You can't change it once you've started."

Valeria and David immediately begin to fight, and I lean against a tree while waiting for them to work it out. They eventually settle on a spot, mainly because Cassia throws herself onto the ground and begins screaming. David concedes to stop the arguing, letting Valeria pick the spot.

I peer through the trees, happy when I notice my kitchen window is just barely visible from where I stand. My excitement falls when I catch sight of my mate glaring at me through the glass, though. She told me very specifically not to give the children axes.

I pretend not to notice her as I show the children how to begin laying down the framework. Their first house will be small, but it's for practice. We'll discuss more permanent options once they're large enough to chop down real trees.

My heart pounds when I eventually take them back to my home.

Vanessa's going to yell at me.

She's full of smiles when the four of us come sauntering inside, but I know it's a lie. I can feel her anger through our bond, and it's confirmed when I walk into the living room and see she's brought the bird figurines out.

Valeria sees them, too, and I'm proud of how well I've trained her when she begins to cry. She loves birds, but she knows to act scared when she sees them in my home.

"Oh, no. It's okay," I coo, rushing to grab the evil objects and shove them deep into the nearest junk drawer. "I'll put them away!"

Valeria gasps and wipes her tears, and I avoid looking at my mate as I pull the tiny being into my arms and rub her back. I don't like fates, but this one's okay.

"Food's in the kitchen," Vanessa says.

Her voice isn't nearly as angry as I was expecting, and when I work up the courage to meet her gaze, I'm surprised to see she's looking at me with a soft smile. I don't trust it.

The kids sprint out of the room at the mention of food, the little goblins already hungry again. I'm going to begin charging Aziel for the food they eat. Maybe I can convince him to hunt me down an ucka in payment.

"I'm sorry," I mumble when Vanessa and I are alone.

She hums, and I stiffen as she approaches and wraps her arms around my waist. This is an attack I'm unfamiliar with, and I remain rigid as she rises to her toes and kisses my lips.

"Did you teach Valeria to cry when she sees those birds?" she asks.

I clear my throat. "No."

The bond between us yanks, signaling I'm lying.

"Admit you're scared of them," Vanessa taunts.

Over my dead body.

"I love you," I say instead.

Vanessa cocks her head to the side, the action so cute, I can no longer hold back. I return her hug, holding her against me. I hate making my mate angry, but the children needed to learn sooner rather than later. It's only a matter of time before they're teenagers and no longer want to hang out with me.

Besides, it's hard to kill demons, so it's not like the axes are a genuine danger to them.

"Gray's going to be here soon," Vanessa says.

I huff, annoyed. The kids are screaming bloody murder as they fight over the food Vanessa made, but I still wish they could stay longer. I love our home being filled with loud children, and I find them a great source of entertainment.

Plus, the more I watch them, the more the Wrath trio is indebted to me. I'll soon be able to ask them for anything I want and they won't be able to say *no*. I'll practically own them. Silas will be my transportation *slave*.

"Would you like to see my bear?" I ask.

Vanessa flushes, but I know it's because she's trying not to laugh at me. Still, she nods, pleasing me with her choice. My bear hasn't seen her in days, and I'm antsy to feel her fingers brushing through my fur. She's gentle with it, and because of her, I'm the softest bear in the pack.

Everybody is jealous of me.

Vanessa and I join the children at the table, and by the time Gray comes to pick his spawns up, I'm practically bursting at the seams to shift into my bear. Gray tries to stick around and chat, but I shoo him away before dragging Vanessa outside.

She's full of giggles, and I join in before shifting into my animal form. My bear is elated, and he circles her legs before plopping onto his butt for pets. I didn't like her petting me at first, the action emasculating, but now I love it.

"Human bears like to catch fish," Vanessa says, running her fingers through my fur. "Have you ever done that?"

I dip my head when she snags a knot. Catch fish? Why the fuck would I ever want to catch a fish? They're small and provide little meat. Charlie has been filling Vanessa's head with everything that human bears can do, and none of their actions make sense. I've concluded that human bears are ridiculous creatures, and I'm amazed they've survived this long.

Vanessa meanders into the forest, heading outside my pack lands, and I follow. This is where the biggest trees live, and Vanessa spreads her arms as she runs her fingers along the bark. Eventually, she reaches one she connects with most, and she pauses to admire it.

I plop onto my belly. She'll be here a while. Vanessa joins me on the ground, her hand still on the tree, and leans against my side.

I've been hiding a tree twice this size from her, the largest in the area, and I've been working hard to build a home around it. She's always asking about that Wrath restaurant we went to, and I know she'll love having a house in the same style.

This home will be large, and I'm making sure to include several extra bedrooms for the many children I'm hoping we someday have.

I curl around her, pleased as my bear begins to purr. When we move into the new home, I will accidentally drop and break her bird figurines.

It's a sneaky move, but I'm a very sneaky male, so I know I'll be successful.

Epílogue

Two Years Later

CHEV

I CURSE, ANNOYED with the size of the small buttons on my new camera. I hate these fucking things, and I bring the device closer to my face to get a better look at the settings.

Vanessa steps into the room, and she leans against the doorway as she watches me struggle to set up my camera and tripod. She doesn't make a sound, but I can tell she's laughing at me. She finds my inability to "properly" use technology entertaining, but I don't see the humor.

It took me weeks to convince Silas to help me pick this camera out. He's not pleased with my reasoning behind wanting one, but he isn't putting up much of an argument.

He knows it's useless.

Gray's one hundred and fiftieth birthday is a big deal, and my present will be the one he likes the most. I've put a lot of thought into this, and even though Gray isn't my favorite demon, I've decided that I like him enough.

"What're you doing?" Vanessa asks, stepping farther into the bedroom.

She's wearing her leathers, and I appreciatively scan her form as she rubs her belly and attempts to balance a mug of tea on top of it. Our twins have made her extra-large, and she's found that leathers are most comfortable to wear in her extended state.

Although a small part of me is convinced she's wearing them to try to weaken my resolve. She knows I'm annoyed by her desire to name one of our babies Birdie, and she thinks me seeing her in leathers will lessen my resolve to fight.

She's right, and I'm unhappy about it.

Vanessa's attention flickers between me and my camera, and I turn back to the device with a low hum.

"I'm taking sexy photos of myself," I say. My present is going to outshine everybody else's. "For Gray's birthday."

I continue messing with the camera settings, trying to remember what Silas showed me. He's good with these things, and I wish I had paid more attention.

"Sexy photos?" Vanessa asks.

I nod, smiling as I secure the camera on the tripod.

Vanessa watches, silently judging as I get into position. I lift my leather skirt until it sits high on my waist, exposing the mate and animal markings on my upper thigh. The camera makes clicking noises as it counts down, and I smile when the warning flash goes off.

The moment the photo is taken, I run to my tripod to see how it turned out.

Vanessa clears her throat. "Is that what you think is sexy?"

Excuse me? I don't like what she's insinuating, and I cross my arms over my chest with a quiet huff. I know what sexy is.

"Gray likes my thighs," I argue.

Vanessa raises a brow and takes a sip of her tea. She's mocking me, and I frown as I glance at the photo I just took. I thought I looked good, but now she's got me questioning it.

"What would you recommend?" I ask.

Vanessa redresses in modest clothing before grabbing the camera and tripod.

"Follow me," she says.

She bundles everything under her arm before making her way outside. I was purposefully doing this inside so my people wouldn't see, and my cheeks turn a bright shade of red as Vanessa storms through the woods with the camera equipment.

A few shifters cast us curious glances, but I ignore them.

Vanessa leads me to the pile of wood I've been working on splitting these past few days and sets the camera up to face it.

"Chop the wood," she orders.

I suck my cheeks into my mouth, unsure how this is sexy, before grabbing my axe and splitting a few logs. Vanessa takes photos of me, near-constant giggles slipping from her lips before she decides she's got a good one.

I drop my axe and rush to her side. "I want to see."

She shakes her head, the evil woman, and begins walking away. I follow, silently noting that she thinks me chopping wood is sexy.

I'm looking forward to seeing what else excites her.

Vanessa leads me to the nearest lake and sits on a large rock on the bank.

"Take off your leathers," she orders.

I hesitate, unsure what she's thinking, before stripping. Vanessa eyes me, and I shift my weight from foot to foot as I await further instruction. We're alone right now, but I can't guarantee that'll last.

I'm sure anyone who stumbles in the area and spots us will be quick to turn around, though.

"Go stand by the water and face away from me," Vanessa says.

I frown. "That doesn't sound very sexy."

I've put a lot of work into Gray's present, and I want it to be good. It took hours to convince Silas to take me to the store and help me pick a camera. He was annoyed when I told him why I wanted it, but he couldn't look me in the eye and tell me it wasn't the perfect present for Gray.

The incubus is a whore, and whores love sexy pictures of shifters.

Vanessa points to the water. "I know what I'm doing, Chev."

Well, who am I to argue with that? I walk into the lake until my feet are submerged. The sun shines on the left side of my body, and I hurry to cover myself when I realize the sun's position casts a shadow of my penis onto the water.

I'm giving Gray sexy photos, not porn.

Vanessa giggles, and I can't help but laugh as I peer back at her. She's still taking photos of me, her smile so wide, I can't help but stare. My mate is so fucking beautiful.

"Remove your hand," she says.

My jaw drops, and I stare at her in disbelief as I remove my hand from myself. Is this her intention? To take photos of me while my penis, or at least the shadow of it, is exposed?

I shake my head and turn back around, letting Vanessa have her fun.

Gray will not be receiving any photos of my penis.

Vanessa continues to giggle as she takes her photos of me, and after a few seconds, I reach down and begin to stroke myself. If she's going to have her fun, I'm going to, too.

The camera snapping continues, and I take great pleasure in listening to her breathing deepen with each movement of my hand. She likes this.

"Turn to the side," she says.

I happily do so, turning just enough that my side profile and the length of my shaft are exposed to the camera.

It turns me on to know I please my mate, and she continues to take her naughty photos until I cum. The snaps increase as I finish in my hand, and I take a moment to catch my breath before making my way to Vanessa.

"Gray's going to love these," she whispers, her voice hitching as I take the camera from her.

I set it aside before dropping to my knees and spreading her thighs.

I'm going to delete those photos the second we're done here.

———————

Aziel hands me another drink, and I try not to look too annoyed as I sip it.

"Only fifteen minutes left," he says, patting me on the shoulder.

I huff. Vanessa had our babies three weeks ago, but she demanded I leave the house to celebrate Gray's birthday. I don't want to be here, a fact I've been quite forthcoming about, but I know she'll kill me if I return home before the two-hour minimum she gave me.

Gray has babies of his own, so I know he understands my urge to be with them. He wouldn't care if I didn't come tonight.

I glance at the clock as Aziel takes a seat on my right. He's been a great host tonight, but Gray did not make it easy for him. The incubus invited about twenty more people than the fifteen he initially said were coming, and poor Aziel had to scramble at the last minute to procure enough food and alcohol.

I can only imagine the earful Gray's going to be getting tomorrow.

"Gray!" I shout.

Aziel gives me a sideways glance as I wave over his incubus. I conveniently forgot to tell him about my present, and I have a feeling Silas will be furious to learn I didn't exactly stick to my original idea.

It's Vanessa's fault.

She gave me all kinds of sweet compliments as we looked over the photos of me pleasuring myself, and I have to admit I looked strong. I'm going to give Gray ten minutes to look at them. Then I'll take them away.

Gray excuses himself from the group he's talking with and saunters over. He takes a seat on Aziel's lap, and I hand over the package of printed images I've been worrying between my hands all night.

"Happy birthday," I say, thrusting them against his chest.

Gray looks confused, his eyebrows furrowed as he accepts them. Aziel cranes his neck to watch as Gray rips open the package, and they both grow entirely still as the first image is revealed.

"*Chev.*" Aziel sighs.

Gray clutches the images to his chest.

"You naughty bear," he teases, flipping through them.

Aziel clicks his tongue against the roof of his mouth and looks away, uninterested in seeing my penis.

I can tell when Gray gets to the part where I turned to the side and exposed more than just my shadow. He's practically vibrating with excitement, and I lean back in my chair with a smile.

I knew he'd like my present the most.

"I want them back in ten minutes," I say.

Gray turns to Aziel, his eyes wide, and Aziel huffs before patting the side of Gray's thigh. Gray's gone in an instant, materializing next to Charlie a second later. He bounces from foot to foot as he whispers in her ear, and she cuts me a sharp glare before nodding and returning to her conversation.

Gray then does the same thing with Silas before vanishing from the room altogether. I don't want to know what he's doing.

"You know he's going to expect this from you every half-century birthday, right?" Aziel asks.

I shrug. "I'll be old by the next half-century. He won't want them."

Aziel turns away. He doesn't like the reminder that my life isn't as long as his, and his jaw clenches as he stares at the wall beside my head. It's simply the truth, and I raise my knuckles and press them to his temple so he remembers he's my dearest friend.

He does the same to me, and I wait exactly eleven minutes before standing and brushing my hands down my leathers.

"Gray isn't going to be giving me those images back, is he?" I ask.

Aziel stifles a laugh and shakes his head. "You gave an incubus intimate photos of a mated shifter's dick. He's going to hoard them like they're fucking treasure."

I shift my weight from foot to foot.

"Don't let him show anybody," I say.

Aziel nods. "Gray would never do that."

He better not. I'll know if he does, and I'll crush him.

I glance at the clock once more, anxious to return home. I have less than five minutes left, and I finish my drink and wait impatiently for my two hours to be up. I'm ready to be with my babies.

Birdie's colicky, and even though Echo is helping Vanessa while I'm gone, I'm sure my baby's been a lot to handle these past few hours. Vanessa's a very capable mother, one of the best I've ever seen, but a screaming baby is enough to drive anybody to madness.

Orson sleeps like a log. My boy is quite content with his schedule of eating, sleeping, and pooping, and I know he's been good for Vanessa.

"It's been two hours," I say, holding out my arm the moment the minute hits.

I could use the portal, but Aziel is quicker.

The wrath doesn't hesitate to grab my wrist, and I squeeze my eyes shut as the party noises vanish and the sound of a crying baby fills my ears. It's heaven, and I beam as I release Aziel and rush to my mate.

This has been the worst two hours of my life, and I'm never leaving home again.

* * *

END OF BOOK 4